TWISTED VENOM

V. W. RAYNES

authorHOUSE®

AuthorHouse™ LLC
1663 Liberty Drive
Bloomington, IN 47403
www.authorhouse.com
Phone: 1-800-839-8640

Published by AuthorHouse   11/25/2013

ISBN: 978-1-4918-3399-5 (sc)
ISBN: 978-1-4918-3400-8 (hc)
ISBN: 978-1-4918-3398-8 (e)

Library of Congress Control Number: 2013919884

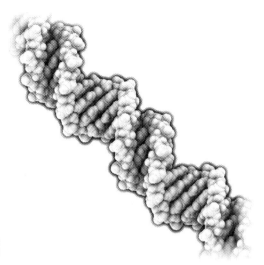

Chapter One

"IT WAS A *SNAKE*," I said, more to convince myself than her. "A fucking *snake!*"

I looked around quickly, wondering if it was said too loudly after having my second drink. But the place was filled with people enjoying their own happy hour and not paying any attention to our conversation. Dru looked at me in her usual calm, impassive way as I was spilling my guts to her. My strange cousin and I had become close in the last year—or as close as time would permit—and she was the only person I knew who seemed reasonably capable of believing my implausible story.

Dru, the professional bank teller by day, transformed into the unconventional counterculture woman by night. It was the unconventional version of her that I'd grown up with. A real tomboy as a kid, she would go hunting and fishing with her father, my uncle Carlos. In high school, she grew into a lanky loner with a talent for math but with no particular ambition to channel it anywhere. We lived thirty miles apart, and I had one year on her. When her family later moved closer to mine, we found ourselves in the same high school, then in the same French class. Now I've got to admit that I, a scholastic overachiever, was a little embarrassed by my cousin, who was considered to be a little on the weird side by most of my friends. But when looking back on it now, I have to admire her for being her unconventional self. She took to wearing tons of smoky eye makeup, with her brown hair long and straight and nails hypoxic shades of blue and purple, before those were acceptable colors. The clothes became dark and darker, with black tights, spiky shoes, and a tendency toward very metallic leather. She wasn't much good at French either, telling me that the old lady who taught the course was gross, coughing green phlegm into a balled up handkerchief—which was true enough. Thirteen years, one transient husband, and two boys later, she'd come to grips with the fact that a more conventional exterior was needed to maintain a living, and she got herself through a vocational school and into a job in a bank.

Now we were sitting at a small back table in Sam's Bar, a nondescript hangout about two blocks from Dru's house—her choice, not mine. She was looking relaxed in jeans and a tight red sweater, her thick brown, now permed hair curling all over the place. Her fingers played with a huge hoop on her right ear, and at least five chains with dangling things jangled on her neck. A small key, evoking a fuzzy memory I couldn't place, was hanging on one of them. We both had our feet on a third chair, but her big platforms took up most of the room. I had to admit, Dru looked good, and it wasn't lost on some guys sitting at the bar. She always managed to stay surprisingly fit, which she attributed to her active sex life—and having big boobs didn't hurt. A guy at one of the pool tables would take a glance over once in a while, I noticed. His head was shaved cleanly, and he looked roughly forty and brawny—and not bad looking.

The middle-aged bartender with a big gut came over, carrying our third round of whiskey-sevens. I'd asked for only a smidge of whiskey in the third one—just for flavor.

"Thanks, Sam." She smiled.

He winked.

This was obviously one of her hangouts.

"OK, hon," she said. "Let's start from the beginning, and tell me all the details before our heads are too fuzzy. You went where and when?"

Her dark eyes looked moist and warm, now concentrating only on me. That was Dru's talent—the ability to become a deep well of understanding and empathy and to tune out extraneous noise.

"Well, I was just going to that meeting—think I mentioned it—the Hematology Society—blood diseases—the one in San Francisco. He was on the plane."

"Yeah." She pulled out a cigarette but just wet the tip slowly with her tongue.

"I was by the window, and he sat next to me. You know me—just kept staring out the window, conveying my lack of interest in my neighbor. Unfortunately, we had to make eye contact and talk when our seatbelts got tangled. Even more unfortunately, he was good-looking. He looked young— early twenties, I guessed, but later found out he was twenty-eight—with hair on the longish side but slicked back, very flat, very white," I said, passing my hand over my head. "Very fair skin. His eyes seemed big, and I couldn't help staring at them. Couldn't tell the color—gray maybe. Very big pupils."

"He sounds very odd-looking," she commented. "Did you have your contacts in?"

"Very funny. But somehow, the combination worked on him. You would have looked twice, Dru."

"So obviously you talked," she said, finally digging in her purse for a lighter.

"Yeah, all the way to San Francisco. He didn't say much at first— seemed almost shy, reluctant to talk, and I didn't ask many questions. But our eyes seemed to—I don't know—click, and talk got easier."

"So you told him you're a doctor."

"Yeah, I got around to that. Told him I was doing an internal medicine fellowship in hematology. He said he was doing research in a genetics lab in Houston. Turns out we were going to the same meeting. Then somehow we managed to talk nonstop all the way to San Francisco—about nothing really, or I don't actually remember what. It was—have you ever just met a guy and had that really nervous feeling with sweaty palms and an inability to really concentrate on what's being said? Like I said, most of it was a vague, jittery conversation until we both settled down a little."

"What was his name? Did he say anything much about himself?"

"Didn't ask his name, and I don't think he mentioned it. That came later, and I'll tell you about it. We talked mostly about traveling, San Francisco, and a little bit about genetics. I thought I'd never see the guy again."

Dru gave her cigarette a big drag and looked at me with a half smile. "You still haven't gotten the nerve to pick up a guy who's interested, have you, sweetie?"

I ignored the remark.

"So how'd you connect in San Fran?"

"Well, we both picked up our bags at the terminal. I had a huge one, and he had a small one. Now I really don't know if I'm remembering this right or not, but it occurred to me later that there was a tag on his bag as he picked it up. I'm not even sure if it was one of those departure/destination tags or an ID tag, but I thought it said Laredo on it, which was strange, of course, since I'd assumed he'd left from Houston. Anyway, we shared a cab downtown—his idea. I got out at the St. Francis, and he went on to—I think he said the Westin."

Dru's cigarette smoke was starting to get my sinuses clogged, but a few more sips of whiskey helped, and we relaxed one more notch. If there was much background noise, I wasn't hearing it.

"So, knowing you, Claudia, you didn't give him your cell phone number, and you thought that was the end of *that*."

"Yeah—and I wish it had been. But I spent the next two days of the meeting hoping I'd run into him walking the halls of the convention center or running into or out of a session. Around six-thirty on Tuesday my last course got out, and I walked back to my hotel—weather was really great that night. Took my time walking by Union Square, stopped in a few stores and browsed. By the time I got to the St. Francis, it was about eight. I was walking around the lobby a little—love the look of the place—and he was standing by the big clock reading a paper and leaning against the wall. I didn't even notice him until he folded the paper and looked at me."

"Not an accidental meeting, I assume."

"No. I knew he was waiting for me. We both grinned like kids."

"That's when you ran up to your room and screwed each other's brains out?"

Her tone irritated me a little, but I ignored it.

"No, we didn't. But what I wanted to say first was how he *looked*. I mean, he was sort of otherworldly sexy, with that slicked-back white, white hair, and he had on a really dark sports jacket with a silvery shirt that seemed to just—*magnify* him. I can't really do him justice, but I swear every female who passed us just stared at him. At the time, I was glad to be wearing a decent black dress and have my hair looking reasonably good."

The picture in my mind suddenly made me very warm, despite what had followed, and a bolt of heat passed up into my head. I took another swallow, shaking my head to clear it, realizing how stupid that was. Dru was very quiet, staring at my glass, a frown on her face. Suddenly she lifted her head and grinned.

"I've got it! He's one of the living dead—a vampire. They're everywhere these days."

I just shook my head, thinking that maybe just going home and sobering up would be a better idea.

"Sorry, kiddo," she said. "What came next?"

"Well, he suggested dinner at a nearby restaurant. I ran up to my room to try and fix up a little first—just swigged down some mouthwash—then we met in the lobby. He took me to a place down the block in a small, nice hotel. Oh, and I finally found out his name is Chance."

"Chance? Did you get a last name, by any chance?"

I gave her a disgusted look, then a pause. "Well, I'm not sure."

"What does that mean?"

"At first I thought he said Munroe, Chance Munroe," I said, remembering the feeling of his hair softly brushing my face as he leaned over and whispered it, gently pulling my long, dark hair from my ear.

"But later when he paid the server, I thought he called Chance Mr. King. At least that might be what he said. I wasn't exactly sober at the time and really wasn't paying much attention at that point. I thought maybe I'd heard wrong."

Dru raised her eyebrows slightly. "What else did he say?"

Her look seemed to change to one of serious interest.

"I'm not sure. We started with some booze, and I got it into my head to order some scotch. Then we got a bottle of red wine, and I finally started relaxing. My mind was getting really fuzzy. I was drinking wine too fast, and I knew it, but I also knew there was no backtracking at that point. We would end up in my room, I knew that, and my whole body tingled when his leg brushed mine and then stayed there. It's a strange feeling to know that you just don't have any willpower whatsoever to change the direction of events, but that's how I felt, along with the feeling that I was spineless."

"What do you mean, 'spineless'? You were just horny."

"I mean that I like to be in charge of my feelings. You know *that*."

Dru was now taking on the air of a shrink, a not quite qualified version.

"OK," she said. "So he really didn't tell you much of anything that you remember."

I thought hard. She was insinuating I was a real dolt.

"All right, let's see. We talked a little about the meeting, and he said he was interested in bleeding disorders—diseases. He said he had, get this, double PhD's in biochemistry and genetics, and I remember asking him from where and don't remember getting an answer. I think the subject got changed. He lost his mother at an early age, and his father hadn't remarried."

"Where does he live?"

"I assumed it was Houston since he got on the plane there, but now I'm not so sure because I can't find him."

"What do you mean, you can't find him?"

"I mean I've checked him out on the Internet, Googled him, checked faculty lists at Houston schools, checked some company directories, checked the phone book, and I can't find a thing—at least not on a Chance Munroe. I need to check out Chance King for the hell of it."

"Well, those're just a few things an amateur would check. It doesn't mean he's not there. Anyway, what next? What happened next?"

She wanted me to get to the good part—what should have been the good part.

"Toward the end of the meal, I couldn't read him very well, not that I could read much at all. I mean—and this is hard to explain—he seemed to get a little jittery. His leg started sort of vibrating under the table, but his eyes were steady, and I wondered if maybe he might be married or something and feeling a little guilty. Anyway, we didn't really discuss it because as soon as we got out of the restaurant, we walked back to my hotel—to the elevator, and I assumed he was coming up to my room. He put his hand on my neck and bent close, asking what room I was in."

I paused, remembering the bolt of electricity shooting through me at the touch of his hand. Dru gave me an empathetic look, like she'd been there before.

"He whispered he'd be right up. I didn't question that—just got on the elevator and went up to six. It did occur to me he might not show up."

"You underestimate yourself," Dru commented, sending a wad of smoke to her side.

"Well, I didn't know what to think, but figured I had enough alcohol on board to cushion the blow if he didn't show. The room was dark. I opened the curtains to let the outside lights shine in and sat in a big chair by the window and waited, getting really groggy despite my anticipation. After a while, I cracked open the window and started checking the street below for a male with a shock of white hair leaving or entering the building, thinking maybe he'd decided to just leave. But then I heard two knocks on the door, and there he was. And there I was, with funny mixed feelings of anticipation and—resignation, maybe? Wanting to do it but not really feeling quite right about the situation."

Not quite knowing how to continue, I took a sip, and Dru nodded me on.

"He walked in and didn't say a word. Just took off his jacket and put it on a chair by the bed. Then he closed the curtains, and we were on each other like two love-starved kids. We kissed hard and long, until my mouth started actually getting sore from doing it, then finally got over to the bed, ripping off the covers. We tore our clothes off—you know, the usual."

I felt foolish talking with my hands and realizing I was pulling at some imaginary shirt, then let my hands fall back on the table.

"But you don't really want to hear every detail, do you?"

"Every fuck-ing de-tail," she said flatly, tapping her ashes in one deliberate motion.

Well, hell—I was there to tell her the whole story.

"We were so hot, we went for each other like two *animals*, writhing and twisting and trying to feel every inch of each other, throwing clothes all over the place. Yet he seemed a little hesitant to actually *do it*, so I tried to grab him and give him some help."

I paused, trying to remember it all.

"He pulled away, like he didn't want me to touch it, and I thought maybe he was embarrassed about the size or something. It wasn't small. He didn't quit, though, and pretty soon I felt something brush my thigh, and then he started making me ready for it. I was ready, all right, and the odd thing is, I'm sure he whispered some Latin-sounding strange words in my ear just before it happened."

"You remember what they were?"

"Not a chance. It could have been *e pluribus unum* for all I know, and that might have been appropriate."

"So you fucked."

She was so erudite. I don't think she got my attempt at sexual humor, either.

"Well, yes, and it felt great. Wonderful," I said, my eyes beginning to water. "We both came, then clutched each other like people do when things feel—well—perfect. Then I felt ready to drift off with him there next to me."

I shrugged.

"So what went wrong?"

"I vaguely remember him getting up and looking down at me. And I looked at him—at his thing—his dick—and I swear it was a snake. At least it looked like one, like a snake head writhing on a stalk, and I saw him put his hand on it to stop the movement."

"You're kidding. You thought you saw a *snake?*"

"Not kidding. And keep it down, Dru."

"So *then* what?"

"I saw it, and I guess things went black. I don't exactly know. The next thing I remember is opening my eyes and feeling pain—bad pain—like my whole lower body was cramping. And I felt wet between my legs. My hand went down to feel it and came back covered with blood. I started shaking, feeling cold and really weak. I was barely hanging on. Someone was talking on a phone—maybe he was on his cell phone. Then he said 'sorry, sorry,' but his voice was dim. I think he was throwing his clothes back on, sitting on the edge of the bed next to me. The room was spinning, and I remember grabbing at the sheets, pulling them up and trying to stuff them into me to stop the bleeding. Then the door closed. I stayed in a little ball on the bed, starting to feel really light-headed and praying that the bleeding and pain would let up, but I was getting pretty damned scared. I could feel blood soaking through the knot of sheets and blanket and knew I needed to get some help soon. Don't ask me how long it all lasted. I remember turning and trying to reach the phone by the bed, but don't remember actually reaching it or making a call."

"Oh my God." Dru's mouth was hanging open, her cigarette slumping in her fingers.

"Well, the next few hours are a blur. I vaguely remember being moved and some murmuring voices. My first good recollection is lying in a hospital bed in what turned out to be an intensive care unit at San Francisco General, but I had a lot of trouble staying awake for a while. People would come and go in a blur. I remember feeling really depressed, looking up and seeing a unit of red cells getting transfused into me and wondering how many of those I had needed. I think I may have asked a nurse if it was compatible."

"You needed a lot of blood?"

"Enough. One doctor told me four units of red cells, several fresh frozen plasma units, and two big units of platelets. She came in to talk about it with me after I was feeling better a few days later. They couldn't figure out any relatives to contact, and I just told them there were none." And that was true as far as my family goes; my mother and father both went in a car crash five years ago.

"You could have called me."

"I knew I'd make it out of there and just didn't want anyone to know, you understand? It wasn't the kind of situation I wanted anyone to know about."

"But didn't you want to get this guy—get him caught before he could leave town? My God, he almost killed you."

"Believe me, Dru, all of that was going through my mind, but in a fuzz. People kept asking me about it, and it just wouldn't come out—I couldn't make it come out—couldn't say it. It was like an unknown something was stopping me."

"I guess I know how you felt. Weird story and all. What did they say about the whole—bleeding thing?"

"I'm afraid I really drove them crazy with that. Oh, they figured out pretty quickly that I had a really bad coagulation disorder, what's called disseminated intravascular coagulation, or DIC."

She laughed. "Of course."

"Well, something triggered my coagulation system to turn on rapidly, and when that happens, the clotting factors get used up, and you bleed. But it wasn't pregnancy related, and that really threw them for a loop. On my exam, they saw a small lesion with swelling on my cervix and a tear or laceration with bleeding and swelling on the vaginal wall and asked me tons of questions about what happened. But I made up my mind not to talk about it and to become the thing that has always really irritated me, the totally uncooperative patient. I'll tell you, that was really embarrassing, and most of my story was the old 'I can't remember' excuse. Really lame. They never knew I'm a doctor; I claimed to be a student, which is partially true. I talked with doctors, a nurse, and some kind of social worker but really told them virtually nothing—just made up my mind to clam up, and there wasn't much they could do about it. After five days, the serious stage seemed to be over, and I signed out AMA—against medical advice—just at the time they were going to transfer me to a regular room. I really hope that I never run into any of those people again. I'd be mortified."

"So you didn't think they'd believe a story about sex with a snake?" she asked sarcastically.

"Hell no. I didn't know what *I* believed. But I do know that what happened to me felt *venomous*—like a snakebite. I want to know what he did to me."

"Well, I don't know how you'll accomplish anything. Sounds like it's over and done, and you don't want to involve any police."

I shrugged.

"Anyway, getting out of the hospital and working on getting home were all I wanted at that point. I needed to get back to the hotel to get some things that were still there and was worried about the room charges. It turned out that the front desk had called for an ambulance, so they cancelled charges after that. Of course, that got me curious about just how the front desk knew I was in trouble."

Dru looked at me, raising her eyebrows and lighting her third cigarette. She was chaining them faster than usual.

"So you really hadn't been able to call 911?"

"No, and have no recollection of being able to do it. I got back to the hotel from the hospital about two in the afternoon and asked a girl at the front desk how I could get some information about what had happened. She sent me to the manager's office. He was a nice guy, but I could tell he was dying to know what had gone on in his hotel. I sure as hell wasn't about to explain the story to him, so I made up a good one about how my pregnancy had gone bad and so on. I didn't mention whether I was married or not, and he didn't ask any more questions. He may not have bought the story, but I thought it sounded convincing at the time. Oddly enough, he told me I looked very pale, like he was worried I'd collapse in his hotel again, but I reassured him I was in great condition. They had put some of my things in storage, and I didn't owe a fortune for the room. Then he asked me if I knew who had called the front desk asking for emergency help in room 688. I looked at him, feeling the blood rush into my head, realizing who had made the call. All I could think to say was that I'd done it. He looked at me, and I could tell he knew I was lying. He just said, 'Funny, I thought our employee said it was a male. Well, glad you're doing better.' I couldn't get out of that hotel fast enough."

"So you came right home?"

"Yeah. I really wanted to try and get some information about Chance, maybe from some list of meeting attendees or something, but the whole meeting was over, and I sure wasn't feeling up to par. I did give the Weston a call for the hell of it, but all they would tell me was that there was no Chance Munroe or Chance King registered there. I threw everything into my suitcases, headed for the airport and got a flight back. Then I had to call the hospital and explain why I needed a few more days off. Of course I had to make up *another* story about getting really sick—maybe from some kind of bite—and still feeling really weak. More lies."

"I wouldn't feel too guilty about that."

I leaned back, feeling exhausted again, and rubbed my eyes. "Soooo, that was two weeks ago. I need to get back to work on Monday. I want to do something about this whole thing, but really don't know how or what, and I want to do it myself. No one else needs to know this story. OK by you?"

"Cuz, you know I can keep my mouth shut, and I will."

"Yeah, that's why I'm telling you and no one else. And what do *you* think about this bizarre story, anyway?"

She leaned her head back, looking about as thoughtful as I've ever seen Dru look, and blew out a long stream of smoke. "Look, I really can't figure out what you actually saw or didn't see. Like you said, you had a lot of booze on board. Obviously this guy hurt you in some way, but I doubt there was an actual *snake* in the room—we'll never know. If he's a science nut, he's probably figured out some bizarre way to hurt women—and I wouldn't be surprised if he's done it before. Anyway, I think you did the right thing, I mean, not telling anyone else about what you *thought* you saw. I would have done the same thing, and believe me, I'd have been mighty pissed. But you got through it, and it sounds like he made a phone call to make sure you didn't bleed to death—which is strange. The guy sounds like he has a conscience, and he was apologizing. Much as I know you'd like to find out more, I don't see how you can, and so I'd just try to forget it and get on with things."

She paused. "And what a waste."

It was exactly what I'd expected to hear, but I'd hoped Dru might be a little more imaginative about what I'd thought I'd seen. She wasn't going there, though, and she was the essence of practicality that night. I was getting tired, sick of breathing smoke, and my mind was bending toward taking her advice.

"Yeah, I've sort of come to the same conclusion even though I'm not happy with it—don't even have time to think about anything but work, anyway."

We left it at that, picking ourselves out of the chairs we'd molded into and saying goodbye to Sam, my new friend. Dru promised to stay in touch and gave me a big hug in the parking lot, and then she waited to watch me leave. On the way home, I started crying again.

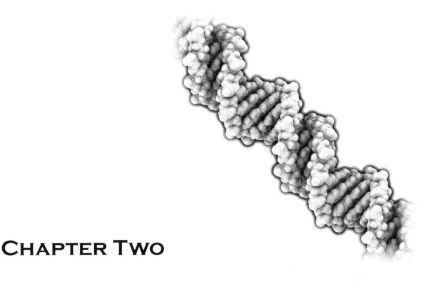

Chapter Two

WHEN I THOUGHT ABOUT IT later, Dru's advice seemed just too hard to take. I simply couldn't buy into the idea that I'd imagined anything. Dru should have known me better than that. My mind was spinning as I drove my Explorer back to the house and got ready for bed. At least it was a Friday night, and the blessed weekend was more recovery time, more time to think.

I slept hard until ten on Saturday morning, when a bright south Texas sun burst through the edges of the window shades and the daylight couldn't be ignored any longer. February in south Texas is a month of constant daily surprises, and this was going to be one of those heavenly warm days that made me want to be out there and definitely not working in a hospital. Of course, a brutal norther, a cold wind from the north, could blow in any time and drastically change things, but it wasn't on the agenda for the time being. I'd decided that this day would be the start of my return to normalcy, a day to begin catching up with the mundane tasks that had been put off since coming home. Unfortunately, laundry was at the top of the list, but at least it didn't require any concentration.

When I'd come back home from San Francisco totally wiped out, I'd grabbed what was needed out of my suitcases and left the dirty clothes inside, shoving the luggage into a closet. Now I started sorting through the rubble, making small piles of them on the bedspread. A plastic bag was among the contents, and it wasn't something that I had packed. After throwing the contents on the bed, I sat down and sifted through them. There was a tiny black button that certainly must have come off the black dress I'd worn the night of the snake. I figured the maid or someone from the hotel likely had found it on the floor and put it into this bag. Also in the bag was the said dress minus the button, along with my underwear and nylons. The final article was a white wad of cotton that when picked up and spread out assumed the shape of a pair of men's briefs, and, despite their history, I had to laugh at the sight of them. Not the boxer kind—the small, sexy kind. Obviously somebody had left in a hurry and forgotten to put them on, and that somebody was named Chance (well, maybe). I was beginning to doubt that *any* of the information that had issued from his mouth was true. A peek inside the crotch revealed no snakes, but there was a small reddish-brown spot about the size of a dime inside the size small Fruit of the Looms. I put the fruit back into the bag and stuffed it into a drawer, not exactly knowing why I didn't just toss the thing.

An hour later I took a frozen pizza from the freezer and put it in the oven, then decided to take the shorts from the drawer, put them in a clean plastic baggie, put the baggie in the empty pizza box and return the box to the freezer. You never know when frozen shorts will come in handy.

The rest of the weekend was spent doing my boring tasks, like paying overdue bills and buying more frozen pizza and microwave popcorn. Dru called late Saturday afternoon and asked how things were going.

"Great," I lied. "Getting back to normal."

"Well, you hang in there. Everything that weirdo told you was probably a lie, so you might as well forget it. The boys and I are going out for pizza tomorrow night if you want to come."

That was about the *last* thing I wanted to do, so I politely begged off. Dru had two boys—Clint, who was six, and Woodie, who was around five. I lost track. If you asked Dru how she named her boys, she would admit to having a soft spot for Clint Eastwood, who she thought was still hot at his age. These turned out to be appropriate names for the boys, since they believed that this was still the Wild, Wild West, and they could behave accordingly. Dru seemed devoted to them, and her allegedly disinterested ex lived with a new female companion and two kids in Minneapolis. Clint and Woodie happened to be my only next-generation relatives, as a matter of fact, so I did my best to tolerate them. Dru talked me into being a last-minute babysitter a few times, so I learned to let weekend calls from her go to voice mail. This time I figured I was safe—obviously still recuperating.

There was a slight pause on the other end. Then she said, "Anything else new?"

"Not really. I just need a little more rest and need to catch up on things this weekend." Well, I guess I could have told her about the underwear but really didn't want to get into that and didn't want her to talk me into pizza with the boys, so we said our goodbyes.

Saturday night I vegetated, reading an unmemorable and stupid vampire romance novel that had fallen into my cart at Walmart. Drinking red wine, I began an inane conversation in my head about why vampires don't have transfusion reactions. Maybe they know how to pick out compatible victims, or maybe they don't have antibodies. I always thought what they sucked up through their fangs went into their bloodstream, but maybe it just goes through the GI tract. But then . . .

The night was full of ill-defined, uncomfortable dreams, and the next morning the only memory of them was a vague notion of a thin chain around a neck, with two pieces of metal gently pinging against one another. The hair of the wearer was stark white and soft, and it brushed my cheek when he bent forward to speak in my ear. I looked right down at the sparkling line of silver as he came near. There was something else about it, but I simply couldn't picture it. Going once again through the events of the rest of that night—for the hundredth time—I just could not remember seeing the chain again or hearing the gentle pinging.

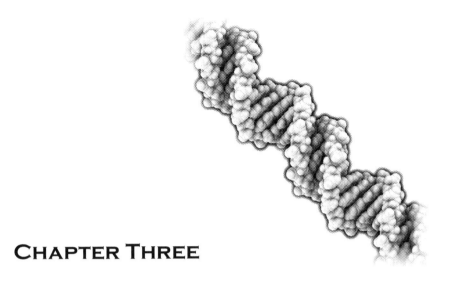

CHAPTER THREE

AND SO IT WAS MONDAY and I was back at the hospital, the big university hospital. The place where serious things happened, things that required my full attention—I knew that, but I was worried. My stomach still felt like a big, dead ball was pulling it down, and depression was a demon lurking in my head. After stashing my purse in the office space that the first-year fellows shared and throwing on my white coat, I forced my brain to concentrate. The time for contemplation didn't last long—it never does on the adult leukemia service. Normally I would have had a resident working with me, but a combination of circumstances had temporarily put them in short supply, so we'd been told. The medical students were at some kind of conference that morning, so I decided to just go ahead with the work up of a new acute leukemia patient, a very nice and very elderly lady who'd noticed some bruising and some strange spots on her skin.

Her CBC had shown no platelets in her blood when her family doctor had done blood counts, and her white cell differential counts noted "suspicious cells," a term that always made me think of cells that were up to no good and probably should be arrested. As it turned out, the cells were downright bad—I counted 56 percent blasts on her blood smear. She let me do a bone marrow biopsy on her, her brittle little bone crumbling and crushing beneath my biopsy needle and hurting her, but she thanked me for doing it. I wondered if I would be so nice when I'm a little old lady getting a biopsy for a terrible malignant disease. I doubted it. Her diagnosis, I told her, would be known by the end of the day and then repeated the news to a few relatives outside the room. The answer was obvious, though.

By the end of the procedure, I felt exhausted for both the patient and for me. Before San Francisco these things had been easier to cope with— just daily required work.

Monday was a specialty conference day in the early afternoon, so I had a quick lunch and got over to the meeting room, where several students, residents, and fellows and the faculty head were already gathered. Dr. Still was the head of the Clinical Hematology department, and he loved to show slides and make us identify little cells. I hated the format—dreaded getting the answer wrong. The day's topic was infectious mononucleosis, and we had to decide if his lymphocyte pictures were representative of the disease or not; luckily my slide was a big old reactive lymphocyte that no one could mistake for normal.

On the way out, among my other partners in training, I ran into Jeff Dunn, one of the other heme (hematology) fellows in the program (there were four of us doing a first year fellowship). Jeff was on the adult leukemia service with me, handling half of the service with an Internal Medicine resident to help him out. He was, I must admit, my favorite of the bunch, probably because he was cute and fun and no stress, since he was dating a hot nurse. Still, I tried never to look at his eyes too hard because they were friendly and a very nice shade of blue. Since he was exactly my height, it was hard to avoid them.

"Hey, welcome back, Claude," he said in his slightly loud voice, knowing that the shortening of my name would irritate me.

For the record, my name is Claudia Ranelli, and I do not like being called Claude. It sounds too much like clod.

Never deterred by my look of distaste, Jeff continued his loud banter. "I thought you had one week off, but here it is two weeks later, and I've been working my ass off taking care of your patients. Did you fall in love with San Francisco or whatever his name was?"

"Believe me, if I fell in love it wouldn't be with a saint. The *city* of San Francisco was just great. Unfortunately, I got a little bit sick and wound up in the hospital for a few days. And keep your voice down."

Since sickness or a family death were about the only acceptable reasons for dumping extra work on your colleagues, I had decided the sick excuse would be the best.

"Sick? You eat something bad?"

He was persistent.

"No. No bad food. I got some kind of bite and had a really bad reaction to it—very strange."

Still not lying. We were in the elevator now, making our way to the oncology unit to see our inpatients.

"Really." He sounded intrigued. "Maybe a spider?"

"Maybe. Maybe Spiderman," I said sarcastically. Maybe Snakeman, I said to myself.

"Where'd it bite you?" He was *so* nosy.

"In a place I'd rather not discuss. Anyway, it's healing and there's no major harm done."

That shut him up for the time being, and he started on introductions to the patients he'd admitted for me and going over their charts. It was two hours before we finished, and I felt guilty for all the time he'd put in covering for me.

"Thanks. I owe you one for all the extra work."

"Well, you can buy me a hamburger after work if you want. Jenna's working the late shift tonight."

I knew he was still curious about San Francisco, but I figured a quick dinner and drink might do me good.

"Sure. I can do that. Any idea where?"

"Well, there's always Charlie's."

Charlie's was an upscale bar/restaurant near the hospital, but I found myself suggesting Sam's, don't ask me why.

"If you don't mind a little smoke, there's a place called Sam's at Broadway and Main. I like the—ambiance."

"Right. I've been there. If you mention ambiance to any of those people, they think you're mispronouncing ambulance. But that's OK. See you there around 6:30?"

"See you there."

I left him sitting at the nursing station and headed for the pathology lab to get the diagnosis on my little old lady from the morning. Actually, her name was Mrs. Sapen. I knew the diagnosis had to be acute leukemia, and the pathology fellow confirmed it. It was bad news, and I spent the next three hours explaining the diagnosis to her and her family. Surprisingly, she agreed to therapy, and so she was started on the hazardous route to survival or death. Then I was more than ready for Sam's.

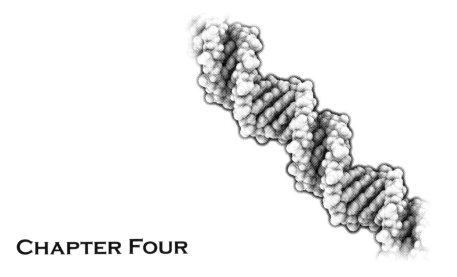

Chapter Four

I STOPPED HOME TO GET some jeans on and got to Sam's Bar before Jeff. The place wasn't very crowded on a Monday night. The table where Dru and I had sat was taken, and I made my way to a far back table by the wall, away from the jukebox and pool tables. This was definitely not a wine place, but I ordered some anyway from a tired-looking waitress. Glancing around, I noticed that the good looking (in a very unconventional way) guy with the shaved head who'd been there last time was playing pool with three other guys. The sleeves on his black T-shirt were rolled up macho-style, and I could tell even from my dark corner that his arms were heavily tattooed. Jeff showed up a half hour late.

Fifteen minutes later we were chomping on hamburgers and playing with our French fries (I never eat them). Jeff was telling me all the wonderful things he loved about Jenna, and my mind started wandering to thoughts of stark white, soft hair and a pair of Fruit of the Looms. My question came out of nowhere—just popped out of my mouth while Jeff was in mid-sentence.

"Jeff."

"Yes?"

"Do you know anybody working in the molecular genetics lab at the hospital?"

His mouth pinched in thought. "Um—I met the doctor in charge of it at a hospital conference once. A guy from Australia—I think Palmer was his name."

"Oh, is he the short guy with the mustache I heard talk at one of our Monday conferences?"

Jeff pondered this for a second and then said, "Yeah—sure, I think that's the guy. Why?"

"Ah—just curious. I might want to do some special testing on an interesting case I saw." I wasn't about to tell him there was a pair of men's underwear in my freezer and that I was considering analyzing them for DNA. It was a crazy idea anyway. What would I say I was looking for? What *was* I looking for? Who would pay for it? That kind of testing was still expensive.

At our little table in the back of the room, I had a view of the bar, partially obscured by Jeff, who was sitting with his back to it. Jeff was well into a criticism of some discordant genetic testing results he'd gotten on a patient, when a striking looking woman in a black bomber jacket walked into the place and sat at the bar. She flung her long, curling hair back and apparently ordered a drink from a bartender I hadn't seen before.

The new patron was Dru, and obviously she hadn't and couldn't see me back in our dark corner spot. I just sat there, half-listening to Jeff and watching Dru drink and chat at the bar. Soon the big bald guy who'd been playing pool went and sat next to her, and it was obvious they knew each other. I didn't think too much of it until I noticed about ten minutes later that he was shaking his head in what seemed to be a very negative manner, and then Dru began gesticulating with her hands in a way that was conveying a high degree of frustration (I think she was pissed). It was obvious they disagreed on something (a lover's spat?). This went on for a few minutes, and he seemed to throw up his hands in disgust. I had a very cousinly curiosity but really didn't want to get involved. If she was having problems with this guy, she hadn't mentioned anything to me, which I found a little disappointing.

My curiosity finally got the better of me, so I asked Jeff if he'd go to the bar and get me another wine (our waitress had disappeared anyway). Jeff was in a very mellow mood by then, and he sauntered over to the bar to get our refills. I caught glimpses of the continuing conversation between

Dru and Mr. Tats at the bar. Jeff was standing almost right next to him, waiting for our drinks to come, and I noticed him taking a long look at Dru and then at Tattoos. Sam appeared on the scene and gave Jeff the drinks.

Jeff came back, sat down and heaved a sigh.

"Here's to curing cancer," he said.

We clinked. I wanted to know more about the sleazy but interesting-looking guy Dru obviously knew pretty well.

"Kind of an unusual-looking guy at the bar, huh?"

Jeff took a big mouthful and swallowed, thinking about the question.

"Well . . . It depends on what you mean by *unusual*. Lots of tats aren't really unusual these days. Have to admit, though, those are some of the best I've seen. Beautiful coiled snakes up both arms. Must have taken days to do, and they look almost real."

This did not make me feel good. I was hoping Dru would meet a wealthy banker and we'd never have to worry about overdrawn checking accounts again. This guy didn't fit the bill.

"Were they arguing?"

"She did not look happy, but I didn't hear them say much. Why the curiosity?"

"Because she's my cousin Dru."

"Your cousin Dru what?"

"Drew you a picture, smartass. Her name's Dru Salinas, which was her married name. Our mothers were sisters."

"Were?"

"My parents died in a car crash five years ago."

"Uh. Sorry. Didn't know that."

"It's OK. Dru and I both grew up here but didn't really see each other much until she got divorced about a year ago. Her ex immediately moved to Minnesota and already has a new family."

"Good-looking girl, although not quite as striking as you."

Never having been one to take compliments very well, I could feel my face heat up—and it was unexpected coming from Jeff.

"Yeah, right," I said sarcastically.

"You're not going over to say hello?"

"Well, no. This doesn't seem like a good time. She'll tell me about it."

Really, I wasn't so sure about that, but time would tell when I talked to Dru again. Then she got up and left in a huff. Tattoos drank a little longer and went back to the pool tables. I thought I saw him take a quick glance in our direction, but his look didn't linger. We found our waitress and left—my treat. Sam was looking down, wiping the bar top, and I walked by without saying anything. Once we got to our cars, Jeff took off, but I sat thinking that Dru's choice of acquaintances seemed a little strange.

The fact was I really wanted to get a better look at Tats; the guy fascinated and repelled me, and I'd had just enough to drink to spur my curiosity into some action. I turned off my car and headed back to the bar again through the back door, heading straight for the women's room as if I'd forgotten to visit it before leaving. This took me next to the pool tables, by the way, but there was no sign of Tats in the vicinity. I did my thing and came out again but still didn't see him anywhere. It was time to give up, go home and get some sleep, so I hurried to the door.

Someone was pushing it open just as I was about to pull it, and the edge caught me right in the head. I saw a few stars for a second, and my purse clunked onto the floor. Tattoos began apologizing, but I wasn't hurt that badly, and we both bent down to retrieve my purse and some contents from the entryway. I was moving a little slowly, one hand on my bruised left forehead and the other trying to pick things up. Tats was handing me a compact and a few coins, and a groggy view of his muscular right arm came into view; I tried not to stare too hard. The snake's tail ended in a point on the back of his hand, and the graceful body wound in even coils up to his rolled up T-shirt sleeve, where presumably the head was hidden underneath. A black band of some sort paralleled the snake in the same coiled pattern, reminding me of something I couldn't place at the time. The big man helped me up, and I saw a very large chest—he was about a foot taller than I was. I looked up at the face. It was handsome all right—that was obvious even in the dim light. But the mouth was almost a lipless thin line that seemed to be smirking.

"Sorry, lady," he said. "I guess sometimes I get in too big a hurry to get in here. You OK?"

"I'm OK—just needs a little ice."

"Need help getting to your car?" He had stone-hard eyes.

"No, thanks." I was already walking toward the parking lot. "Thanks anyway."

"Well, hold on a sec," he said, pointing a finger in the air.

I got in the car and started the engine, blinking my eyes and trying to get them to focus properly. Tats emerged from the back door and ran toward my car, holding something in each hand. My stomach gave a lurch until he got near my window and I realized it was a cloth and a bottle of beer. He signaled me to roll down the window, so I did, and he offered me both, but I just took the cloth, which had ice in it. I thanked him and drove off, steering with one hand, holding the cold ice on my forehead with the other. My head was throbbing. I wondered what Tats had been doing outside the bar.

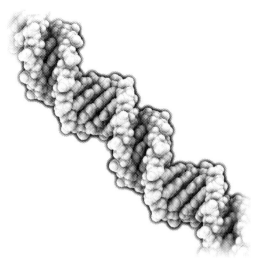

CHAPTER FIVE

IT TOOK ABOUT FORTY-FIVE MINUTES for me to drive home, back to the only permanent place I'd ever known. It was the two-story brick Tudor where I grew up, in an old independent upscale neighborhood in the middle of the city. Having left town for my residency training, I had returned for my fellowship, moving into the empty place after the car accident. It was too big and in serious need of updates, but it was paid for, and I couldn't bring myself to sell it. Despite my mother's sometimes-wild spending habits, my parents had also left me around three-hundred thousand in a bank account and a small insurance policy. Dru calls me incredibly lucky.

The place has two old fireplaces that I love, one in the living room and one in my father's office/study on the first floor, but I have never gotten past artificial logs and started an actual real fire. I still use my own bedroom, but the cheery yellow walls have been replaced with black wallpaper that has golden sun faces on it. It reminds me of a slightly spooky Venetian *carnevale* and is strangely soothing.

I put my Explorer in the attached garage and went in the house and up to the bathroom to assess the damages. A rather dejected-looking woman who reminded me of my father stood at the mirror, her long, dark hair looking a little stringy and the greenish eyes looking slightly bloodshot.

The straight bangs were wet on the left side, and I pushed them away to examine a nice bruise on my temple, but nothing to write home about—nothing to worry about. A glass of wine and a hot bath would make things better, and I got ready for both, settling with relief into the almost painfully hot water. My hand went to my right shoulder, gently feeling it with my fingertips, just as I always did in the bathtub, touching the old slight ridges and furrows of the burned skin. At the age of five, I made the mistake of pulling on the handle of a pot of boiling water on the stove. Luckily for me, only my right shoulder got seriously burned; I rarely wear anything that shows it.

My cell phone rang in the distance, but it was downstairs, and I ignored it. When I checked it before bed, there was a voice mail from Dru. All she said was "Call me when you get a chance," in a nondescript voice. Figuring it could wait, I crashed into bed.

My head greeted me the next morning with a slight throb in the left temple, but it was tolerable, and I smeared a bunch of concealer over the bruise. At least it wasn't a black eye. I put on my usual blouse, sweater and pants—my wardrobe was pretty minimal. I had no time or inclination to buy much.

It was another busy day on the leukemia service, and I ran into Jeff during morning rounds, but there was no time for shooting any bull. Driving home later, I realized I hadn't remembered to call Dru, but the phone rang before I could dial her. It was Dru, sounding out of breath and unlike her usual laid-back self.

"Cuz, I'm really, really sorry, but I've run out of willing babysitters tonight, and I desperately need someone to watch the kids for a few hours. You know I wouldn't normally ask you to do this, but could you please, please do me a huge favor? The kids are already fed and just need to get ready for bed in a while."

What could I say? It's not like I had a social life. A quick stop at home was just long enough to change and pick up a book. Dru still lived in the small, two-bedroom bungalow she and her ex had bought in a '60's style neighborhood north of downtown. Forty minutes later, I pulled up to her place, wondering what her urgent business was. Another meeting with Tats, maybe? I wanted to ask her about him—some other time. I needed to warn her about running into him in doorways.

Dru was halfway out the door as I was walking up the stairs to it. She looked preoccupied and in a hurry.

"The kids ate—I already told you that. Their pajamas are on the beds—just put them on and get them to bed when you can."

That didn't sound encouraging.

"Help yourself to anything you can find in the fridge. I'll be back as soon as I can."

She was gone before I could get a word out. I'd wanted to tell her what my hourly rate was and that she probably couldn't afford me.

Inside, Clint and Woodie were in their room playing with their Wii game-thing. They were doing the bowling game and forced me to play with them. Now I'm not a bad bowler, though I seldom bowl now, but I used my best form to toss the ball with the little remote device and did miserably. Clint and Woodie just threw their arms in the air with wild gestures and hit a strike or spare most of the time. Go figure. They laughed at all of my gutter balls, and I became their favorite relative.

After I had finally talked them into getting ready for bed, Clint let me put his pajamas on him with little trouble. I was beginning to think kids were OK after all. Then Woodie took off his clothes and ran naked into the hallway bathroom. I waited patiently for him to do his thing, but after waiting about five minutes I went to check on him.

Little Woodie's sense of modesty obviously had not kicked in yet, since he just gave me a big grin when I opened the bathroom door and found him standing in front of the toilet holding his little wee-wee. I couldn't help laughing at the sight of him. He shook off his little organ, and then he proceeded to do a very strange thing. He held it between his thumb and small forefinger and began guiding it in a slithery, circular motion, or as much of a motion as the small organ would permit. I just stood there, watching with some fascination. He looked at me for a reaction, and when he didn't get a reprimand, he continued, adding a few vocals to the performance.

"It's a *snake*, Auntie Claudia, a snake. The snake's gonna *bite* someone. Hiss, hiss, hiss."

My stomach did a flip.

Trying not to sound too serious, I asked, "Where in the world did you hear that?"

He thought a second and finally said, "I dunno," and shrugged his shoulders.

"Did you hear it from Mommy?"

He just giggled and sidestepped me at the door, running back into the bedroom. I followed, and he began fumbling with his pajamas, eventually getting them on. It became clear that the subject was changed as far as he was concerned, and I gave up asking, not wanting to push the issue with him or mention it in front of Clint. But where in the hell had *that* come from? I wondered. When they were finally in bed, I turned the light off and closed their door nearly all the way.

Suddenly my hunger had vanished, but I scrounged around and found an open bottle of white wine, then sat in the living room, thinking hard and drinking the wine too fast. Surely Dru couldn't have told Woodie about what had happened to me, I kept thinking.

Impossible.

But it couldn't be a coincidence, could it?

No way.

Then he had heard it from someone else.

Who?

I'd need to ask Dru. When she walked in that door, I'd have to say, "Dru, did you know, by the way, that your five-year-old son thinks his little pecker is a snake that bites people? How'd he get *that* idea?"

The absurdity of it all made me laugh softly, and I got another glass of wine, drinking more slowly with the second, thinking that probably babysitters shouldn't get drunk. I looked around the room but didn't see anything of much interest. Being unable to concentrate on reading, I noted Dru's closed bedroom door, suddenly wondering if it might be locked.

A minute later, I got up and tried it. Closed, yes. Locked, no. It wasn't an open invitation, but, hey, cousins share things. I opened the door and found the light. The ceiling fan was still on, creating a soft breeze in the room, and the bed still had the bright blue spread I remembered, with clothes scattered over it in no apparent order. The closet doors were open, and a few shoes were spilling out. I sat on the bed, thinking of some of our silly times together growing up, then got up and looked at her chest, seeing only the usual things on it. It had six large drawers, one partially open. I closed the open drawer neatly, lining it up in its proper place; then

I opened it. I then proceeded to open them all and look around, feeling wildly guilty about the whole thing, not knowing what the hell I was looking for. At one point, I checked on the boys again to make sure they were asleep. They were.

Back to the drawers, and nothing exciting until I ran across a box in the sixth and largest drawer, a pretty lacquered black and red box with a red tassel on the lid over the keyhole that was immediately recognizable, since I had one exactly like it—a gift from our uncle to each of us when we were small. The box was from Japan—a music box that played a plinky Japanese melody. I shook it gently; there were things inside. Not knowing if it was wound up or not, I took the box into her bathroom and closed the door. The box was locked, and the top wouldn't budge despite some gentle prying and jiggling of the lid. It occurred to me that I'd seen the key recently—it was the small one I'd noticed on a chain around her neck when we were at Sam's, and she probably still had it on. I wondered why. It's not like the lock was very sturdy, but I didn't want to break it. But then, mean auntie that I am, I figured if I *did* break it, she'd probably think Clint had done the deed.

I looked at the back of it, remembering some intricate metal hinges attaching the lid to the bottom. They were attached to the bottom of the box by the tiniest of screws that could be unscrewed if only one had the tiniest of screwdrivers, like the kind that are used to fix sunglasses. I didn't have one but *did* have a possible substitute in my purse—a Swiss army knife with several little gadgets on it, the most important of which I'd thought was a corkscrew. I walked to the couch and got it, then pulled out the smallest blade and tried it on the screws. It worked, but the first screw was short, popping out and bouncing off the floor and into oblivion. Good work. I was more careful with the other three screws, letting them fall onto the bedspread where they could be retrieved. The bottoms of the hinges were free, and I pulled the lid gently up from the back, the front lock preventing me from getting much of an opening. After some shaking of the box, a fine silver metal chain partially dropped through the narrow opening, and I used my fingers to gently pull out more of it. Several inches came out, but then I had to pry the opening a little more to get some larger pieces of metal out. Then the whole thing was in my hand—a delicate chain holding two pieces of metal, each about two inches long.

I pulled the chain up in my hand, letting the pendants swing freely. They gleamed and pinged against one another, sounding almost musical. The feel of soft white hair brushed over me, and I felt dizzy. The pendant to the left was a series of four arches, all the same size but of alternating colors of silver and gold metal. The pendant to the right was a snake, its head at the top—mouth open wide, large fangs showing—his body a series of arches like the other pendant. I put one in each hand and brought the two pendants together. They locked into one another, forming a perfect, though bizarre, double helix.

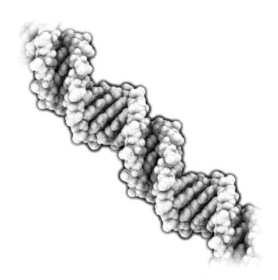

CHAPTER SIX

I FORCED THE NECKLACE BACK into the box through the crack and spent the next half hour getting the hinges back on, minus one screw. My brain was a bag of frustration trying to handle the tiny screws, but the small pair of forceps embedded in my army knife helped to hold onto them. The hinge that was missing a screw was a little wobbly, but I didn't think Dru would notice or she would think it had come out on its own. I shoved it back in the drawer and returned to the living room couch, my glass loaded up with more wine, which she probably *would* notice was nearly gone.

I was hoping it would help me think—or just not care about what was going on. It did neither, and I felt like a kid who'd just lost her mother and dad for a second time. Quirky though she was, I'd trusted Dru, maybe trying too hard to replace the feeling of family that had been lost. After all, childhood friendships and promises can only go so far; then girls grow up, and the one thing that can break a trust comes along with a force that's impossible for some of us to fight.

Men. A man. However you want to say it, the trust becomes a fragile thing and becomes secondary to any sexual relationship. That *had* to be what happened to Dru. But how did it all fit together?

Did she or did she not know Chance?

Where did Tattoos fit in?

Should I or shouldn't I confront her with all this?

Where the hell was she now? What was so damned urgent?

Enough games. I would load it all down on her when she walked in the door.

Waiting, I tried in vain to read. Finally at midnight I tried her cell phone. It went to voice mail, and I didn't leave a message—she would know why I was calling. Sometime after that I dozed off, worried about being too exhausted to work in the morning and a little worried about her. At two a.m. I awoke and left a voice mail message for her to call me right away.

Nothing.

At ten to four her car pulled in, and she walked in the door with her head down and her long hair in a tangled mess. Her smudged lipstick made her lips look big and grotesque. Her eyes had a pleading look.

I didn't say a word, waiting for an explanation.

"Please. I'll talk to you tomorrow. I just can't go into it right now. Are the boys OK?"

That question scared me a little.

"Yeah—fine. I was just worried sick—you didn't return my calls."

"Sorry. I really owe you. Let's talk later."

I gave up, too tired to argue, more than relieved that she was all right.

"OK, later. I need some sleep, anyway."

As I walked out to my car, the air now felt pretty nippy, and the wind was blowing hard from the north. I got on the highway, not looking forward to the forty-minute drive—maybe a little shorter at four in the morning. The satellite radio was tuned to an investment channel, and it finally dawned on me that the conversation was centered on the Indonesian stock market. I leaned forward to turn the channel and found some ancient rock station I hoped would make me feel better and wake me up a little.

A bike swung into my rear view mirror, following closely on my tail, the roaring sound startling me for a second. I slowed down, thinking it would pass me by and be on its way. Instead it just stayed on my tail, irritating me with its intrusion into my thoughts. I slowed even more, but it didn't budge. That got me worried, and I accelerated fast, sliding over to the middle lane, going about 75. The bike followed me, not missing a beat. I kept up the pace for fifteen minutes, frequently changing lanes, only to see that the bike was always there, closer behind than ever. I tried to glance at the driver—it had to be a male—all in black. Black leather jacket, black helmet. Strangely, he had glasses on in the middle of the night.

Not sure what to do, I took the exit to my block, and he followed. Just what I was afraid of. I sped past my house, not slowing down in front of it and headed toward an icehouse that was open all night. Pulling to a stop in front of it, I jumped out of the car, ready to run inside.

The rider slowed down and glanced my way before speeding up again. He flipped off his glasses, but I couldn't make out his face. All I saw was a glimpse of white hair as the bike passed under a streetlight and made its way down the road.

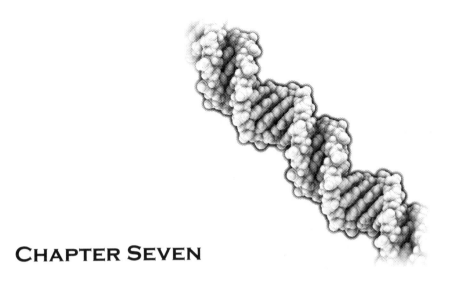

CHAPTER SEVEN

I LEANED AGAINST THE CAR in frustration. It had to have been Chance, but certainly not pure coincidence. So he was here. Friend or foe? He'd scared the crap out of me, following on the highway like that, so maybe the latter. I wasn't going to figure it out parked by an icehouse, so I finally got in the car and drove home, constantly checking my rearview mirror and seeing no bikers. Some of the extra-early morning commuters were making their way to work already. I jumped out to open the garage door (my father had never put an automatic opener on it), then drove in and closed it immediately. It was getting to be daylight already, and the worst of my paranoia was over. Still, I checked all the locks on the doors and windows before getting in the shower, having given up on getting any real sleep.

Just because I was extra-tired, the leukemia service went bonkers that day. Three new acute leukemias (acute leuks, as we called them) all needed long workups, lots of lab work and bone marrow biopsies. Mrs. Sapen had spiked a temp and didn't look good; in fact, she was pretty much disoriented. She asked me not to pull her teeth out, but they were sitting in a little container on her nightstand, so I said I wouldn't. Her daughter gave me a sad little smile, sitting by the bed holding her mother's hand. If nothing else, this profession sure takes your mind off your own problems.

At 12:30 I broke for lunch and saw Jeff and Jenna sitting in the cafeteria. In the midst of walking to another table, figuring they'd like some privacy, Jeff waved me over, and I thought I saw Jenna give him a funny look as I put down my tray.

"God, look at you," Jeff piped up. "Where'd you get that nice bruise on your forehead, and haven't you gotten any sleep lately?"

What a great guy—my pal Jeff. But that remark made Jenna perk up nicely.

"I ran into a door, and no." My mood wasn't improving. "Still want to eat with me?"

They laughed, and Jenna, once again feeling confident in her superior degree of physical attraction, excused herself to get back to the nursing station, but not before planting a sweet little kiss on Jeff's cheek. No engagement ring yet, though, I noticed.

"Seriously, though. You doing OK?"

"My weird cousin Dru talked me into babysitting last night, and she didn't show up until four this morning. Then some weirdo on a Harley or something chased me home on the interstate. I got no sleep at all, and I really did get hit by a door. I have three new acute leuks today, and I'm tired. That's all." And I said it all in a very calm, soft voice to show how well I was coping.

This elicited from him the pity that I was fishing for, and he offered to do the two bone marrow biopsies that hadn't been done yet. The guy was a saint. By seven o'clock I was home and exhausted. Dru hadn't called, but that would have to wait.

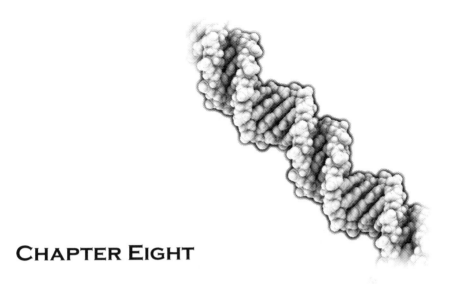

CHAPTER EIGHT

BY THE NEXT MORNING, I felt much better and made a concerted effort to look reasonable. A silky blue blouse might do the trick, and some creamy stuff shined up my hair. The forehead looked better after some concealer, and I combed my bangs over the bruised spot. At work, I had no new patients and spent the time following up on the old ones. There was some serious scouting to do.

At 3:30 I took the walk down several hallways to the molecular genetics lab. This area was part of a subspecialty department that had grown rapidly in the last several years, now with its own chairman and several technologists and researchers. Actually, it was in a new addition to the hospital, and the old painted walls gave way to bright murals and shiny marble floors. Ostensibly, this was a trip to check on some results on my patients, though it would have been just as easy to call for them. A sign in the hallway pointed to the Department of Molecular Biology, and I followed it to a set of double doors with a simple Laboratory sign on it. I walked in with my white coat on and didn't spot anyone who resembled a clerk. Two technologists were working at long counters that looked like an accession and processing area. The room wasn't large, and two doors led down hallways to other areas of the lab. A skinny woman in purple scrubs with stars on them looked up from her monitor and asked if she could help me.

"I'm looking for some molecular results on one of my patients, Mary Sapan—a BCR/ABL. I'm sure the FLT-3 and NPM aren't done yet."

This slush of alphabet soup was thrown in so she would immediately understand that I was no slouch in the field of molecular genetics. I saw her glance at my name tag, though, just to be sure I was official.

"Hold on a sec, and I'll check." She sat down in front of a monitor, pecking in the information.

Standing behind her, I watched her pull up my patient on the screen. A tall man came in through the hallway door, and I recognized him as someone I'd seen in the hospital a few times before, a striking-looking guy (forty-something?) with curly, slightly longish gray-black hair and brown eyes. Well built. Uh-Oh.

"Emily," he said, nodding as he passed by us, but he glanced at me.

"Hi, Dr. Palmer," was her reply, and my helper watched him make his way down the hallway before she got back to me.

So that was Dr. Palmer. And my dear pal Jeff had deliberately let me think he was the short guy with the mustache.

The tech gave me one result and said it would take a week for the rest. I acted surprised. It was a positive BCR/ABL result for the Philadelphia chromosome translocation.

"Are you sure this is right? This leukemia doesn't at all look like a Philadelphia-positive acute leukemia, but I don't have any other genetic studies back yet."

She hesitated, and then went back to her screen to check again.

"Yes, that's the result, but if there's really a question about it, I could check with Dr. Palmer."

Bingo. That's what I'd had in mind. She disappeared down the hallway and re-appeared about three minutes later.

"Why don't you explain it to him—he might want to repeat it."

"Sure," I said, following her down a hallway lined by doors to specialized parts of the lab, past a door labeled "Cold Room," and finally to an office at the end of the hall. The plate on the door read "S. Palmer, MD, PhD, Director of Molecular Biology." A smaller sign beneath read, "Genes Make the Man." It sounded a little sexist to me, but I was ready to give this guy plenty of leeway. Unfortunately, my knees felt like rubber, and my stomach was churning. Two reasons: One, I wasn't exactly telling the truth about the lab result. It was probably correct, but I'd ask them to repeat it anyway, and believe me, it made me feel mighty guilty. And two, I didn't really have an exact plan. Admitting to this guy that there was a pair of frozen shorts I wanted tested sitting in a pizza box in my freezer was not something I was ready to do.

He was sitting at his desk and stood up when I walked in, introducing himself as Stephen Palmer and reaching out his hand for a shake. Emily exited when he glanced at her. The accent was there; Jeff had mentioned he was Australian. His hand felt big and warm—like Australia. I sat in the chair across from his desk and introduced myself.

"Claudia Ranelli—thanks for taking the time. I'm a Heme fellow. I just had a quick question about a test—a BCR/ABL—but I really don't need to waste your time about it. Emily said you could repeat it, and that would be fine." I was talking fast and losing my cool. The whole thing felt like a mistake. Behind him was a wall of the usual certificates and degrees from his training, one from Johns Hopkins and one from MD Anderson. For some reason, I'd assumed he'd trained in Australia.

"Believe me, it's not a problem. Obviously it's really important to get that one right. We'll re-run it first thing in the morning. Do you want it re-collected?"

"No. Don't bother; I drew it myself."

I really didn't want the poor lady stuck again.

He seemed to be looking at me a little too intently, as if trying to make out the color of my eyes or something. I realized what was coming, and my head got hot.

"Are you by any chance related to Dr . . . ."

"Yes," I interrupted him, nodding my head rapidly, fighting off the mist trying to get into my eyes. He sat back, obviously realizing it wasn't my favorite question. I pulled it together and sat up straighter.

"It's all right. It still takes me by surprise that so many people knew him."

"He was certainly highly respected—one of the best in his field. I heard him speak several times. Personally, I think his book was greatly underappreciated; I read it more than once."

That was a lot more than *I'd* done.

"Really. I hate to admit it, but I just don't know that much about his work, strange as it may sound. He was gone a lot and didn't talk about it at home. I've barely glanced at the book. I've always figured it was beyond *my* comprehension."

"Well, I'd be happy to explain some of it to you sometime, if you're interested. It's fascinating work."

I was beginning to relax by then. The guy was actually very nice. Did I dare look? Trying to do it as discreetly as possible, I glanced at the left hand. No—no ring. Not always a reliable finding, but sometimes it was indicative of the marital status.

"Divorced, no kids," he said, and we both laughed while my face got red. Obviously, I wasn't going to pull any wool over this guy's eyes.

We chatted a few more minutes, and he showed me around his research lab, where I recognized one of the third-year Heme fellows. It seemed I really *had* taken up enough of his time by then, and I went back to the hospital, with Dr. Stephen Palmer promising to call me with the results ASAP. When I left, my spirits felt slightly buoyed for some inexplicable reason. I certainly hadn't accomplished all I'd set out to do, but something told me there might be another chance.

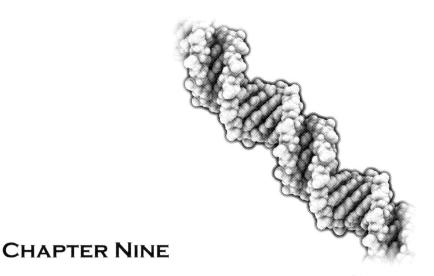

CHAPTER NINE

WHEN I DROVE HOME THAT night, I still felt an inexplicable high after talking with Dr. Stephen Palmer, until I started to recount all of the things I needed to worry about. There was Dru. We had to talk. Answers were needed. If Chance was around, I was determined to confront *him*. But not that night. I drove into the garage determined to have a relaxing evening and to avoid answering any phone calls, text messages, e-mails or voice mails—to have some peace.

After catching up on bills, I had a nice dinner of wine and popcorn. My phone didn't ring until nine o'clock—the landline—and I hesitated, listening to the flat female caller ID voice pronounce "Palmer, Stephen." Despite worrying about sounding like a wino, I answered on the fourth ring.

"Hello, Claudia?"

"Yes," was all that came to mind.

"Well, this is a little awkward, but I was wondering if perhaps you might like to join me for dinner on Saturday night—that is, if you don't already have plans. I'll have test results by then, and maybe we can discuss that along with some lighter topics."

He didn't waste any time. But I sure wasn't in any shape to get into anything other than dinner and some conversation. I needed an out.

"Ah, it just so happens that my social life is not overwhelming right now, and Saturday night is free. Can I meet you somewhere?"

Not subtle, but safe.

"Ah, sure. That would be just fine. I was thinking about a small place at Marshall and Haven called Renoir's. Do you know it?"

"Yes. Sounds great."

We set the time for eight. Then I began to worry about it. My plans included bringing home some sterile gloves and other supplies and making my sample more presentable, if it even got that far.

I wandered into my father's office, a small room off the entryway that had the second fireplace in the house, a nice room that I had seldom been in except to dust. The smell of his pipe tobacco still lingered—maybe in my imagination—and the room made me sad. I'd avoided going through most of the shelf and desk contents with the exception of finding papers and documents that were really necessary, but now I sat in his desk chair and looked around. Four boxes in the corner still held some of his work office contents that I hadn't gotten around to putting away. My high school graduation picture was on a bookshelf, along with one from their wedding. A few sticky notes with some scribbling on them were still stuck to the corner of his desk. I walked over to the bookshelves and browsed the books I'd glanced at many times before—mainly fiction, oddly enough, for a man who was so into science. He loved to read Sherlock Holmes, and the complete collection was on a shelf. I'd given away most of the books from his work office. Two copies of his book were on the middle shelf, where I knew they'd be. They were heavy volumes with a blue cover inscribed with the title *Mechanisms of Mutation Induction in the Human Genome*, by Antonio Ranelli, PhD. I pulled out the copy on my left, opened the cover and saw the inscription. It was to me, Claudia, with his love. I'd never read the book, never even tried to get to it; it intimidated me, and my mother had called it a waste of my time.

"Get a life," she'd said. "Don't waste it in some lab playing around with rats and flies."

In fact, I'd studied only the minimum amount of genetics needed to get my training, knowing the avoidance was mainly because I figured I could never match his stature in the field, afraid that I'd be a real disappointment to both of us. So I took an entirely different track to a specialty that was oriented more toward real people, so I thought. I wouldn't be holed up in some lab for most of my life, as my mother would have put it. It had been obvious that my mother spent much of her time resenting the long hours he put in at work and traveling, but then that might be expected of someone who lived to go out and socialize. How they paired up was a puzzle to me, but she was pregnant when they got married. Also I never figured out how much she resented giving up most of her career to be a wife and mother. To her credit, she never said a word that made me think she regretted having me.

Thumbing through the book, I saw nothing that seemed unusual; I'd need to ask Stephen Palmer what was so impressive about it. On page 319, a purple sticky note was stuck to the side of the page. Scribbled on the note was what looked like the letter M, and under it was the word "modification."

The phone on his desk rang, scaring me out of my silent concentration. I slammed the book shut and checked the caller ID. It said "Wireless Caller." The number didn't look familiar. I let it go to voice mail, but whoever it was left no message. It could have been any kind of benign call, but my paranoia was replicating itself at a high rate. I walked over to my father's safe behind one of the doors on the bottom of the bookshelves—the combination memorized years before. I pulled out the gun. It was a black 9mm Beretta with a brown handle, and on the handle was a little brass plate engraved with the name *A. Ranelli*. He'd taken me to shoot it once, and I hadn't been too bad, but that was at least five or six years ago, and I had no permit to carry it. After turning off all the house lights and double-checking the door and window locks, I went up to the bedroom and locked myself in. I put the gun under the mattress on the far side of the bed.

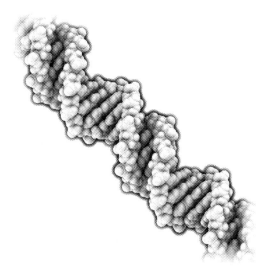

CHAPTER TEN

FRIDAY WAS A NICE DAY with some breathing room at work, and I had lunch with Jeff and a second year fellow, Julie Jennings. Jeff called her JJ, and she called him JD—his life was plumb full of J's. I didn't know Julie that well, but she knew how to keep a conversation lively, and her gabbing helped to keep my mind from veering to painful thoughts. She was from Oklahoma, apparently from a well-to-do family in the oil business, as they say, and she was definitely out to find Mr. Right—or probably Dr. Right, who knows? Anyway, she didn't make any secret of it around us, as she interrupted our deep conversation about the length of bone marrow biopsy needles.

"Now there's somebody I'd sure like to invite over for dinner," she commented, looking at the far end of the cafeteria where people were walking in with their trays.

Not facing that direction, I didn't feel like turning around and staring at anyone.

Jeff piped up, "Oh, Palmer? I don't think he's so hot. You like 'um that *mature*? I heard he's kind of *kinky*. Heard the ex-wife accused him of some weird stuff."

I dropped my fork.

"What do you mean, weird?" I asked, trying not to sound too interested and hoping Stephen Palmer wasn't on his way to our table. It wasn't likely, but you never know.

"Don't know exactly—just the rumor mill. I got it from Jenna, who claims it's not firsthand information. She didn't name her sources."

Julie put her chin on her hand, still apparently following the movements of Stephen Palmer.

"Well, hon," she said to Jeff, "I think I can handle that. I'd sure as hell like to give it a try—and find out the meaning of kinky."

By then, it was apparent that there was no need to worry about Stephen joining us, and I sat back and listened to a little more banter between Jeff and Julie, wondering if he might be a little jealous of the imposing guy who was the head of molecular biology. Julie had suddenly become a focus of my scrutiny, and I found myself looking for faults that would make her unattractive in his eyes. She was a tall girl, with lots of wavy brownish-blond hair and nice, big eyes that were actually a beautiful shade of blue that glistened when she was in an animated mood, like most of the time I'd seen her. Twenty pounds or so looked like excess baggage to me, but then some guys like that—and plenty of it was in the boobs.

Jeff gave her a smile, leaning back in his chair and crossing his arms.

"Well, I dare you to ask him out—or over—or whatever. And find out about the kinky part."

Julie just smiled back at him, got up and walked off toward the door. I turned around for the heck of it to see if she'd stop by Stephen Palmer's table, but she kept on going. He was deep in conversation with another staff doctor. As we walked out, I kept Jeff chatting, pretending that I didn't know my Saturday night date was in the large room. Besides, what would I have done? Smiled? Winked? My Saturday night plans were better kept to myself.

Before leaving for the day, I managed to grab a specimen bag and some sterile gloves and scissors from the nurses' station.

At home that Friday night, I crashed after watching some weird movie on the Sci Fi channel. A late night call to Dru's cell phone again went straight to voice mail.

"Hey there, what are you Druing? Give me a call."

It was an old joke between us, and it was my way of letting her know I wasn't still mad and really wanted to talk.

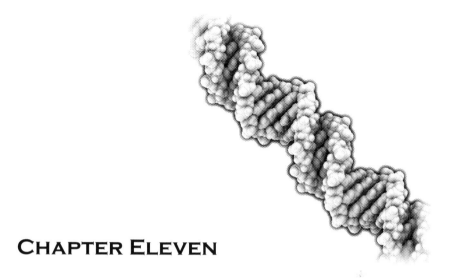

CHAPTER ELEVEN

MY TREMENDOUSLY BULGING AND PAINFUL bladder finally forced me out of bed late on Saturday morning, after a fitful dream about running into strange restaurants and finding they had no bathrooms. Later I grabbed a cup of coffee and perused my closet for something suitable to wear to a high-end restaurant like Renoir's. This felt pretty much like a waste of time, since I only had two dresses that I liked, one black and one purple—for some reason, the idea of wearing a dress was stuck in my head. The black was the one I'd worn in San Francisco, and the thought of wearing it was not particularly appealing. It had been dry-cleaned and the button replaced, and I pulled it out for the hell of it, examining the skirt carefully for spots. None was apparent, and I threw it over a chair. I pulled out the purple—not quite as depressing as black—and gave it a quick pressing.

Later, when I was checking my cell phone, there were still no messages and no e-mails from Dru. Lunch consisted of a few nibbles, and then I finally decided to open the freezer and get out the pizza box. The shorts were still in their plastic bag, looking a little stiff. Lord only knows what they had touched by that time, but still I put on the gloves and unfolded the shorts to find the spot. Using the sterile scissors, I cut as wide a swath around it as possible without giving away the fact that this was part of a man's underwear. They might guess that anyway, but why make it easy? I stuck the piece into the specimen bag, sealed it and put it back in the freezer in the pizza box, where it would stay until Monday—if things worked out.

After showering and dressing, I thought the woman in the mirror looked passable. The dress was a little low-cut, but on me the cleavage was really minimal. My hair was long and shiny-dark, and I figured I could let it fall into my cleavage if a need for modesty overwhelmed me. A short gold chain around my neck with a man in the moon on it and finally some small gold hoop earrings were my last attempt at image improvement. I was as nervous as I ever get. Before leaving, I grabbed some black-framed glasses that really do nothing for my vision, but a sudden urge not to look too overdone came upon me. I didn't want him to think I was on the prowl. Call it self-defense.

Renoir's was a good five miles from my house, and normally the interstate would be the logical route to take, but that night I'd thought of everything that had happened and decided to get paranoid again. I backed out of the garage and onto the street, looking around for a while to see who or what might be in the neighborhood. It was dark and a little hard to see, but no unusual vehicles were apparent in the vicinity. I just really did *not* want to be followed on this particular venture. Obviously being no expert on ditching a follower, I thought I did a pretty decent job of weaving around some of the local streets and alleys before assuring myself that no one was following. Then I took some smaller roads all the way out to the restaurant, adding at least a half hour to my drive time. By 8:05 I was at the restaurant and parked in an inconspicuous area of the lot. Then the glasses went on.

I'd been to Renoir's a few times before with my parents on some special occasions. It was set in a woodsy strip center, with a somewhat plain-looking exterior, but the inside was quite posh, with long, blue velvet curtains and a deep brown and blue carpet. White tablecloths, of course, and several sparkling glasses and silver were standard. And it was dark and quiet, with tables set into nooks and corners for plenty of privacy. Perfect.

Walking in, I didn't see Stephen in the entry. The maître d took me to his table in a quiet corner, where Stephen stood up to greet me. He looked awfully good in a dark sport jacket with a white shirt, the collar open at the neck, as he shook my hand and seated me. I decided to ditch the glasses.

He steered at the start; I went along for the ride. A nice bottle of red wine helped me get relaxed; it was his favorite from Australia.

"Ah, before I forget. Your patient's test turned out the same result."

I tried to act surprised and suitably contrite for making him repeat the test, but I had the strange sensation that maybe he could see right through all this. Just a feeling. I changed the subject.

"So, how did you say you knew my father?"

This wasn't my favorite subject, but I was curious.

"Well—yes—I met him at a dinner meeting the first time. We were at the same table, and I was still a resident. This was at a meeting in Boston, quite a while back, of course. He made quite an impression on me. I believe he was working for a private laboratory by that time. What was the name of it?"

"EraGen Labs. He was there . . . a long time."

Until he died.

"Oh, of course," he said. "They have a branch here."

"Yes, he opened it. He was at the university for a while many years ago, but he left to work with them. How long have you been here?"

"Not quite three years now. I was at Hopkins for a while. I left after my divorce; it's easier that way." He gave a small, wry smile.

Yeah—especially if you're into perverted sex. Still, he seemed pretty normal. His brown eyes looked soft in the dark light, reflecting the deep color of the wine. I kicked myself for getting way too distracted and soppy.

We had a superb dinner. There's no recollection in my mind of what I ate, but it was great. I asked him about Australia, growing up there— then told him of some relatives there I'd never met—in Perth. My dad's cousins, maybe. Word was they owned gold mines, and I was anxious to meet them. He laughed—he had a great set of teeth. Into my second glass of wine, the nerve to bring up my question finally surfaced.

"Dr. Palmer . . ."

"Stephen," he gently corrected.

I took another sip.

"Stephen."

He nodded, probably thinking I was drunk.

"Suppose, just suppose that . . . Well, this is really more than a supposition. I happen to have a sample—I guess probably a pretty good but *small* fluid sample—*probably* body fluid, that is—anyway, a sample that might prove really interesting with regard to genetic findings. Well, I'm not *sure*, but it *could* be. Really interesting."

I think I winced. Did that sound stupid, or what?

"You're talking about a human sample, I assume?"

"Human? Yes." I nodded my head. "It *should* be human. But that's one of my questions."

I hoped it was human. He sat back.

"And what do you think might be so interesting about it?"

This was making me feel like I was in a father-child conversation, and he was being very patient with his seven-year-old.

"I think the sample might show one or more very unusual mutations—on the other hand, it might be totally normal. I really think it's worth checking out, at least with some kind of screening test."

"And is there anything else you can tell me about this *unusual* sample?"

He seemed to be enjoying questioning me about it.

"Not right now." I tried to convey a pleading look.

"That's not much information to proceed on. So you want to confirm it's human DNA, if the sample contains DNA, that is—and, it would probably be a very small quantity. Proving it's normal is a much tougher proposition because you're talking about looking at the entire genome, a much more complicated and expensive undertaking."

I guess I gave him a disappointed look.

"We could start with the human question, though. I suppose I could do the daughter of a colleague a favor. We could do a quick screening test that takes a couple of days to detect the presence of variations in nucleic acid sequences, if that's what you'd like. If that's positive, though, you're going to need to tell me more, because the testing gets a lot more complex from then on. Where's the sample?"

"In a freezer. I could bring it in on Monday. Could we keep this—confidential?"

"Of course."

That was too easy. He sat back and was quiet for several seconds. It occurred to me that he'd just realized what I'd been after from the beginning.

The conversation became a little stilted after that. Just before we got up to leave, he said, "Thank you so much for sharing your Saturday evening with me. You'd probably prefer friends your own age. I've actually been seeing a woman for the last several months, but she's out of town this weekend."

This hit me like a ton of bricks, and I started to feel sick to my stomach. We left, and he walked me to my car in a deserted part of the lot. It was dark. I must have looked totally depressed. Actually, it was a strain fighting off tears.

We stood by my car, and he turned me to face him.

"Claudia," he said in a quiet voice, putting his hands on my shoulders. "You have the air of a very sad person, someone carrying a large burden that she doesn't really want to talk about or share. I heard how your parents were killed, and I'm sure that's incredibly difficult to get past, especially when someone brings up the subject of your father. But this thing with the sample testing—you're being very cryptic and probably less than honest about it, and if you're in some kind of trouble, I hope you can eventually tell me about it. I'll do it, but I'd appreciate some honesty from you when you're ready."

A tear slipped out, making me feel incredibly stupid and embarrassed. I dropped my head down, and he wrapped his arms around me, giving me a big, warm hug, which I appreciated—and gave back. I guess I wanted mounds of pity and got it. He gave me a soft kiss on the forehead, wiped my eyes with a finger, then the hug went on. I wasn't sure what to do next, but the seconds went by, and I decided to un-hug and just go home. One can take only so much pity. As I looked up to say good night, his lips moved down to my mouth and began a long, slow kiss that started some dormant hormones roaring through me. It lasted more than a minute, and then he pulled me even closer, and we could really feel each other. I finally had to break away. Not that I wanted to, of course, but my body wasn't healed—not physically and not even mentally, although the former was the larger problem. I put my hands on his arms to try and let him feel that my reluctance in going further wasn't because I didn't want to.

"I really appreciate the dinner tonight," I said and hoped it didn't sound gushy. "I guess I *am* still pretty depressed about them, but I've got some other problems that need to be worked out. Maybe you could give me some perspective, but I just can't bring myself to talk about it yet."

He nodded in seeming understanding, but who knows what he was thinking.

"Bring your sample in Monday morning," he said, as he closed my car door for me.

I drove off, leaving him walking back to his own car, then took the smaller roads back to the house, pounding my hands on the steering wheel in frustration. I wanted a warm body near me in the night, and his would have been comforting, indeed. Such is the fate of the snake-bitten.

Once home, I drove into the garage, then pulled down the door, thinking I needed to stop putting off my overdue project of installing an electric door opener—the next Saturday, maybe. The door was halfway down when the roar of a bike barreling down the street hit my ears. As I ducked under the closing door, I saw him speed by. Maybe I saw the shock of white hair—or maybe just imagined it. I slammed down the door and locked it.

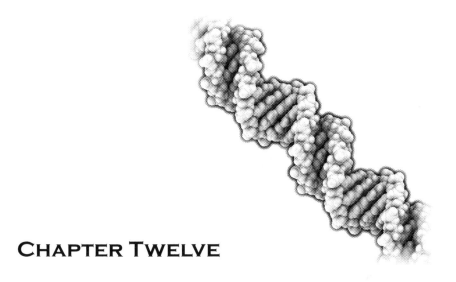

Chapter Twelve

I HAD A TOUGH TIME getting to sleep that night. I finally got up and took some over-the-counter sleeping pills. Sunday was spent dragging around the house without showering or washing my hair, looking like some witchy creature from Harry Potter minus the mystical powers. I made a face at the reflection in the big hallway mirror, then peeked outside and noticed the front and back yards were getting full of leaves and made a mental note to worry about it. Dru still wasn't answering phone calls, so I tried a text message and e-mail. We hadn't gone this long without talking in quite a while.

Wandering back into the study, I started mindlessly dusting the shelves, then got to the boxes in the corner and decided maybe it was finally time to start going through them to see if anything was worth keeping. I took everything out of four boxes and began sorting things out on the floor. There were books, file folders, loose papers, some ring binders, several CDs, a calculator, and some desk paraphernalia. A framed picture of the three of us in the middle of St. Mark's Square was the same as the one sitting in their bedroom—a small girl stood in the middle, looking like she was afraid of the pigeons. My mother looked angelic, with a white lace shawl draped over her long dark hair. My father had a mustache and looked like a native Venetian. The books and picture went on the shelves; the files were left on the floor to go through when I felt more like doing it.

By Monday morning I was feeling a little less funky and managed to get myself suitably cleaned up, but almost left the house without my sample and had to run back to get the pizza box while the car was running. I took out the plastic bag and put it inside another bag with some ice in it, figuring to drop it off at Stephen's lab first thing.

At work, I stuck it in the big pocket of my white coat and headed for the molecular lab as soon as rounds were over. Wouldn't you know, only a technician was there; she informed me that Dr. Palmer wasn't in yet. Not wanting to leave it with her, I carried it around in my bulging, cold pocket. There were two new admits to take care of and no time to make it to lunch before the Monday conference was ready to start. I hadn't had time to review any of the cases and prayed Dr. Still wouldn't call on me to say anything intelligent. Jeff caught up with me just before we went in the door, and we sat together in some side seats I hoped were obscure. The room was a small semicircular amphitheater, with the speaker standing at the bottom of several tiers of seats. Jeff had a crumbly cookie at the bottom of his lab coat pocket, and I gulped it down gratefully to keep my stomach quiet. Julie and two residents sat down one row from us.

Dr. Still came in and started a discussion on acute myeloid leukemia with some colorful pictures but didn't dwell on it for long. I hadn't noticed until then the tall, attractive doctor in the white coat sitting across from us and down in the first row—Stephen, wouldn't you know. Still flicked on the lights, and I saw Stephen looking at us with no apparent facial expression. I looked back, then looked down as Still introduced him and he gave a talk on molecular testing in acute leukemia.

His talk was smooth and succinct, lasting a reasonable thirty minutes. I was impressed, and Julie looked like she was drooling. Still talked for a few more minutes, and Stephen sat through the rest of the conference, looking our way once in a while. Still gave us a break and didn't ask any questions. I decided to look down at my lap most of the time. My pocket was getting wet.

Jeff and I were close to the door and left together, walking down the long halls and chatting.

"Is it my imagination, or was he staring at us?"

"Who?"

"Palmer."

"Dr. Palmer?"

"Yessss. You know who I mean. Do you know him? Weren't you asking about him the other day?"

"Yeah. You said he was a short guy with a mustache."

"No, you said that."

"Well, you led me to believe that."

"So, did you go and talk to him?"

"I stopped by his lab last week."

He looked down at my coat.

"Your pocket's all wet."

"So are you."

He gave me a friendly nudge on the arm and went toward our office. I finished what I had to, replenished the ice in the bag, and finally around five o'clock called the cell phone number Stephen had given me on Saturday night. He was in his lab and asked if I could stop by around six. There was plenty to keep me busy until then. This time I knew the layout, and at six I walked past the main lab entrance and around the corner to a single door marked *Private, No Laboratory Entrance*. He'd told me this was the other door to his office, and I was glad to avoid going by Emily or any of the other techs who might still be there. I'd ditched my wet white coat and put the bag in my purse. Immediately following my quiet knock on his door, he opened it and led me to the same guest chair I'd been in before. I gave him the bag.

"It's a piece of fabric with a brownish spot on it—maybe blood or some other fluid? It's been frozen, but lord knows what it's come into contact with before then."

"Claudia," he said, "I'm doing this as a favor to you, and the results are just between us, if there *are* any results. I'll run it myself as an unknown. I'm sure you're familiar with any patient confidentiality issues."

"Of course," I said. "This is purely out of interest. No one's confidentiality is at stake."

He just stared at the bag and said he'd take it to the lab and be right back. Just then his cell phone went off, and he pulled it out of his pocket to check the call, then apparently let it go to voice mail. He opened the door to the lab and closed it behind him. I waited about ten minutes, hearing remnants of a dim conversation coming from the lab. He came back in and closed the door, then sat on the corner of his desk, right smack in front of me, folding his arms on his chest, shaking his head like a scolding father. I didn't at all like being in the position of having to look up at him.

"I'll see what I can do with it."

Feeling too stupid to ask any questions, I just sat there. But he had a quirky little smile on his face, and when I noticed it, my face started to heat up.

"I just have one question about the sample," he said in a very professional voice. "Are they Jockeys or Fruit of the Loom?"

I gave up trying to get anything past the man and put my forehead in my hand and laughed. What else could I do?

He stood up, and I had the feeling something was about to happen between us, but there was a knock on the hallway door to his office, and someone tried to open it. Apparently it was locked on the hallway side. Stephen shrugged his shoulders and got up, moving around the desk to open it. When he did, a tall redhead with skin-tight leggings, tall boots and a short jacket with fringes was standing there, one arm on the doorframe and the other on her hip.

"*Stephen*," she began, and then paused when she saw me sitting there. He turned around and excused himself, and they went into the hallway. All I could hear were a bunch of frantic whispers, mainly from the feminine side, and something about many phone calls and being worried sick. I wasn't sure whether to sit it out or leave through the lab door, since this was obviously the woman in his life who'd been out of town for the weekend—or maybe not. Who knew? There were probable many women after him. He finally came back in, and she followed behind, smiling nicely now.

"Sorry," he said. "I'm going to need to get going. Oh, excuse me, Ronnie, this is Dr. Ranelli. She works in the hospital."

He sounded nervous.

I smiled, pretending we were all just good buddies.

"Nice to meet you, Ronnie. I'm just on my way out."

But my mean streak suddenly popped up. In as serious a voice as I could muster, I looked at Stephen and said, "I'll have those tests finished for you in just a few days. Don't worry. With any luck, it's nothing contagious."

Stephen looked at me and rolled his eyes. Behind him, Ronnie gave him a very questioning look. Smiling, I walked out the door to the lab. Emily was at her monitor again, but she was obviously more interested in what had gone on down the hall. She watched me leave his office and walk by her, and I could see her catching a glimpse of Stephen and Ronnie still in the office.

"Holy shit," she whispered, as I walked out the door.

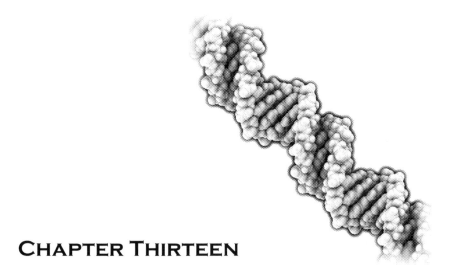

Chapter Thirteen

I DROVE HOME, CHASTISING MYSELF for spending so much time lately thinking about Stephen Palmer, who appeared to have as much female companionship as he wanted. But still, his help was needed in order to get some answers. Also, I'd about had it waiting for Dru to get back to me and found myself driving in the direction of her house. The traffic was heavy, and I got there at 7:30.

From the street, the house looked dark, but I walked up to the door anyway. No one answered the doorbell, so I walked around and peeked in the windows but couldn't see much. A look in the garage window, though, revealed the absence of a car. I decided to call her at the bank the next day and catch her at work.

The next afternoon, Jeff covered for me while I kept an appointment made with a gynecologist when I got back from San Francisco. I needed a follow-up exam, and she was a nice lady, probably in her sixties by now, who'd been a family friend for a long time, Dr. Katy Maxim, but I'd always called her Dr. Katy. I believe Dr. Katy helped my mother push me out. She was in private practice, gynecology-only now, and her office was in a strip center near downtown. I hadn't seen her in years but decided it was preferable to see a doctor in private practice for this particular visit, rather than a university doctor. It looked like she and her tastes hadn't changed much. A tall, slender but sturdy lady, she still wore her hair in a little bun on her neck, only now the hair was a blend of silver and deep brown. Her eyes were still the clear, alert jade color that I remembered, her face not pretty but pleasant and reassuring—her demeanor relaxed but confident. Her speech had always suggested the trace of an English accent to me, but I really didn't know much about her past. Never any lipstick.

She performed the exam with her nurse, and I heard her take a slight, rapid intake of air after she put in the speculum.

"Does that hurt?" she asked.

"No."

Not anymore. She took the Pap smear and some cultures. I had asked her to do cultures and testing for the usual transmitted diseases, including blood for HIV. So far, she hadn't asked why.

We met again in her office a few minutes later. She looked at me expectantly, so I asked, "So how does it look?"

"It's healing. There's no infection that I can see. With any luck, you'll still be able to have kids. What happened to you?"

"It's a weird story, but believe me, it won't happen again."

She looked at me, obviously hoping for more but willing not to push it.

"Do you need birth control?"

"No, but I'm almost out of pills, so give me more, just in case I get lucky."

"I'd definitely suggest a different partner."

That's what I liked about her—she was my idea of a true, non-intrusive professional. I left with my prescription, some samples and a promise from her to call me when the results were in. She also said to call her sometime if I wanted to talk or get a bite (to eat).

I liked Dr. Katy, and she had always seemed to like me. She had been some sort of friend to my parents, especially my father, but I don't think she ever knew that I had seen her with him in his office one night when my mother was out of town or gone somewhere; I don't exactly remember. I was supposed to have been in bed but went downstairs after hearing voices, catching a glimpse of her with her hand on his, the two of them standing by the lit fireplace. Aside from a few covert-looking glances between the two, I never saw or heard anything more that would suggest an affair, but I believe that Dr. Katy, who married only briefly, probably very much liked my father.

After the appointment, I remembered to call Dru's bank and ask for her. The manager informed me that Dru had the week off and wouldn't be back until the following Monday. I stopped in the office to drop off my coat and purse and scrambled back to the ward to catch up on things. By six o'clock I was making my way back to the office and found Jeff sitting at his desk, his cell phone to his ear in an intense conversation I tried my best not to overhear. Actually, someone else was doing most of the talking.

"Yeah. Well I . . . But that's not what I said."

"I do."

"I'm not sure that's a good idea."

"Look. Let's talk tomorrow. Someone just walked in."

Sure, blame me. He turned the phone off and had a sour look on his face, which I decided to ignore and got my stuff together to go home.

"I don't feel good," he announced. "I'm constipated, and my beer and pizza levels are dangerously low."

"Well, I don't do enemas, but you know a nurse who could help you with that. I could start an IV and give a beer infusion."

"The nurse and I have a problem, as you just heard. I could really, really use a friend for a quick beer and pizza tonight. Think of all the favors I've done for *you* lately."

"Oh, God, I'm really beat. Tomorrow's a work day, and I'm on call this weekend."

He gave me his most pleading look.

"Oh, all right. But it needs to be fast. And don't expect a bunch of sympathy."

"How about if we stop at that bar you like. Sam's, right?"

I thought about it for a second. That might not be such a bad idea. It was certainly a possibility that Dru might be there. We decided to meet at Sam's.

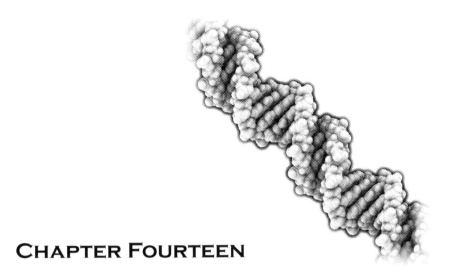

Chapter Fourteen

SAM'S WASN'T PARTICULARLY BUSY ON a Tuesday night, and it didn't take me long to figure out that Dru was not around—neither was Tats. The only person I recognized was Sam himself, who seemed to be chatting with some guy at the bar while wiping some bar glasses. Sitting at the same table we'd sat at the last time, I ordered a beer, looking at my watch periodically to assure anyone interested in watching me that I was certainly expecting some company. Twenty minutes later, Jeff still hadn't shown, and I was wondering if something at the hospital had held him up. After ten more minutes, I called his cell phone. No answer. Surely he knew enough to let me know what was going on.

Since I wasn't in the mood to start eating alone, I got up and walked to the bar. When Sam put a beer in front of the guy sitting there, I gave him a little wave and sat down on a stool.

"Sam," I said, putting on my best bar-friendly tone, "I don't know if you remember me, but I was in here one night with my cousin Dru."

"Oh, yeah, sure I remember. The whiskey-sevens. Ya need another one?"

His double chin bounced a little when he talked.

"No thanks." I laughed. "I've got a beer. But I was just wondering if you'd seen Dru here lately—haven't heard from her and . . ." I shrugged my shoulders, not knowing exactly how to put it. He stared at me for a second.

"Dru? No. Ain't seen her in, oh, maybe a week. At least. She comes in once in a while, but she ain't a regular."

He started to concentrate on drying the glass in his hand, like it was a cherished piece of fine crystal.

"Well—how about the guy she hangs around with sometimes?" This was a stab at the truth. I'd obviously only seen her with him once. "The guy with the snaky tattoos on his arms? What's his name?"

Sam slowed his wiping and seemed to glance around the big room for a few seconds. He shook his head.

"Think I know who you mean," he said, giving the air in front of him a pensive look. "But I'll be damned if I know his name."

I didn't leave the bar with a feeling of much satisfaction. Sitting back down at my table again, I checked my phone, but still no calls from Jeff. After another thirty minutes, I finally gave up. The waitress who'd served my beer showed up, and I paid her off, but before leaving, I caught her on the way to one of the tables and asked her about the big guy with the snake tattoos. She told me they called him Jonesey but she'd heard somebody call him Jer or Jerry. I don't know why—maybe it's my honest face—but she added, "He gave me a credit card once, and if my memory serves me right, and sometimes it does, honey, the name was Jeremiah King. The name stuck with me for some reason. He was good-looking and just didn't look like a Jeremiah."

Yeah, it fit a nice bullfrog but not a guy with snakes.

I left with more things to worry about. Not to mention the fact that Jeff hadn't shown up or called, but the name King had popped up again. A common enough name in the area, for sure, but was it pure coincidence? Chance King instead of Munroe? Jeremiah King. Leaving through the back door, I gave Sam a little wave but really wanted to give him the finger. I opened the door to a major downpour of rain and got soaked running to my car. Once on the freeway, the visibility was miserable, my wipers frantically in motion but unable to keep up with the torrent. I realized I should have waited for it to ease up.

My phone went off, but I couldn't be distracted with the call. Several cars had pulled to the side, but that looked a little hazardous too. My stomach was flipping out as I strained to make out the white lines on the highway. A big truck in front of me took the next exit, and what looked like a bike took its place. I could barely see the taillights as it swung in front of me, but then it turned its hazard lights on. It was impossible to make out the driver, let alone tell whether he had white hair sticking out of his helmet, but I had the feeling he did. Following at a safe distance behind, I decided to find out.

A minute later, he took my exit, and it became obvious he was headed for my neighborhood. I followed him down the streets to my driveway, expecting him to turn in and finally let me get a look at him. Instead, he took off down the street, gunning the bike. I thought maybe he gave a wave, but visibility was still bad. It wasn't a good night for pursuit, so I gave up any thoughts of that.

When I got in the house, my phone made the little text message noise.

"Cuz," it said, "Back in town in a few days. Sorry for no answer. Don't talk to anyone. D."

Well, that was just great. Now I was really worried. I dialed her cell number, but of course she didn't answer—then I checked my voice mail. There was a message from Jeff.

"Sorry, Claude," he'd said. "Something came up. Talk to you later."

Right. I went to bed, disgusted with everyone.

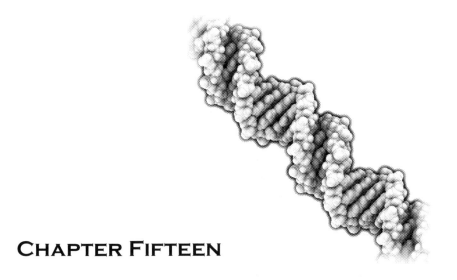

CHAPTER FIFTEEN

GETTING INTO WORK AS EARLY as I could make it on Wednesday, I was anxious to give Jeff a hard time about standing me up and wondered if it had to do with Jenna. Love has a habit of overriding common courtesy. After a donut and coffee in our little office, by 8:30 I had to give up and start rounds with a new resident who'd come on the service. He was a tall guy named Luis, who immediately apologized about not knowing much hematology. I told him he was at the right place to learn quickly and wasn't complaining. We made our way around the ward, and Jeff's resident was there—but no Jeff. I had to ask.

"Jeff around this morning? I need to talk to him." I tried to give it a serious medical tone.

The guy shook his head, looking a little frustrated.

"Haven't seen him, haven't heard from him. Maybe he forgot to mention an appointment or something." He shrugged and moved on down the hall. There wasn't much I could do at that point but finish rounds with the resident and get him up to speed on my patients and the therapy protocols. Around noon, Luis stayed to read protocols, and I went to grab some lunch. Stopping by the lab where Julie was doing some research project, I got her to go with me. I wanted company.

We got to the cafeteria, and she must have put ten things on her tray. The girl had an appetite. I had some soup.

"How's it going?" I asked, great conversationalist that I am.

"*Bor-ing*. Not one good-looking guy around that lab." She stuck with that theme for a good five minutes. "Next year I'm going to try and get a spot in Palmer's lab. At least I'll have some good scenery, even if I don't know jack about molecular genetics."

"Go for it," I said. "But put on some tall boots, tight pants and a fringy jacket. That'll get his attention."

She gave me a questioning look, but I pretended it had just come out of the blue.

"I can do that," she said, and I believed she would.

It was time for a change of subject.

"Jeff hasn't shown up yet today. He wasn't supposed to be off that I know of."

She stopped shoveling.

"Are you worried? You sound worried."

"No. Just pissed. And curious."

"What's been going on? You two aren't—" She gave her face a funny little contortion. "Are you?"

"*No*. Nothing like that. It's just that I walked into the office after work yesterday, and it sounded like he and Jenna were arguing about something on the phone. Then he sounded like he wanted to talk, so we made plans to meet somewhere for a beer."

"OK. Then what?"

"Well—I got there and waited—over an hour, then finally left. My phone rang when I was trying to get home in that torrent of rain we had, and I had to wait until later to take the voice mail. He just said something had come up and he'd catch me later."

"Huh," she laughed. "Something probably came up with Jenna, and I bet she had a good time with it."

"Yeah. That's the last time I commiserate with *him*."

"Let me know if he doesn't show up or call today, though. I can sound out Jenna when she comes in for her shift, if she's working today."

I went back to work, and Jeff didn't show. At five o'clock I called Julie, and she got back to me a half hour later.

"Well, hon, I talked to her. The news is strange. She hasn't heard from him since he left work yesterday, although she's not too surprised after the argument they had. But she's worried now, since he's obviously not at work. She's tried calling and texting, but no answers. She plans on stopping by his apartment when she gets off, or earlier if she can find someone to cover for her. For the hell of it, I checked with Still's secretary to see if Jeff had called in or scheduled time off, but she said no. She asked me to get back with her tomorrow if he couldn't be contacted. I also took the liberty of checking with the other local hospitals, but no one was admitted with his name or description that I can tell. So there we are."

"Ugh," was all I could say, feeling guilty that she'd done all that when I was one of the people working most closely with him. Not to mention the fact that I might have been the last person to see him. Julie realized that.

"By the way, I didn't mention to Jenna that you two were meeting last night. No point in bringing that up right now. He'll probably show up later or tomorrow, and we can give him hell for getting us worried."

"I'll kill him."

I worked late, spending time getting the new resident familiar with the patients and workflow—worked until I was so tired I could go home and crash from exhaustion, too tired to think about missing doctors or cousins or of bizarre sexual encounters.

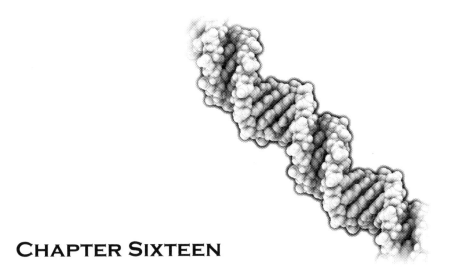

CHAPTER SIXTEEN

I GOT IN EARLY AGAIN on Thursday, anxious to hear any news. About anything, really. Stopping by Still's office, I found it still locked, so I moped around our office for a while. There was no sign of Jeff. After staring at his desk and empty chair for a while, I got up and took a closer look. The desk was littered with his usual junk: books, mail, lab and other reports, some charts, and a few sticky notes with writing that could hardly be interpreted. Stuck on top of a pile was one of those "While You Were Out" notes, and I wouldn't have paid much attention to it except that it was dated for "Tues PM". Under that was a local phone number. It could have been Jenna's.

I copied it into my phone notes, just for the hell of it, then rounded up my resident, and we spent four hours doing rounds, which were interrupted by one admission. In an unusually helpful gesture, one of the senior staff was helping out Jeff's resident. When I finally got the chance to stop by Still's office again, his secretary, Linda, was on the phone looking frazzled. She signaled me to wait a second and then finally got off after five minutes.

"I'm sure you're wondering about Dr. Dunn," she said, giving me a sympathetic look. "Dr. Still plans on meeting with you and the residents soon for an update on coverage if he doesn't show up, but about all I can tell you is that we haven't heard a word about his whereabouts, and we plan on talking with his parents today. We'll contact the police if necessary, and we're hoping for the best. We really appreciate the extra work the rest of you are putting in." She gave me a little arm squeeze.

I went back to work, and ten minutes later Julie called me.

"Hey," she said. "Can you get a quick bite?"

"I've had one of those, thanks. Could we get some food instead?"

She sounded confused, then laughed unconvincingly. Only Dru could appreciate my biting humor. We met in the little hospital coffee shop for pastry and coffee. I wondered if I was talking to Julie too much—I really hardly knew her. She was sitting at the counter when I got there, dunking a huge thing dripping with white frosting and cinnamon into a cup of coffee.

"What's up? Don't tell me *that's* your lunch."

"No. Dessert. And no good news, I'm afraid."

My stomach curdled. "Tell me."

"Well, Jenna said she went to his place last night—she has a key, by the way—but there was no sign of him and no car. He doesn't have a home phone, so there weren't any messages she could retrieve. She talked to a few neighbors, but they didn't know anything. She wants to notify the police, but I think there's probably not going to be a need for that."

"What do you mean?"

"I mean, and you must swear to keep this to yourself . . ."

"Yeah, sure."

"Well, my daddy knows a lot of people, and frankly, neither one of us is shy about taking advantage of that sometimes."

"Annnd?"

"Well, he knows one of the high-up mucky-mucks at the local police, and he got me some inside, very confidential information that'll likely be in the news as we speak, anyway."

She polished off the pastry and gave her finger a big suck.

"It seems the police found a badly mangled car that went off the road and down a steep hill into a woodsy area between 281 and Kendalia. Seems the license plates are registered to Jeff. Funny thing is, the car is empty. Nobody inside or nearby, far as I know."

"I wonder what he was doing out that way? Any blood inside? Any signs of trauma?"

"Don't know. That's all I heard."

"Guess I should tell the police about my conversations with him last night."

"Well, I'm not so sure I'd rush into that. We have no idea of the time frame of all this. That could put you right in the middle of a big investigation if this turns out to be something unusual, and there's really no need for that. After all, you had nothing to do with what may have happened to him. Think about it."

I was. But his phone would have my number under the recent calls list, and his phone could possibly be found. It might be important to know what time he'd called.

I worked late again and drove home feeling as dark as an old bloody emesis. And alone.

There was a message from Dr. Katy on my home phone—I was probably getting special treatment because of the old family-friend status.

"Hi, Claudia. It's Dr. Maxim—Katy. Just wanted to let you know your lab test results are normal. The Pap's not back yet. I hope you're doing well. Give me a call when you get a chance."

That was good. No AIDS, no bad diseases. She sounded nice and maybe a little concerned, but I didn't feel like talking to her. Ten minutes later my home phone rang, and the caller ID said "Palmer, Stephen." I picked it up while walking over to pour myself a glass of wine. I anticipated an uncomfortable conversation.

"Claudia. Stephen. Can you talk a second?"

"Sure. I just got home. Trying to wind down after a heck of a day."

"I'm sure it was. I just heard about your friend Jeff on the news. What a strange story. They found his car in a ditch? God, I hope he turns up—alive. I guess that's not the greatest way to put it, but it sounds like there's no sign of him so far."

"My God, I hope he's OK," was all I could think to say. My depression level was rising quickly. He picked up on that.

"Are you doing all right? I know this has got to be hard on you. Do you need to talk? It's difficult being alone sometimes when these things happen."

"I'm hanging in for now, thanks. Concentrating on work is not easy."

"Listen. I've got some test results I'd like to discuss with you, but I'd really rather do it in person. And I'd like to see for myself how you're doing. What's a good night for you? Tomorrow night? Saturday night? Just tell me, and I'll make the time."

I wondered what the deal was. Was fringy Ronnie out of town again? Was it a fatherly concern? Feeling a mean streak, I suggested Saturday night, to totally break up his weekend. He took the reins from there; I figured I owed it to him.

"Good. Meet me at the lounge at the Exeter. Is about eight-thirty all right?"

That was a small, quaint old hotel downtown, and a bit of a drive, but the atmosphere might be a nice change. Anything might be a nice change. Without a pause to think about it, I agreed.

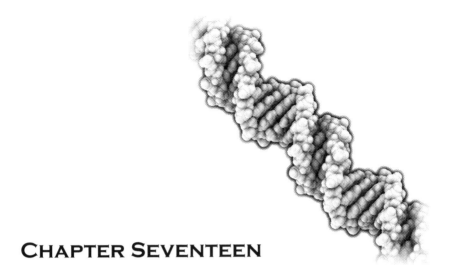

CHAPTER SEVENTEEN

FRIDAY WAS CRAZY. WELL, WHAT did I expect? Jeff was officially missing, and our shared office space was closed off, since his desk was being examined by some detectives who were nosing around. At Still's office, various people were milling in and out or just standing around, scrounging for information or wondering about being questioned. Julie and some other fellows and residents were standing at Linda's desk, so I waited behind them, anxious for some news. Julie finally turned around and spotted me.

"What?" I said, shrugging my shoulders.

"Not much." Her eyes looked baggy and tired. "Seems like info is hard to come by. Our boy hasn't shown up anywhere. To top it off, no one can get a hold of any relatives. His father is on his records as his closest relative, but the phone number belongs to somebody who doesn't know either one of them. They're working on it."

"No brothers or sisters?"

"Nada. Did you know much about him?"

"Not really. I think he said he was an Army brat—moved all over the place growing up. Did he say his father retired in Houston? I just don't remember for sure."

"I really barely knew him either," she said. "Funny thing is, Jenna doesn't seem to know much more than we do. She has no idea where his family is. Says Jeff claimed they didn't get along all that well."

"So what's happening?"

"The detectives here this morning are going to interview some of us, including you, I'm sure." No surprise there. "You'll get a page to go to the conference room in Still's office. No telling when that'll be. Still's working on a new schedule for coverage. I'll probably get bumped back to the wards at this rate." She shook her head and left me there.

Dr. Still himself walked in a few seconds later and made a little finger gesture for me to follow him into his office. I sat in the familiar purple leather chair I'd been in when interviewing for the fellowship position eighteen months before. He was a pretty good-looking guy of about fifty, medium height, with white hair and a receding hairline—and always a snappy dresser. And then there was the personality—a sense of humor that sometimes bordered on the obnoxious, but it kept the students, residents and fellows in stitches when someone else was the target for embarrassment. Luckily his biting humor and questions were generally directed at the males in the groups, I suppose to dodge any problems with sexual harassment issues.

That day, he was in a rare serious mood. Of course, we discussed how worried we were about Jeff, but Still was consoling me about the shortage of coverage for the service and thanked me for working so hard. He told me about the police interviews that day.

"I know you're seeing patients all weekend," he concluded. "The senior staff and I will help to pick up some of the workload for the time being. Just to show our support, I'll take call this weekend if you come in and do rounds with me on the patients."

I thanked him profusely, since I'd been scheduled to be on call. Being able to sleep through the night would be a big relief.

It was two-thirty in the afternoon before I got the page for my police interview. Wiping my palms on my coat, I headed into the small meeting room adjacent to Still's office, where Linda had directed me.

"There's two detectives in there, Garcia and Schmitz. So far, everyone's come back out alive." She smiled.

Very funny.

They were seated at the far end of the long conference table, a chunky guy with brown hair wearing a sports jacket, and a dark-haired woman in a navy pantsuit, sitting with a small laptop propped in front of her, typing quickly. The guy did most of the talking, motioning me to sit in a chair by the door. The glass-topped table felt cold through my white coat, as I rested my arms on it. A stethoscope was draped around my neck (which I never do), just to remind them how busy and important I was.

"Dr. Ranelli?" the guy began. "We're detectives Schmitz and Garcia, and we'd just like to ask you a few questions regarding your colleague, Dr. Jeffrey Dunn. We understand you've worked pretty close with him. I assume you've heard that he's missing, and his empty car was found in a ditch outside of town."

"We're hematology fellows on the same service—ward, that is—so I've seen him just about every day lately, if that's what you mean by working closely."

The guy obviously was going to do the talking.

"So, when did you see or speak with him last?"

My stomach started knotting. "Tuesday. Tuesday after work." I decided it was best to plow right into it. "We'd both finished seeing patients and doing our work for the day. Actually, he asked me to meet him for a drink at a place here in town—and get something to eat. I agreed, and we made plans to meet at Sam's Bar. I got there before he did, waited over an hour, but he never showed up."

Then I explained about the missed phone call from Jeff and the voice mail message. I took out my phone and showed them the message. He listened to it, and his partner took some notes after looking at my phone.

"And you haven't seen or heard from him since?"

"No—nothing."

"So what do you know about this—doctor colleague of yours? Where was he from? Any relatives? Anything unusual?"

"You know, I talked to him quite a bit on this service, but to tell you the truth, I hardly know anything about his personal life or family. He just never said much, and I didn't ask. He has a girlfriend, as I'm sure you know by now. We had no personal relationship outside of the hospital, except that we had a hamburger one time at Sam's about a week ago. Most of the time we talked about our work here."

They asked a few more questions that got us nowhere, and I was beginning to relax a little. The guy looked up and smiled benignly.

"So who do you know who might want this guy *dead?*"

My stomach flipped.

"Dead? Is Jeff dead?"

The guy put up his hand toward me, palm facing outward in a calming gesture.

"Sorry, doctor, calm down. I'm just asking a question. Right now we have no idea about his whereabouts or physical condition. Do you know of anyone who might want to harm him?"

That sounded like one of those baiting questions—the kind they ask the guilty guy on the TV shows.

"No. Like I said, he didn't talk much about things outside the hospital. But I sure as hell hope he's all right."

"We'll be in contact if need be," he assured me as I got up to leave. "Call me if you think of anything more." He got up and handed me a card.

I stuck it in my pocket without looking at it.

"And I'd sure appreciate knowing if you turn up anything, Detective Schmitz."

"We'll be in contact with Dr. Still," he assured me. "And I'm Garcia, by the way. My partner is Schmitz."

Schmitz finally looked up and gave me a little wave as I started walking out the door. I stopped suddenly, remembering the phone number I'd jotted down.

"I just remembered something. Did you find a sticky note in our office—on top of a pile on Jeff's desk? It had a local phone number on it, and it was dated from Tuesday. I saw it there yesterday."

They looked at each other, and finally Garcia spoke. "We did find a note with a number on it. Do you remember the number or did you recognize it?"

"Not really," I said. "It had no prefix, I remember, so it seemed local."

That was true. I didn't remember the number, but it was in my cell phone notes. I figured it was enough that they'd found the note, and I decided to leave it at that, anxious to get out of there and not wanting them to think I'd been snooping around Jeff's desk like some jealous girlfriend.

I worked nonstop with the residents the rest of the day in order to catch up, and Still actually found us later on the ward so we could familiarize him with some of the patients. It was eight-thirty before we made it back to see if our office was once again useable. It seemed all visitors had gone, and no one was around the place. Exactly what they'd done around Jeff's desk wasn't really apparent, except that things were arranged differently, and one drawer was slightly open. I sniffed around the desktop, afraid to touch anything. The note with the phone number that had been there on Thursday was indeed missing.

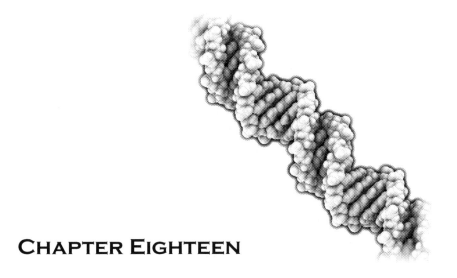

CHAPTER EIGHTEEN

I WAS UP AND READY early on Saturday but didn't go into work until later than usual, which made me feel unbelievably antsy and worried about my patients. Dr. Still called, and we agreed to meet for rounds later in the morning. The garage door guys showed up around eight-thirty to put in the automatic door opener, and a security system company showed up around nine. After getting them started as quickly as possible, I took off, leaving the whole house to them, along with my cell phone number. I grabbed my standard silk blouse number two (this one in Emerald City green) and a little bit of jewelry (my mother's pearls and earrings) and shoved them into the car, not knowing if there would be time to get back home and change before meeting the wizard.

Finally on my way, the local radio announcer reminded me that a norther was due to blow in that afternoon, and I'd forgotten to bring a decent jacket. I decided not to worry about it.

Working like crazy, Still and I did quick rounds (he was in a hurry too), getting orders written and reviewing labs and x-rays. It wasn't as fun as it used to be. Around twelve-thirty, Julie showed up on the ward, asking if she could help with anything.

"What in the world are you doing here today?" I asked, surprised to see her.

"Oh, I had to come in and read data on some tubes I started incubating yesterday, so I thought I'd stop by and see how it's going here. Got time for a quick lunch?"

"Oh, God, I'm snowed, and I'd really like to get out of here today."

But she had a disappointed look on her face, and she hovered. There was obviously something on her mind—maybe she wanted to talk about Jeff. Anyway, I gave in, and we headed for the cafeteria and sat droopily in a far corner.

"Heard anything new?" I asked.

"Nothing. And I don't think they've found any family yet. Weird."

She didn't look up at me, and her appetite wasn't the usual ravenous. It surprised me that she'd get so depressed over Jeff. She nibbled a little more, then finally asked, "You seeing anyone lately?"

Uh-oh. Now how in the hell would she have heard anything already? Deciding not to go there, I played dumb.

"No, not really." Whatever that means. "How about you?"

"No. You *know* who I'm interested in."

That I did, and the conversation was getting me a little irritated. It really was my business, not hers. And it wasn't actually a relationship at that point.

"You mean Palmer? Have you invited him to dinner yet?"

For some reason, this seemed to tip her over the edge, and she looked up at me, her blue eyes transformed into cold agates.

"Yeah, as a matter of fact I have, and we had a great time and fucked each other's brains out. Want the *details*?"

I looked at her, almost gagging on my food, astonished at the transformation.

"Just stay out of my way," she added. "You got that, honey? There's no way you could hold on to him."

My head suddenly felt like a hot furnace.

With that, she grabbed her tray and got up to leave, but not before her iced tea spilled and splashed all over me. She turned and left, her face crimsoned with jealousy. I still couldn't figure out how she knew—really couldn't believe she'd seen Stephen. After trying to dry myself off with a paper napkin, I sat there, still surprised at her vehemence.

Then my knife and fork started vibrating, and I watched her forgotten cell phone moving along the table, an iPhone in a pink rubber case. Don't ask my why I did it—it was unusual behavior for me, but she'd pissed me off. Picking up her phone, which apparently wasn't locked, I looked at the caller and number displayed on the screen. It was no one I recognized and not a hospital call, and I let it go to voice mail.

Then I looked at the number from Jeff's desk I had stored on my phone and used her phone to dial it, using the caller ID blocking on her phone. It rang six times before there was an answer. Finally a female voice sounding pretty lifeless said, "To proceed, please enter your sequence."

I held my breath, but no sounds ensued, and after several seconds there was only a dial tone. I put her phone back on the table and left, but not before deleting the number from the Recent Calls list. I went back to work, wondering if maybe she'd follow me to see where I was going that night, but that seemed a little extreme. The thought of calling Stephen and telling him I just couldn't make it occurred to me, but I wanted some information from him, and I was determined to get it.

It took me the whole afternoon to get through everything, and by six I was sitting in the office I'd shared with Jeff, feeling exhausted and still wondering why Dru hadn't shown up. Another call to her went to voice mail—again. The garage door guy had called and said he was finished. The security people said they had some more wiring to do and would finish on Monday, so they'd left and locked the doors behind them.

The hall by the office was empty and quiet, and I got up, closed the door and looked at Jeff's desk again. The charts that had been stacked up were now gone, presumably filed away where they belonged. A few books were still sitting on top. Grabbing a Kleenex off of my desk, I wadded it over my fingers before opening the drawers—which were pretty much empty except for a few loose hospital-issue pens and some paper clips. I closed them the way they'd been. The books were professional standards, the top one a clinical hematology text. Sticking out of it was a makeshift bookmark looking like some kind of schedule. I opened the book and looked at it—just last season's football schedule from A&M. Had he gone to A&M? Maybe he was just your average male football fan—there were plenty of those around. Some of the capital letters were underlined, but there seemed no rhyme or reason to it. Still, the oddness of it gnawed at me. Finally giving up, I closed the book but then pulled out the schedule and stuck it in my purse, feeling a burst of sadness for whatever ill had befallen my friend. My eyes were getting foggy.

I decided against driving home at that point. I ran out to the car and got my change of clothes, freezing in the arctic air that had blasted in. I ran up three hospital floors to the operating rooms to change in the female doctors' "lounge," which is a nice word for an old bathroom and shower with a tiny little sitting area that housed two worn couches and a small television. Various green scrubs and some paper booties, caps and masks were in their usual spots, rumpled and spilling from some shelves in a corner. The place was deserted. I flumped on the couch and turned the TV on to catch the news, sitting in a half-daze, listening for anything about Jeff. My phone made the text message sound.

"so sori bout lunch. Pls frgiv this idiot. Talk soon. J."

Well, of course I forgave her, but at that point I was feeling a little guilty myself and didn't really want to talk any time soon.

"frget it," I sent back, and put my phone on vibrate.

A shower seemed like a good idea after a day of spilled tea and some heavy sweating under my white coat—the armpits were bad. I found a small stick of slightly used deodorant by the sink and smeared it on when I was through. Looking around for something to make me smell better, I was disappointed to see that no one had thought to leave some perfume, so I sprayed on a little air freshener left near the commode, which made me smell fresh but a little piney; then eventually I was on my way downtown.

Being in a continual paranoid state, I drove around several blocks and down a few alleys before heading toward the hotel; I couldn't see anyone following and finally parked in the underground hotel garage. The hotel bar was a sleekly remodeled place done in black, white, and silver and overlooked the lit up river. The bar lights were dim, and I had to wander around for a few seconds, finally spotting Stephen sitting in a very relaxed pose on a black leather sofa in a far corner, his arm over the back, the other hand holding a cell phone he was staring at. An empty chair was next to it. My first major decision: couch or chair. I headed for the chair, and he stood up, jamming his phone into his pocket and giving me a half-smile as I dropped into it. As usual, he looked good but casual in some khakis and a blue shirt open at the neck.

"Green suits you," he said with the same half-assed smile.

I wondered what he meant by that.

"Sorry about making you drive all the way over here, by the way, but some friends of mine are staying here for a meeting, and it was handy for me. I met with them this afternoon."

"No problem. I like this place." I really did.

"I'm having a single-malt scotch," he said, raising a small cocktail glass that looked half empty. "Ever had one?"

I had, and surprised him by ordering a Glenlivet, neat.

"My mother's favorite," I explained. "She'd leave them around the house, and I'd sample them." I immediately regretted putting it that way— it sounded alcoholic-like, but he didn't seem to ponder the statement.

"Sorry I never met her. I heard she was a beautiful woman and very talented."

I was also immediately sorry to have brought her up at all. The scotch came, and I took a big sip, then had to stifle a cough as the strong stuff hit my throat.

"Well, yes—I guess. My father met her on a trip to Europe. She was teaching music and singing with an opera in Rome. He loved opera and met her at some kind of reception."

"So she was Italian?"

"From way back. But her family was from Argentina, and they moved to Florida when she was growing up. She spoke Spanish, Italian, and English. Before you ask, I can't sing a note, by the way. Didn't get that gene."

"You received your share of good ones." He gave me one of those smiles they call "warm." We needed a change of subject.

"Sooo," I said, cradling and squeezing my glass with both hands, "what's the word on my sample?" I was feeling stupid again, but the scotch was helping.

"Your sample." He sat back and looked thoughtful, swirling the liquid in his glass. "Your sample may be very interesting. I was able to extract some DNA."

"Really."

"In my lab, I have primers for the TP53 gene, the tumor-suppressor gene or so-called 'guardian of the genome' because its protein product helps to repair damage to DNA and to inhibit cancer development. I'm sure you're familiar with the cancer prognostic tests looking for TP53 mutations."

I struggled to think clearly through the scotch effects and managed a reasonable reply. "Sure. It's part of the workups for chronic lymphocytic leukemia and multiple myeloma, for example. A TP53 gene mutation is associated with a worse prognosis."

"Well, it just so happens that TP53 has also been used for animal species identification, so I did PCR amplification of the sample with some TP53 primers, then electrophoresed and analyzed the amplicons—the product."

I waited. "And?"

"It looks human."

Well, what had I expected? Honestly, I felt a little disappointed that it was ordinary human DNA.

"But I also found something more interesting."

Another pause, and he shook his head slightly and looked at me. I gave him a questioning look back, but my mind was already racing, predicting his next statement.

"This sample—this DNA—looks like it has an abnormal TP53 gene." He shook his head again. "I can't be sure—I can't say anything for sure. I'd need more sample—with the person's consent, of course. But you *know* the implications of the presence of a mutation."

I had a pretty good idea. Chance could have some type of malignancy or be at a high risk of developing one. It was all hard to believe.

Stephen broke into my thoughts. "Claudia, do you know who this sample is from?"

"No, not really," I lied. He looked perplexed, and I felt unbelievably guilty. "Sorry, Stephen. I just can't say anymore. But if I find out more information, I'll do the right thing, believe me."

Whatever *that* was.

"So there's no chance of getting more? I'd like to do more testing or some sequencing on it. Is this person still healthy? I'm interested in this mutation."

"Sequencing," I said, my mind starting to churn.

"Yes, sequencing, Claudia. As in adenine, cytosine, thymine, and guanine—and combinations thereof. But I need more sample. Any chance of getting some?"

A twinge of an important thought flitted through my mind, but it was gone before I could hold on to it. Scotch makes thought pathways very slippery. I forced myself back into the conversation.

"A *chance* of getting more?" I said, looking at him and smiling at the irony of the question. I shook my head. "That one was difficult enough to—*come* by, let alone get another one." But then, I thought, there was the guy on the bike who had followed me.

"Well—maybe there *is* a chance. I'll let you know," I said.

He looked at me, and I could guess he was disappointed and frustrated with my responses. A cloud of silence enveloped us for a minute while we sipped some more, and I felt myself sliding into a pit. Finally, he leaned toward me, his elbows on his knees.

"Claudia, I hope you don't take this as unduly critical, but I'm concerned about you. You have the air of someone about to enter into a deep depression, and I think you need to concentrate on some positive things in your life. You're a brilliant, beautiful woman with all sorts of possibilities in front of you. Make the best of it. Go after your demons or just leave them behind."

I cringed as he changed the nidus of the conversation onto me. An unexpected jolt of electricity shot through me as he gave my knee a squeeze, then sat back and ordered another round as the waitress in the short, tight skirt came by.

I thought about what he'd said.

"You're right. But things seem to have snowballed lately—out of my control."

I didn't really want to bring up Jeff, but that was certainly an opening.

"Yes, I know it's been very difficult for you at work with the disappearance of your partner." He paused and looked at me. "Were you two very—close?"

I looked back at his eyes.

"Jeff and I were friends. That's all. *Are* friends. He has a girlfriend, a nurse.

They got into a spat the night he disappeared, and I was supposed to meet him for a drink. He didn't show. He called and said he couldn't make it. That's the last I've heard from him."

"Look, there's nothing you can do about that situation; we can only wait and see what turns up—hopefully nothing tragic. You've told the police what you know, and now we hope for the best."

Well, not exactly everything.

My cell phone was in my pants pocket, and it vibrated, taking me by surprise and causing me to slosh a little of the precious liquid onto myself. Besides that, my eyes had gotten a little moist talking about Jeff and my miserable life in general. Stephen gave me what looked like a pitying look, and I pulled out the phone to see who'd called. Another text from Julie, of all people, wanting to know if we could meet for a drink. Yeah, what a great idea. I put the phone away and ignored the text. I had to quickly dig out a Kleenex to wipe my nose.

Stephen stood up and took a step to my chair, grabbed me by the arms and sat me down right next to him, pulling me close to his chest with his right arm. And like some little kid, I started crying again. I really had to get past that stage and toughen up. On the other hand, he was stroking my hair and saying something in my ear that made my skin tingle, so pity didn't seem so bad at the time. Pulling myself together after a minute, I glanced around, hoping I hadn't drawn any attention from other patrons at the bar—but it wasn't busy, and no one seemed to notice.

Stephen was talking into my ear in a low voice, obviously trying to get me to relax, talking about Australia (had I been there?) and describing the Sydney Opera House (your mother would have appreciated it). There was no way I could totally relax, not with his arm around my shoulder, wondering what his next step would be and how I would react. I was getting to the bottom of my second drink and running out of questions to ask about his home country. It was time to make a decision, and I decided it would really be best for both of us if I just got up and drove home while I still could. Like a mind reader, he seemed to anticipate this and spoke up first. He turned me toward him, forcing me to look at his eyes, sparkling in the dim lights.

"I really don't think it's a good idea for you to drive home."

He waited for my reaction. I couldn't make up my mind about what to say, so of course, like some stupid zombie, I said nothing.

"I'll be right back," he said.

I knew where he was going, and five minutes later, he was back.

"All I could get was a parking lot view, but I have a feeling we won't notice."

My hormones were working, but all sorts of old nemeses were rearing up, making me lose the self-confidence I felt was needed. Especially where he was concerned. It was so much easier to be around someone my own age, someone doing the same things, someone I could relax with—like Jeff, I thought, then realized I was being a coward and that Stephen was worth the effort.

I don't even remember walking to the elevator and going up to the room; I didn't want to remember the last time I'd done this with a man. Twice bitten? I didn't think so. Surely my luck couldn't be *that* bad.

The room was dark, with shards of light angling in from outside, and we left it that way. Then we simply turned and melded into one another, in a long, slow kiss from which there was no turning back. I don't remember breathing, and my body just responded willingly as I let him take charge.

He unbuttoned my blouse and pushed it off, then my bra. His hand cupped my breast, then my nipple, and I pushed it against him, taking a deep breath, suddenly feeling wanton. I felt his fingers rise to my shoulder, then linger and dwell on my burn scar and held my breath. His lips brushed gently over it, then up to my neck, and we were past the burn, not thinking about it again, kissing hard and long.

I unbuttoned his shirt, throwing it across the room, then wrenched his belt off and unzipped his pants, thrusting my hand into his underwear, grabbing his penis in my hand and messaging it until he groaned. It was more than a handful and extremely ready. He fumbled with my pants, and I finally helped him with the side zipper, then he pulled them down hard, along with my underwear. His fingers moved up between my legs, beginning to get me ready, but suddenly I could tell I was tight as a vise.

I glanced down, almost afraid of what I'd see. I slid my hand back around his wonderfully normal human organ that was soft and hard in just the right places and a size even Julie would appreciate, then wondered why I would even think of Julie at that point. He worked his fingers inside me until I could finally feel myself relaxing, opening up and aching for those particular muscle spasms imparting the feeling we live and die for.

Wet and craving him as he pushed it inside me, I held still at first, until he drove me crazy and I said, "I want you, Stephen." He began moving faster, and just a small touch from his fingers threw me into huge spasms, and I could feel him do the same. Sex has always been better for me when my hold on a relationship is most tenuous, and this was the best I'd ever had. We finally both lay back, panting, sweating and laughing a little. I could see him fairly well in the half-darkness—pretty hairy, but there was nothing I didn't like. After a few minutes of catching our breaths, he spoke.

"So how are you feeling now?"

"Actually, much better," I said, pulling a few strands of hair out of my mouth in the sexiest way I could muster. He laughed, then rubbed a finger along my shoulder and kissed it.

"What happened?"

For some reason, I was no longer feeling at all self-conscious about it. It certainly hadn't ruined my life and never would.

"Well, did you ever have the urge, when you were little, to pull on the handle of a boiling pot on the stove, just to see what it was all about?"

"No."

"Apparently I did, although all I remember are some vague memories of pain and being in the hospital. It kind of soured me on cooking."

"That's all right. There are some things you're very good at." And his fingers continued on down, rousing us both once again, this time more slowly, with incredible tension building until the end. And I felt no pain; no blood oozed out, and I felt well again. Shoving my demons into some thoughtless recess in my brain, I let myself totally succumb, at least for the night, to a man I barely knew but trusted. I could retrieve my perspective tomorrow, I thought, and it would come all too soon.

We slept sporadically, waking twice more to do the physical love thing, and when I got up to shower at six, Stephen joined me. I had to go back into the hospital to round on patients again or Still would start getting a bunch of phone calls. I left while Stephen was still getting dressed, but his shirt wasn't on yet, and he displayed two nice scratches I'd left on his back. We were both looking very sober, neither of us really understanding why, except that our relationship had taken an inexorable turn.

"We really need to have a serious talk about what's bothering you, Claudia," he said, looking at me hard. "No more putting me off if you value this relationship. I only want to help you."

Wondering what in the world I'd be able to tell him, I nodded, then left to retrieve my car and get back to work so I could finally get home from work. Suddenly I missed the house so much I could hardly concentrate on driving.

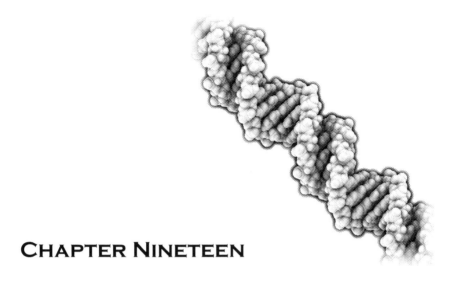

Chapter Nineteen

IT TOOK ME MOST OF the morning to get through rounds, forcing myself to concentrate on everything that needed to be done to prevent fires before Monday. A few of the patients were chatty, but my brain was lacking the ability to listen and retain, and nothing seemed to stay with me for more than a few seconds. Later I stopped at a few exotic places, like the grocery store, that I didn't visit very often.

I finally got home, feeling like I hadn't cleaned up or slept in days, despite the morning's shower with Stephen. After jumping out of the car, I just about pulled out my back giving the garage door its usual yank and forgetting that it was now locked. I found the opener in the house, then spent a few minutes marveling at the new technology. A long, hot bath came a little later, a soak in the boiling-hot water that nearly put me into a coma as it drained away all my energy. I got out, put on my bathrobe and went downstairs into my father's office, sitting on the chair with a light beer and rocking it once in a while (the chair). Some classical music was soothing, and I closed my eyes. When I opened them, they went to the familiar bookshelves, the blue genetics books standing out slightly from the darker ones on either side. My mind was slogging along through a haze, with no particular path in sight.

Genetics, I thought, talking to myself out loud and looking at the book. I should read it. How good was he at it, really? Nucleic acids—I liked the clickety-click sound of the words. Did Stephen think I didn't know what the hell they were? I knew what they were. Made from bases, plus sugar, plus phosphate. Mix four bases thoroughly and they will know how to complement one another, magically. Twist two strands in a right hand helix around the same axis, and voila—DNA. Does adenine like to be with thymine, guanine or cytosine? Can't remember. A + G might be right. I scribbled it down.

"That leaves C + T. That looks right."

I stared at the letters for a second until I realized what I needed to do. It should have hit me when I saw it the first time, if I'd been smart enough to see it.

I retrieved my purse, pulled out the football schedule, and looked at the underlined capital letters. I wrote down AGATTCC and stared at them.

A genetic sequence? Maybe.

"Please enter your sequence," the voice on the phone had said. When I felt like it, I might try it, I thought, but I was too tired to get further than that.

A half hour later, Stephen called my home number; to my chagrin, I realized I'd been waiting for the call. We chatted about nothing memorable at first, and I considered telling him about the phone number and the sequence message, and then decided against it for no apparent reason. Maybe another time, depending on how the relationship went. He finally did say that the night had been special and that he hoped there would be others—in other words, I wasn't just a good piece of DNA.

That made me feel better.

"Oh, by the way," he said. "I picked up a little something for you today. Feel free to stop by my office and pick it up tomorrow."

I wasn't sure if this was good or bad news.

"Really. Can I ask what it is?"

"Oh, just a wonderfully musky-smelling perfume I think you'll like. Honestly, Claudia, you're a wonderful woman, but I'm just not crazy about the smell of pine trees right in my face when I'm in bed."

There was a moment of silence on my end.

"I feel your pine," I said lamely. "Next time it's musk."

Later, I was charging my phone and noticed there was a new text message.

"Ambac wil call u"

Who the hell was Ambac, I wondered in my stupefied state of mind, thinking it sounded like a bank or insurance company. Then I saw that the message was from Dru—who apparently was finally back. From where? I really don't like texting all that much.

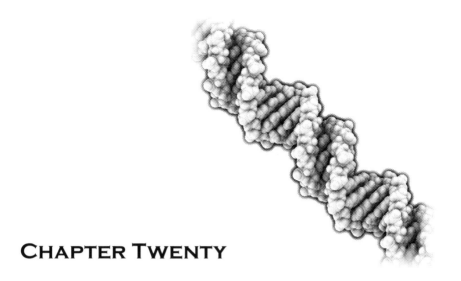

Chapter Twenty

MONDAY TURNED INTO A REAL juggling act. I tried to get through rounds as quickly as I could, but that wasn't really feasible with a fairly green resident and now a new medical student. Mrs. Sapen was doing reasonably well with her chemo but needed another bone marrow biopsy. My resident wasn't very good at doing the procedure, it turned out, and I had to start over on the patient's other iliac crest after the failed first attempt. Another leukemic had spiked a fever, and one had a bad episode of GI bleeding. I felt like a prisoner shackled by my patients, then felt guilty for thinking that.

Giving up on getting any lunch, I ducked out to make a quick trip home around noon. The alarm system guys were finishing up, and I needed to see them. Jerry, the chief installer, showed me the control panel, explained the system and gave me the little book that drives sane people mad. I managed to program in the new code, set it and get back to work, just slightly late for the Monday conference.

When I walked in, the lights were out. Still was picking on a new resident, and I could feel him blushing without even seeing him. I groped my way to a chair in the back row and sat, not really able to concentrate on anything Still was saying. The lighting came back up when he was finished with his pictures, and I noticed Julie sitting a few seats over from me. She turned and gave me a half-smile, looking what I took for penitent. Stephen wasn't in the room, from what I could tell. When we broke up, Julie caught up to me in the hallway and grabbed my arm.

"Claudia, I just really need to tell you what a jerk I was."

Her fingers went to her forehead. "Didn't realize I could be such a bitch. You know, if you're seeing him, that's your business. I have to tell you though, I'm not giving up yet."

I liked her again, even felt a little sorry for her.

"To tell you the truth, I *have* been seeing a little bit of him." Well, really, all of him. "But who knows if it'll go anywhere." I shrugged my shoulders, thinking that projecting my lack of self-esteem might put us on better terms. I changed the subject.

"Heard any more about Jeff from your source?"

"Not much. They've searched the area and come up with nothing. I think they found some blood in the car. They're trying to confirm whether it's his. Doesn't sound good so far."

We went our separate ways back to work.

At six o'clock I got a call from Stephen, then made the trek over to his office, heading for the hallway door to avoid the ubiquitous and nosy Emily. I looked at the door and couldn't help picturing the vision of tall, leggy Ronnie seductively leaning against the doorframe. Surely I was currently the drab version of that apparition, in my dowdy white coat with its droopy and ink-stained pockets. I quickly unbuttoned it, pulled it off, rolled it into a ball, and stuffed as much as possible into my purse. I'd worn a halfway decent looking skirt that day—all my pants needed washing.

Stephen looked fresh and relaxed, like his day was just beginning. I stepped in and noted the closed door leading to the lab. Closing the hall door behind me, he turned and pulled me to him, hard against his chest. His lips felt hot as they locked over mine, and I started to let myself melt into the fire before pulling away and looking questioningly at the closed door to the lab.

"Locked," he said reassuringly, not letting go. "And Emily's on vacation, thank God."

"Does she keep a close eye on you?"

"I think the woman *somehow* knows everything I do. She's a gossip and a pain in the ass."

I wondered if perhaps she knew Julie.

"You're probably great gossip material."

"I'm trying to be," he said with a smile. "If you'll just be quiet for a while."

"I just stopped by to pick up my gift," I said.

He relented and pulled a small box out of a desk drawer. He opened it and took out a new pretty crystal bottle, removing the stopper and setting it on the desk. Then he gently steered me to a half-sitting position on the edge. Paralyzed by anticipation and an overwhelming need, I watched as he wet his fingers with scent, then came to me and slowly drew them down my neck lightly, then down to the bottom of the V in my sweater, and I felt myself heating up. Relentlessly, his fingers slid down and crossed over to caress my right nipple, and it swelled and ached under the touch. He pulled his hand away and added more of the scent to his fingertips, then knelt down, putting them on my right ankle. The fingers drifted up my leg until the whole hand grasped my thigh, and he stood up, his fingers now working to get my underwear off. I felt them fall to the floor and could barely breath as the fingers explored my opening. My hands came up, wrapping around his neck, but not before knocking some Petri dishes off the desk, sending them clattering to the floor. I held my breath, looking over at the lab door, but Stephen ignored it, unzipping his pants and sliding inside me before I could worry about it. From then on, I was hopelessly lost, and I wound up lying on the desk in a pile of papers until we both finished, which didn't take long. We were both exhausted with relief, and I was a mess. Stephen pulled a lab towel out from another drawer in his desk, and we cleaned off; then he tossed it in the trash. I wondered if the towels were there for this particular use and began to feel uncertainty gnaw at my gut. Stephen looked at me.

"Claudia, your mind is an open book, at least to me. I keep towels in my drawer for other reasons. Sometimes I spill coffee. Sometimes I dust the place, since no one else does."

He pulled me close again.

"And sometimes I fantasize that you'll stop by and we'll need one like we did today."

I laughed. If he was a liar, he was a good one. His mind was still a mystery to me.

We just stayed that way for a while, relaxing in the post-climactic release of pent-up needs. Stephen finally stepped back, but not before stepping on a Petri dish and breaking it on the carpet. We got down to pick up the pieces, and I noticed his hair was starting to get thin on top—so he wasn't perfect after all. I felt better.

"I'm famished," he said, looking at me. "For food."

I was suddenly feeling the same, and a huge craving for pasta inserted itself into my brain.

"There's a small Italian place a couple of miles from here," I suggested, before he could bring up an alternative. "Why don't you follow me there?"

Ten minutes later we were on the road, and there was a sleek, new-looking black Maserati convertible on my tail. I wondered whether Stephen made more money than I'd thought or if he just spent it all on that car. Pulling into the back of the restaurant, I suddenly realized that I'd forgotten about potential stalkers, but there were no bikes within sight or hearing range.

The place was quiet on a Monday night, and the owner, Joe Picci, who'd known my father for years, waited on us himself. I'd always thought of him as Mr. Peachy in my child's brain, and he usually had a sweet, peachy demeanor to go with his frequent smile. I'd heard my parents say Joe was from Chicago, and I knew my father played poker with him and some other pals, but my mother spoke of him with some disdain in her voice, calling him a shady teamster leader (what was that?) that she didn't trust. Joe Jr. and Frank were his two sons, but I saw neither of them around the dining room. I introduced Stephen as a "friend" to Joe Sr., who gave Stephen a longish look-over before shaking his hand and smiling. We ordered a bottle of Joe's best Chianti and two big plates of spaghetti *al dente* with sausage, and it was all heavenly, sipping the wine and talking until my phone went off and I looked at the caller's name.

"I'd better answer this," I said apologetically. "It's my long-lost cousin." I swiped the phone on.

"Dru."

"Cuz," she said in a soft, fast voice. "I need to talk to you—soon. It's important."

"Like *how* soon?"

"Tonight—*please*."

I wasn't happy, but obviously she had me worried, to say the least. And I really didn't want Stephen worrying about it.

"Where, when? Are you at home?" I looked up at Stephen trying to look frustrated and apologetic, like my cousin was just a common pain in the ass.

"Yes, but not here. Your house around eleven, maybe later. I'll call you."

"That's my bedtime, you know." She was sounding a little desperate, and I couldn't help being a brat.

"I'll talk to you in bed, if that's what you want. Just make sure you're alone."

"Right. What else is new?" She didn't need to know about Stephen.

"Sorry. I'll talk to you later." She hung up.

"I need to talk to her later tonight," I said, shaking my head and putting the phone away. "She sounds a little worried about something, Lord knows what. She tends to blow things out of proportion."

We had a great dinner, but somehow the night had taken on a hugely disappointing turn. By nine we managed to squirm out of our chairs and leave.

"Talk to me," Stephen whispered, as he gave me a hug and a peck on the head before climbing into the pristine red leather seat of his car.

Some day, I thought. I wondered if Ronnie had already sat on my side of that car.

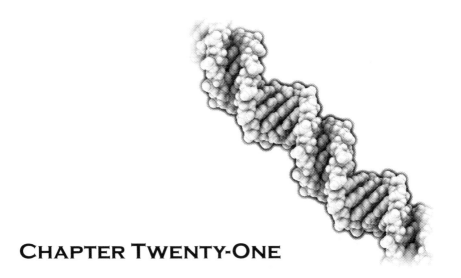

Chapter Twenty-One

I WAS IN THE FORD driving toward home, and it was a little after nine. Something made me reverse course and head toward the freeway, toward Dru's house. Why not, I thought. I didn't want to wait for her to show up if we could get things over with sooner. I was also wondering about the boys. She hadn't mentioned where they would be when she left the house later. I was a few blocks from her place when my cell phone went off again.

"Claudia."

It was Dru, and she rarely called me by my name.

"What?"

"I just can't make it tonight. Something's come up. I'll have to call you back tomorrow." She sounded breathless, talking in a soft voice I could hardly hear, and there was a funny lisp to her words.

"Dru, what the *hell* is going on? This is crazy. And where are the boys? Are they OK?"

"They're OK. Talk later." She hung up again.

I was really pissed by then and was already turning onto her block, a quiet '60s era neighborhood with small one-story houses and no heavy traffic. It was dark, and the street wasn't very well lit, but I saw Dru's garage door opening, which was funny because her car was parked in front of the house with no apparent driver in it and no lights on. After turning off my lights, I pulled in behind a parked car across from the house. It was hard to see them, but Dru was standing near the open garage door talking to a tall male figure in dark clothes. She looked like she was running her hands through her hair, then waving them in the air. He put his arm around her shoulder and hugged her to him. Then he disappeared into the garage and came out on a bike, pulling a helmet over his white hair and taking off at a slow, quiet speed. She watched him ride down the street in my direction, and I ducked my head down, though he could easily spot my car if he was looking around.

When the fading noise of the bike confirmed his departure, I raised my head and saw Dru disappear into the garage. I ran out of my car and across the street, yelling Dru's name, then ran into the garage just as the door was closing—but she had already gone into the house and closed the door. I yanked on it, but she'd already locked it.

"Dru," I yelled. "It's me."

"What are you doing here? I told you I'd call you!"

"Dru, you really need to talk to me. Unlock the door, and let me in. This is nuts!"

"Claudia, I really cannot let you in. Please. Just go home, and I'll call you." She sounded like she was crying.

"I can't. I won't. I need some answers. I'll stay here all night if I have to. Maybe I'll call the police. Fuck you, Dru." I sounded like *I* was crying. I yanked on the door again. There was silence.

"I mean it, Dru. I'm not leaving," I said in a softer voice.

"Claudia, for your own good, you need to leave right now. I'm serious. You don't want to come in here. It's much better for you if you don't."

I should have taken her advice, I suppose, but it didn't feel right, and I had to know. I desperately wanted an explanation for what I'd seen that might make me feel better, if that was possible.

"Dru, I want to know exactly what's going on. Let me in—please."

She unlocked the door as I was still hanging onto it, and I teetered backwards as she pushed it open, just catching myself before falling. Recovering, I walked into the kitchen. Dru was standing just inside, and I put my hand to my mouth when I saw her face up close. There was major swelling on the right side, and her right eye was getting puffy and closing, beginning to turn color. She had a long cut on the right side of her neck, not deep, but blood was still oozing from it, and she grabbed a cloth from the table and dabbed at it. I guessed she'd look a lot worse the next day.

"What the hell happened to you? Did Chance do this to you?"

"Chance? I guess you saw him leave. Hell no, he didn't do it. He saved my life," she said in a hoarse voice.

I grabbed some ice out of her freezer and wrapped it in a cloth for her to put on her face.

"Well, who did it? Aren't you going to call the police? File charges? What's the deal?" I flung my hands in exasperation. "You probably need to go to the ER."

"I'm OK, I'm definitely OK. Just some bruising and a little cut. And no police, absolutely *no* police."

"Why not? And where are the boys, by the way?" I couldn't get the questions out fast enough.

"The boys are in a safe place. That's all I can tell you, because I don't want anyone to know where right now. In fact, *I* don't even know exactly where, and that's the way it'll stay for now."

She put her hand on her head, and I pushed her gently onto a kitchen chair, looking harder at the face and neck, but she was squirming like a little kid. I cleaned off her neck, and she flinched at the touch, faint bruises showing on both sides. A small bandage from my purse closed the cut well enough. I noticed red welts on her wrists, and the left one looked abraded but not bleeding.

"Would you get me a swig of vodka, please? There's some in the fridge," she pleaded in her gravelly voice.

"Dru, I don't think booze is a very good idea right now."

She gave me a disgusted look and started to get up so I gave in, pouring her some in a small glass with lots of ice. I let her sip for a while, then eventually I couldn't sit still any longer and started pacing the floor of the small kitchen. Finally I stopped and looked at her.

"Dru, this is disgusting. This is crazy."

"Don't worry, it gets worse," she said, her speech getting very thick now with the swelling of her lips. "I suppose you might as well see this, but *do not scream.*"

She got up, turned and walked toward her bedroom down the hall. She opened the door, and the room was a huge mess. The bedding was crumpled around the bed, and pieces of clothing were thrown everywhere. The exposed sheet on the bed was the highlight of the room, with a really big glob of blood nearly centered on the bed. The closet door was half off its hinges.

I wanted to stop and run out, but kept following her, like a lemming headed for the cliff. She led me through the open bathroom door, and I watched her throw back the shower curtain and stand back for me to see, catching my breath as she did it and half-expecting to see something really bloody. Her hands looked shaky, but her face looked sturdy when I glanced at it. Of course, there had to be a body in the bathtub—just my luck.

It looked huge in the small tub, but I couldn't register the gist of it at first. It was wrapped in a big, opaque piece of plastic tarp or something like that, with wide strips of painter's tape holding it closed tightly around the body, like a big plastic mummy, its head propped against the back wall over the tub. I squatted down to get a closer look. It was a big white male with no apparent hair on his head and faint slithering tattoos up his arms.

"Tats," I whispered.

"You know him?"

"I was eating with a friend at Sam's one night, and I saw you talking to him at the bar. Later I ran into him in the doorway going out."

"You never asked me about him."

"Never had a chance."

Why was I feeling like we were having a normal chat about boyfriends, I wondered. We were staring at a dead body in my cousin's bathtub, and my mind was going into a disconnected mode.

"He was going to kill me." Her voice was steady and low, and she was staring straight ahead. "He tied me to the bed. Chance came in and they fought. Chance killed him. Did you know he's very strong? You wouldn't think he could survive against this big thug, but Chance is really very strong." She looked at me and added, "He's coming back soon to get rid of this thing."

"How'd he kill him?" I wasn't sure why that was important, but I asked anyway.

"Came up behind him while Jeremy was working on me. Bashed him on the head with a hammer, but it didn't quite knock him out. Chance got me partly cut loose with the knife Jeremy had, and I kind of got out of the way. Jeremy went after Chance, saying Chance needed to be straightened out about what needed to be done. Chance punched him in the face, and Jeremy rolled back on the bed and turned and grabbed me, locking his hands around my throat. I thought I wasn't going to make it."

Her hands rubbed her neck, where purple bruises were getting darker. "I'm not exactly sure what happened then; I was starting to black out. I remember a big weight hitting me, and Chance seemed to be on top of both of us. I heard a big grunt, and when I could finally see again, Jeremy had the knife sticking out of his chest. He was staring at the ceiling, trying to move his lips. He shook his head, looked at Chance and tried to say something, but that was it."

"So why didn't you call the police? Instead you wrapped him up? What are you thinking?" My hands were flying around again.

"Chance wrapped him up. And he asked me not to tell anyone."

"And you thought that was all right?"

"I trust him. Besides, he said it was dangerous for me and the boys if certain people knew Jeremy was dead. He said he would take care of it."

"You *trust* him." I couldn't believe it. "You trust the weird guy who nearly killed me in San Francisco? How long have you known him? You were just pretending to sympathize with me when I was telling you about it, *weren't you?*"

She looked at me and gave a big sigh.

"Cuz," she said, I only met him about a week . . ."

Lights flashed by the windows, and the sound of a car's motor came from the front driveway. She broke away, heading for the kitchen again.

"He's back," she muttered as she left. But she gave an abrupt turn and said, "He's a good guy. Don't mess this up. You insisted on coming here, so just listen. Please."

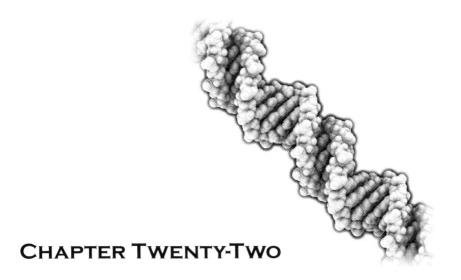

CHAPTER TWENTY-TWO

I LEFT THE BATHROOM. STANDING by the open bedroom door, I could hear Dru open the kitchen door, then the sounds of the garage door opening. A car door slammed, and the garage door went down again. I felt frozen in place, listening for the first sounds of a conversation coming from the kitchen. Some garbled words were exchanged, and a minute later the two of them came down the hallway, Chance's leather boots making a heavy noise on the wood floor. I stood aside as they walked into the room.

Chance came in first, dressed in dark denims with his hair pulled back and tied with a leather string. He stopped and looked at me, not seeming at all surprised and apparently not afraid to look me in the eyes. I crossed my arms on my chest and raised my eyebrows with a questioning look.

"Sorry," he said. "There's really no time to go into it right now. I need to get rid of *that*—for *all* of us." He jerked his head toward the bathroom. "We really could use some help."

Dru nodded her head, giving me a serious look. "More later," she said.

I wanted to turn off my motor and thought functions and crawl into a bed, but instead I followed them into the small room. Chance grabbed the top of the wrapped body and dragged it out of the tub; then he had Dru and me carry the bottom part. It was disgustingly heavy and awkward, and

I almost laughed absurdly when Dru and I got stuck trying to get through the small bedroom doorway at the same time.

We wound our way out the doors and down the hall to the open kitchen door and into the garage, luckily with no obvious spillage of body fluids that I could see. Apparently Chance was better at packing up dead bodies than he was at sex—or maybe it was just sex with me that was the problem. The car turned out to be a dark van, the kind that doesn't have back windows. We got the body into the back of it onto a big tarp, and Chance jumped in and did some more wrapping with Dru's help. I was looking out of the garage window at the street, wondering if some secret enemies or law enforcement people would descend upon us at any moment—and listening to the crinkle of a body wrapped in plastic. Outside, it just looked quiet and dark. "I need to get rid of it for *all* of us"— what the hell had *that* meant? I wondered.

They jumped out of the van, and Chance slammed the doors. I followed them into the kitchen, and we all washed our hands in the sink, like we'd just finished a satisfactory surgical procedure.

The procedure was a success, and the patient died, I thought.

Chance had a serious but determined look on his face. The gray eyes were alert, almost glowing, as they darted around the room, then fixed on me, then on Dru. I couldn't help staring at that extraordinary face, remembering the effect it had on me the first time. To Dru, he said, "I need to get going. You know what to do."

Dru nodded and started to say something, but he cut her off.

"I'll talk to you in the morning. Have you got a gun?"

"Just a sec," she said, running back down the hall toward the small laundry room. She returned about thirty seconds later with a gun in hand. She unlocked the safety and checked to see if it was loaded like she'd done it a thousand times.

"I can use it," she said to Chance.

He nodded and turned to leave. He looked at me. "Listen to your cousin—please."

Dru followed him out the door, leaving me standing there, listening for sounds of the van driving off. After five minutes, it finally did. Then the garage door closed, but Dru didn't come into the kitchen. I finally walked into the garage, only dimly lit from the kitchen light. She was sitting in an old lawn chair smoking a cigarette, the gun cradled between her legs. I thought I saw a glistening look in her eyes, like people get when they're very close to crying, but not quite.

"I didn't know you could use one of those," I said.

"Cuz, I'm afraid there's a lot you don't know about me."

"Apparently."

She stood up and squashed the butt out on the floor, like she was killing it.

"That's the last of those I'll be having for a while, unless you've changed your mind about letting people smoke in your house."

"I guess that means we're going to my house."

"Chance said I can't stay here. We need to hunker down at your place until he takes care of things."

"What things? What's going on?"

"Damned if I know much, but I'm scared. And you should be too, from what he said. We'll talk when we get there. I'll pull my car in the garage, and you can help me put some stuff in it."

She ran out to the street and pulled her car in.

"I can't leave it this way," she said when we walked into the bedroom. She started straightening up the furniture and tried to re-align the closet door. Then she ripped the bedding off the bed, but there was still a big red bloodstain on the mattress. She made me help her flip the mattress over and gave me clean bedding to remake the bed while she grabbed a suitcase and some plastic bags and started loading some of her things. She put the bloody laundry in a big lawn bag. Dru was moving at a furious pace by then, washing down a part of the wall that had some blood spatters and making me wash out the bathtub. I didn't care; at that point, I only wanted to be told what to do.

She ran around the house, apparently searching for a few things she couldn't do without. Some pictures of the boys, her computer, a glob of papers in a kitchen drawer and from bedroom shelves. She grabbed the jewelry box from her bedroom drawer. We finally got what she wanted into her car.

"Dru, I don't want that damned bedding at my house," I said, when she threw the lawn bag into the car.

"I'm dumping it on the way. Forget about it."

She sounded irritated. So was I.

"What about *his* car? How'd he get here?"

"On a bike. The one you saw Chance on. And don't ask me what Chance was driving 'cause I don't know. I'm going to have to assume he's taken care of it. Now. You go. I'm coming soon." She walked to the fridge and took in a mouthful of vodka, then offered me the bottle. I shook my head no.

We looked at each other for a second, and a nauseating wave swept over me at the sight of her sad, misshapen face. I gave her a hug and went to my car, tears starting to stream out for both of us.

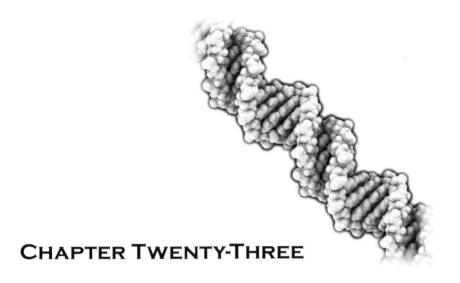

Chapter Twenty-Three

IT WAS AFTER MIDNIGHT WHEN I began driving home, but my numb mind left me no recollection of that drive. I'd had neat little plans about my life, carefully orchestrated and organized with some hard work thrown in, only to have them flushed down the bathtub in one unlucky night. Weird bites I could survive; abetting in a killing, though one in self-defense, was leaving me gasping for air, gasping for some relief from my longing to just curl up and hide.

I got to the house, turned off the alarm, and ran up the stairs to my bedroom. The gun was still under my pillow, and I grabbed it, then walked through every room, checking closets and under beds, behind chairs and curtains, under sinks, anywhere anyone could hide and some places they couldn't possibly fit—with no idea whom or what I was looking for. My sanity eventually returned, and I made room for Dru's car in my garage, throwing junk into corners; it would just fit, I hoped.

After putting the gun back, I walked down the hall to my parents' room, where I'd decided Dru would stay. I pulled the fancy bedspread off the big master and shoved it in the closet, replacing it with a dark down quilt they'd sometimes used. Walking into the big closet, which was still packed with my mother's gowns and clothes (some useful), I pushed as much aside as possible to give Dru some room. Some shelves behind one of the rods held totally impractical shoes in various colors that I had adored on my mother, as well as some likewise beautiful purses that you could almost fit a piece of Kleenex into. Stashed at the end of one shelf was a tall, disheveled stack of papers and files I'd not noticed before. I grabbed them and went downstairs, throwing them into the unread stack in the corner of the office, then ran back up and started emptying drawers, throwing things haphazardly into an armoire that wasn't packed full yet.

Then I ran back downstairs and poured myself a glass of my mother's scotch, a bottle of Macallan that hadn't been touched in five years—well, none of her bottles had. I poured it into one of her expensive crystal glasses—a little dusty, but who cared? I took it to the kitchen table and sat, waiting for Dru, listening to the sounds of nothing but a stray branch tapping against the window and an occasional hum from the fridge. I began to calm down and wondered if that was the start of my career as an alcoholic—beginning to see what my mother liked about the stuff. I thought about my dilemma—that was a nice word for it. Two choices seemed relevant: one, go to the police and tell them everything; or two, don't, and live up to the consequences, if there turned out to be any. Also under two, if that choice prevailed, was the proviso that I understood I would go on living without feeling incapacitating guilt, regret or foreboding. Whichever, the choice could wait at least until Tuesday, which actually had already started.

Then there was the problem of Stephen. It seemed like we'd said goodnight in another lifetime; I wasn't optimistic. There was no way I could involve him in the mess I was in, didn't even want anyone to know I'd been seeing him. Did Chance know? I didn't think so, but who knew?

Chance was a huge question mark. He'd nearly killed me, but he saved Dru's life. He had a lot of questions to answer, as did my loving cousin. Maybe I did too. Invariably my mind would go back at unbidden moments to scenes from San Francisco, as though I were a concerned observer of each segment of memorized video, beginning with the plane ride and ending in bloody pain. Still, the scene of sitting closely in a dark restaurant and feeling soft hair—hearing the gentle clinking of silver on silver while feeling a searing warmth would always be juxtaposed before the thought of pain and dread. He hadn't seemed bad; I'd thought I knew, could detect, good people.

TP53. I'd forgotten about that. Did he have the gene mutation? More than one mutation? He looked pretty healthy, as far as I could tell. If he really *was* trained in genetics, he'd know what that would mean, but I doubted that much of what he'd told me was really true. I wondered if there would be a chance to talk about it.

It was close to 1:30 when Dru finally showed up and we got her car into the garage.

"I'll unpack it tomorrow," she said, standing by her car with a nightshirt in one hand and a Spiderman backpack in the other. "I really need a shower."

We dragged ourselves upstairs, and I showed her the spots carved out for her things. She was no stranger to the room; we'd played in it several times as kids, putting on my mother's clothes and makeup when she was gone. Dru went to take her shower, and I went to my room to change for bed, giving my face a quick wash and taking a birth control pill, the latter feeling like a waste of time at that point. Padding back to Dru's room, I sat waiting for her to reappear; there were questions to ask.

Five minutes later she emerged from the steamy room wrapped in a white towel, with another one wrapped around her hair. She fell into the armchair opposite mine and draped her legs over the side, letting out a big sigh. I stared at her. Something slithery was hanging around at the bottom of her towel.

"Dru. What's *that?*"

"What?" she said, acting clueless.

"That blue stuff. Under your towel," I said, getting up and pointing to her groin.

"Oh, that." She gave a big sigh, then stood up and lifted the towel. "A present from Jer." She lifted her eyebrows and gave me an "oh, well, the deed is done" kind of look.

I was staring, repelled and fascinated, at an elaborate serpent coiled around her pelvis, the end of it on the right side and the head with a protruding tongue centered over her pubis, looking like it was about to take a bite. Shades of black, blue and green melded in a very intricate pattern to form the creature that encircled her like a small garment. Even I could tell a very skilled tattoo artist had done it.

"*Why? Who?*" I asked her. "Didn't it hurt like hell?"

"Cuz, if we're gonna talk tonight, I really need a cigarette."

I let her smoke, and she drew a long one, held it in, and said, "By the way, I've taken a leave from my job. Actually, I don't know if they'll even take me back, but that's that for now. And it'd probably be best if you did the same."

"We'll see," I said, knowing I couldn't stay home.

"Jeremy did it," she said, putting her head back and staring at the ceiling. "I met him at Sam's, oh, maybe about nine months ago, not long after the divorce was final. I was lonely—started seeing him. He said he did some ranching, had a place by Devine, but he came into town on business a lot." She made a quote around "business" with her fingers.

"What's the deal with the snake fetish?"

"Oh, that." She shook her head. "He said he was just fascinated by them. Called himself a herper. He'd go on hunts, I guess with other herpers, for rare kinds, like an unusual king snake, I think he said."

"What's a herper?"

"Well, I don't know the exact definition. I thought it might be someone with Herpes. But my real take was it was this group of people who hunted and liked snakes and maybe some other—unusual—reptiles." She shrugged her shoulders.

"Oh. Like amateur herpetologists, probably not professionally schooled."

She nodded. "Anyway, he was great at sex, had a great body and a big dick, and he was nice to me at first. It wasn't until a couple months later he started getting a little weird. I should have dumped him, I know, but instead I just let him pull me along—with him and his bad habits both. We drank and smoked dope a lot—he had a big stash of the stuff at the ranch, along with coke and some other junk."

She looked at me. "Yeah, I know. I was stupid. Left the boys with a lot of babysitters. We'd get drunk and stoned, and he started doing the tat on me, put coke on the needles. He said he was a self-taught artist, called himself *horishi* or something like that, like the famous Japanese tattoo artists—told me he'd done his own arms, and I guess he was talented in his own weird way. But he said his works were unique. They were a tribute to a new breed, or something like that."

"A new breed of what?"

"Snakes, I guess. Or maybe a new breed of artists? I'm not sure. Maybe some of those snake hunters he hung around with were part of the same breed. He even wore a snake charm on a neck chain."

"What happened to it? Was he wearing it tonight?"

"No. It came off one night in bed, and I found it in my sheets the next morning. I was going to give it back, but things deteriorated between us right about then. He started getting rough, and he was scaring the boys."

I guessed that explained Woodie and the peewee snake. Also the necklace in Dru's jewelry box. She was slumping down in the big chair and yawning like crazy.

I wondered how she could be sleepy after everything that had happened.

"He'd tell them they'd find snakes in their beds if they didn't behave—scared the shit out of them. One night he hit me hard, and I couldn't go to work for two days. I finally reached my limit with him . . ."

She was silent and melancholy for a minute, and I got up to turn on the ceiling fan to disperse the smoke a little. When I sat back down, Dru was asleep, her head slouched on her shoulder. Grabbing the butt from her hand, I took it to the bathroom. A prescription bottle was sitting on the sink, and I picked it up. A bottle of Ambien prescribed by Dr. Katy.

I managed to get Dru into the big bed and let her sleep, then went to my own room to see if I could do the same. It was already four a.m. I lay in bed, staring at the dark, wondering why Tats hadn't tried to kill Dru sooner, if that was what he'd had in mind all along. Maybe he wanted to have some fun first.

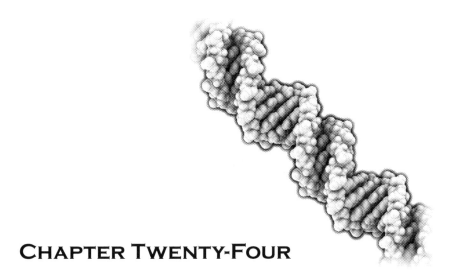

Chapter Twenty-Four

I DIDN'T GET ANY SLEEP worth mentioning that night. I desperately wanted some help, like the Ambien Dru had used, but I'd never liked the idea of sleep meds, even if I thought they would ease the anxiety that felt like a knife in my stomach. I got up at six, as usual, and got ready for work, then peeked into Dru's room. She was still out cold, and I let her stay that way but left her a long note on top of the instruction booklet for the alarm system. I hadn't had time to read it and hoped she wouldn't open a door before looking at it.

At work, we started rounds, and it was obvious that Luis was a quick student and becoming an actual help on the service. He was apparently spending a lot of time reading, and I had to make an effort not to get irritated when he started asking questions I couldn't answer. Actually, I did get irritated. Also, I desperately wanted to see Stephen and just pour out all that had happened, but fought the urge the whole day, waiting to see if he would call me first. He finally called toward the end of the day, in a much better mood than I was.

"You sound different," he said. "Everything go all right with your cousin last night?"

Where to begin? I'm not a natural or even a half-decent liar.

"I think everything's under control," I managed.

Now that we were rid of that annoying Tats.

"Dinner tonight, then go to my place?"

If only, I thought.

"Really wish I could, but Dru's staying with me for a few days. She's had a rough time lately, and I need to give her a little attention. How about a rain check?"

"All right." I could feel his disappointment, which surely couldn't possibly exceed mine.

"By the way," he added, "did you hear about the nurse in the ICU, Jenna Downs I think her name is? Didn't she know your friend Jeff who disappeared?"

Now what, I thought.

"She's Jeff's girlfriend. What about her?"

"I only have some second-hand information, but apparently she's quite ill in the MICU, I think admitted Sunday night. Some strange malady, I hear, that no one's quite figured out yet."

We agreed to talk the next day, but I didn't like the sound of the news about Jenna and made it a point to stop by medical intensive care before leaving for the day. It was on the sixth floor, and I found her there in a private room on the unit, sedated and asleep. I picked up her chart by the bed and read, then accessed more results at the nursing station. She'd presented to the emergency room late Sunday night in "acute distress" with a rash on her legs, low blood pressure, a rapid heart rate and evidence of kidney failure. She was admitted, and lab results showed a blood coagulation disorder with low platelet counts. So far, the cause was unknown. An infection was suspected, but workup for an infectious agent was negative—in other words, they were scratching their heads for a cause. Since then, the rash had progressed at an alarming rate, now involving her arms, chest, and face. She'd been getting antibiotics, steroids, and heparin, but so far without a good response. And insulin. She was a juvenile diabetic, it turned out.

I looked at her face closely and realized it was covered with bluish splotches. I felt her hands and feet, and they felt cold. The chart didn't mention any signs of trauma, and I looked her over briefly without seeing any. I don't pray often, but did my best to say I hoped this wouldn't progress to something much more awful, not knowing what to make of her bad luck.

The internal medicine resident taking care of her walked in, a tall guy with curly black hair and an expression that read "I wish I knew what the hell I was doing with this one." I introduced myself as a heme fellow interested in her coagulopathy, and we chatted for a while.

"We think it's an unusual reaction to *something*, not sure what. No infectious agent has shown up yet. Of course, her diabetes isn't helping things, but it's under reasonable control. Maybe a medication triggered a reaction. We think she'd been using a non-steroidal anti-inflammatory, maybe some acetaminophen—nothing terribly unusual."

"That purpura looks bad," I said.

"We're doing a skin biopsy first thing in the morning."

I left just as an elderly woman was walking toward Jenna's bed, looking very upset.

Heading for home, I realized I'd totally forgotten to call Dru to check on her. I walked into the house, and the alarm system was on. Good for her, I thought, but she wasn't around anywhere downstairs and didn't answer when I called. The sounds of an aria were blaring from the stereo system in her room. I walked upstairs, feeling a few small butterflies flitting around in my stomach. One may have been called Madame. Dru wasn't into opera, at least as far as I knew.

Her door was closed

"Dru, are you in there?"

"Yeah. Sure. Come on in." Her voice sounded thin but relaxed.

I opened it. She was sitting in one of the big chairs, bare feet and knees pulled up and a beer in her hand. Her hair looked long and clean, but her face was still swollen and discolored. She was wearing one of my mother's gowns, a pretty mid-calf blue one with silver sequins and some delicate feathers all along the hem—and several feathers scattered on the floor.

"I've always liked that one," I said, sitting down in the other chair.

"I think you need one, too." She got up slowly, losing a few more feathers, and went to the closet. "We'll dress for dinner."

"Right."

She brought out a long red one with a plunging neckline and lots of sequins.

"Dru, that weighs a ton."

"That's OK. We're not going far."

It wasn't my favorite dress, but it brought back a memory of Dad and me sitting in the audience facing a small stage on a medium-sized cruise ship in the Mediterranean. I was about thirteen, watching the brunette soprano on the stage, her thick hair piled elaborately on her head. She wore the red dress, and her ample chest filled out the deep neckline, showing large cleavage. The voice was pleasant, with an impressive range. She was animated, with a thin, red transparent shawl draped over her shoulders, throwing it this way and that as she sang. Her stage antics embarrassed me, but the audience loved her, happy with the well-recognized songs. But then, I'd always felt ambivalent about my mother.

I humored Dru and put the damned thing on, tripping over it as we made our way downstairs. She set the table in the dining room with a tablecloth and the china and silverware from the cabinet after putting some frozen dinners in the microwave. After lighting the candles in the center, she put her gun down between them. I got a decent looking bottle of red wine from my father's wine refrigerator in a tiny basement-like room off the kitchen he'd called his wine cellar—not an easy task in that dress. She wanted to crank up the music, but I reminded her it wasn't a good idea. We put our entrees on the china and ate our dinner in silence for a while, until the wine started kicking in.

"Chance didn't call me today," she said, leaning back and pulling the hair from her face.

"Great." Not good news. "So, by the way, where'd you meet him, anyway?"

"It was a Monday, a little over a week ago. Carey and I went to lunch at the Hyatt by the bank."

Carey was also a bank teller; I only knew her by name.

"I noticed a white-haired guy walk in and sit at the bar area at the far end of the room. Couldn't see the face, but the white hair was obvious. I thought he was an old guy, 'til later he turned around and walked toward the restrooms. He walked right by our table and looked at me, and I figured there couldn't be too many people around matching Chance's description. You're going to think I'm crazy, but I got up, saying I needed the restroom in a hurry and following him."

I just shook my head.

"He was standing outside the doors—expecting me. Said he needed to talk to me alone, it was important, and could I put off going back to work for a little while. I said OK. I mean, what harm could he do in a public place like that? Besides, he really seemed—nice."

I looked at her. "You mean you also found him to be incredibly sexy, and you wanted to find out if his dick really was a snake."

She gave me a half-grin. "Maybe that too." She sighed, leaning back. "Why don't we continue this by the fireplace?"

We cleared the table, and I lit a fire. After replenishing our wine supply, we sat with the dresses pulled up around us, our feet bottoms meeting in the middle of the couch. I got the feeling she wanted to make foot contact.

"I didn't go back to work that afternoon; Carey made some excuse for me," she said slowly, pausing and sipping between sentences. "We stayed and talked a long time. He said Jeremy was a close relative of his—I just assumed probably a brother. Anyway, he called Jer a maniac. Like I wasn't already finding that out for myself."

"He said Jer wanted to hurt me—and you, too, and anyone close to us, probably. I asked him why, but he didn't say exactly. Said it wasn't our fault or even Jer's fault because Jer was raised in a weird environment of hatred and maybe jealousy and was probably a little shortchanged in the brains department. So it sounded to me like there is someone older behind it. A weird father, mother—or both? He didn't say. Just said I should get the boys to a safe place and not to see Jeremy. Said he thought he could get Jeremy under control and take care of things for us. Well, that got me plenty worried, and I believed him. Turns out it was the truth."

I looked up at her, saying nothing.

"Well, dammit," she said defensively, "give me some credit for being able to read people by now. The guy was sincere. I saw him again the next day, and he showed me a picture of him and Jer together when they were younger. And he told me some pretty sickening stories about what Jer had done—he even showed me a knife wound on his thigh he said was from Jeremy. So I took the boys where they'll be safe."

"Why didn't you tell me?" I asked, feeling more than hurt at being left out of the loop, after I had confided the whole San Francisco ordeal to her.

She looked at me with what looked like a little regret.

"I don't know. It's complicated. There I was, believing the guy that you said almost killed you, actually feeling kind of sorry for him, and I knew Jeremy really was a scumbag. Dangerous to boot. I just wanted to get the boys safe without having to explain everything to you right away, and I had my hands full getting that accomplished. He told me he was keeping an eye on you, and you'd be safe for the time being."

"What about the police? We could have talked to the police if he was that dangerous."

"Chance said no—in a way that made me believe him. He said the police wouldn't be able to protect me, and I was better off with him keeping an eye on me. He said things might get even more dangerous if Jer got arrested or if Jer knew Chance was helping us."

"This is bizarre. So someone else would come after us? Is that what he was saying?"

"I guess so. Anyway, I got back in town last Sunday night, and Chance called and said things were under control, at least for the time being. I was relieved and went out after work on Monday for a few drinks with friends. I wanted to call him, but he'd blocked his number when he called me, and he'd warned me absolutely not to call him."

I shook my head. I had the feeling she really wanted a good look at Chance—at all of him.

"I drove home after having a little too much beer, pissed off at Chance for not calling me again and feeling really lonely and afraid all of a sudden. That's when I called you to come over. I really needed to tell you everything at that point."

She dropped her forehead onto her hand, elbow propped on the couch back.

"Unfortunately Jeremy showed up after I called you. I didn't even know he had a back door key, and he came in so fast I couldn't react. Stupid, stupid me. I should have been prepared." She shook her head.

"He gagged me and tied me to the bed. He found a bottle of whiskey and started talking, like he wanted to give me a good explanation of things before getting down to the dirty work of killing me. All I really remember is trying to nod a lot, like I wanted him to go on talking—I really need a smoke."

She looked pathetic, so I hitched up my dress and ran upstairs to get her cigarettes. After lighting up, she went on.

"So get this, cuz. The guy takes off all his clothes and starts playing with himself while he's ranting like a lunatic. Every now and then he comes over to me and rubs himself against my leg, which I let him do, hoping to distract him. It's damned hard to concentrate on what he's saying, but I remember him calling Chance a whimpering wuss. He says something about venom being king and that he won't betray a great scientist. He says some garbage I can't understand, but then I figured I was done for when he pulls out a knife and says I have always had to go, unfortunately, just because of a stupid relative, but it was fun while it lasted. That's when Chance showed up, thank God, and the rest was a mess."

She took a deep drag and blew it toward the fireplace, then looked at me and said, "And Chance said that word of Jeremy's death cannot get out."

I looked at her, knowing what was coming next.

"So, cuz, since I don't really have any other relatives of any interest, it sounds like you're the cause of all this mess."

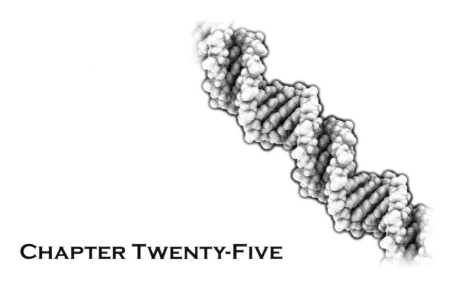

Chapter Twenty-Five

THAT I WAS CONNECTED TO the mess came as no great surprise to me after following what Dru had said, but her conclusion and the way she said it annoyed the hell out of me.

"Dru, you know damned well this isn't my fault. The question is, who *is* trying to get us killed, or whatever the plan is for me. An older relative of Chance and Jeremy? A scientist, I guess, or a so-called scientist, if we can believe Jer's rantings? Now who do you think would know a scientist?"

"Hell . . . ementary, dear Watson," she slurred.

"Hellementary is right. Obviously my *dad* knew plenty of scientists. And don't call me Watson."

"OK. Watson a name, anyway?"

She could be quick when she wanted to be.

"Seriously, Dru. Why doesn't he want you to call him? If he doesn't call soon, we need to find out whatever we can. *Tout de suite. Comprende?*"

"He just said it's not safe for me to call him. This is horseshit," she said, slapping her cell down on the sofa table. "I hope he's still alive."

"If he is, his prognosis may not be too great anyway," I said, thinking about the TP53 gene mutations Stephen had picked up in Chance's DNA.

"What do you mean by *that?*"

I explained the testing that had been done on Chance's underwear—not mentioning Stephen by name or our relationship; it seemed safer for him to remain an unknown in our current pickle.

"So what does that mean? Does he have *cancer?*" she asked, obviously concerned.

"Not necessarily. But he could get it, or have an undiagnosed form of cancer if he hasn't been checked out. Hard to say right now."

She looked thoughtful.

"You know, cuz, I wanted to ask him why he did that to you in San Fran—or *what* he did, for that matter, but he looked so sad I didn't do it. I know he regrets whatever happened."

I let that go by without a comment.

"When you talked to him, did you notice if he was wearing a silver necklace? The one like Jeremy was wearing?"

"I didn't see one," she said, "but he was wearing a leather jacket, and I could have missed it. He asked me last night about Jer's pendant, though. I told him I had it, and he said to hold on to it."

"Chance was wearing one that night in San Francisco, or something like it. Maybe they were both part of some strange cult or something. DNA and snakes. What the hell does *that* mean?"

She sat up straighter, her eyes bigger and brighter. "We need to find out more. About your dad, his work, any run-ins he had, enemies."

"That's what I was talking about, Sherlock. I'll see what I can find out at work tomorrow. Maybe you could go through some of the stacks of papers and boxes in Dad's library, and I'll open his safe for you. There's also his computer in there."

"We're probably running out of time," she said, looking stern. "You should be spending full time with me on this, not running off to work. Tell them you're sick or something."

"You're right, but . . ."

I was thinking about the cascading problems at work and the strangeness of them.

"But what?"

"Well, some pretty unusual things have gone on there recently, and I need to stay in touch with what's happening."

She raised her eyebrows. "Like what things?"

I told her about Jeff and his disappearance, the phone number I'd found in his book and what I thought was a genetic sequence and about the call I'd placed on Julie's phone.

"Whoa," she said. "I guess *you* deserve to be Sherlock. So he hasn't turned up yet?"

"No. Didn't you hear it on the news?"

"Haven't had time for any news, except today I started listening for news of any missing tattoo artists. So your work buddy is missing, but we know nothing about the circumstances except that he was in his car driving somewhere after cancelling his date with you. Also, he makes phone calls to strange numbers that ask for a genetic code—we think. Maybe that was just some kind of game he was playing."

I shrugged. "The police interviewed me after he disappeared. They saw the note with the phone number on it; it was in plain view on his desk. Maybe they've come up with something. At this point, it might be better for me to go to work and not say I'm sick. I don't want police showing up here. Oh, and just to top it all off, Jeff lived with a nurse, Jenna, who got admitted to the hospital with a really weird disease last Sunday night. Maybe an unusual infection they haven't pinpointed yet or a strange reaction to something, but she's not doing too well."

We sat in silence for a while, finishing off the wine, then finally rousing ourselves to go upstairs and ditch the dresses. Dru carried up her gun and threw it on the bed. We watched the news in her bedroom, and I noticed she had put wood bars in the windows, even though they were locked. An extra dead bolt was on the door. She took a long shower, and I straightened my mother's closet, hanging up the dresses and picking up feathers. I went and put a nightshirt on, washed up and went back to Dru's room, where we sat on the bed, piling up a stack of pillows behind us.

"Did you take an Ambien?" I asked.

"No, Sherlock."

"I see you got them from Dr. Katy. I didn't know you used her for an OB-GYN. She didn't deliver the boys, did she?"

"Nope. But when my doc retired, I decided to see her. I remembered her from way back when, and she never charged me. I guess she knew I was from the poor side of the family." She gave a deep sigh, staring at her broken fingernails. "I suppose you know I was jealous of you for the longest time—our mothers being sisters and all, but yours being this talented singer married to a scientist and my mother cleaning houses and married to a handsome guy who couldn't hold a job. I was glad when she moved to Florida."

"So how's she doing now?"

"She's dating some guy there—he seems decent. Funny thing is, Dad's kind of turned his life around—actually just bought a small ranch by Langtry."

"You never told me that." The fact is, I've always liked my uncle Carlos but hadn't asked about him lately, since Dru hadn't seemed anxious to discuss her parents. Since my parents died, I'd always communicated with him through Dru.

"You were busy. Besides, there was really no good reason for you to know."

We talked for a while longer about foggy memories of growing up.

"Cuz, why don't we both sleep in here tonight?"

I didn't want to be alone either, but I ran to my room and grabbed the Beretta from under the pillow, wanting my own gun nearby.

"Cuz, "she said before her eyes closed, "I'm worried about you going off to work tomorrow. This weirdo, whoever it is, could follow you and—who knows what. Watch your back, as they say."

"I will." But I had no idea how to manage that. "I think I'll take Dad's Beretta with me."

"You don't have a permit to carry, do you?"

"No, but there's nothing I can do about that now."

"I miss my boys," she said, and grabbed my hand before falling asleep.

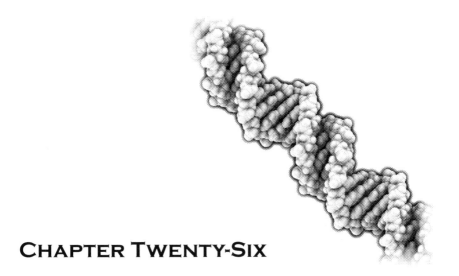

Chapter Twenty-Six

Back at work early Wednesday morning, I was dreading all of the things I needed to fit into a tight schedule. The Beretta had been in my purse, but I couldn't get caught bringing it into the hospital, so it stayed under the front seat of the car.

Luis helped me get through the day, and we were lucky enough to get no new admits. By mid-afternoon I had time to stop and see how Jenna was doing, and it was not good at all. Looking up her records at the nursing station, I saw that she'd had a skin biopsy that morning, but results wouldn't be back until the next day. Consults from renal, infectious disease, endocrine and dermatology services had been requested, some of them already charted. The note that morning from the attending doctors mentioned that her distal extremities were looking cyanotic and dark at an alarming rate, a condition they noted as resembling purpura fulminans, etiology indeterminate so far. I hadn't finished reading when I caught a glimpse of the resident from my last visit and grabbed him before he could head down the hall.

"You think she has purpura fulminans?"

He nodded a yes, looking perplexed. "Cause unknown."

"I guess you totally examined her for any areas of trauma, scratches, anything?"

"Yeah—." He hesitated, apparently unsure if he should go on. "You're from Hematology, right? We'll need a consult from your area, STAT."

"I'm not on the consult service right now, but I'll get someone here ASAP. What were you going to say?"

"We think we see some needle marks on her arm that shouldn't be there—maybe." He shook his head. "Her tox screen shows a trace of barbiturates, but likely not enough to explain things."

"So you think she was using something IV?"

"I can't say for sure; they're just a few small marks, really hard to see. Of course, there could have been some more obvious antecubital marks, but she had IVs put in there right away in the ER. No recent hospital admissions anywhere else that we know of for her diabetes. We're trying to get ahold of the med containers, vials, syringes she had at home." He shrugged and shook his head again.

"I guess you know she was dating Jeff Dunn, one of the heme fellows who disappeared recently."

He nodded. "But it doesn't look like a suicide attempt, at least not that we can tell. It *is* pretty weird, though."

I left the station with a bad feeling for Jenna's fate, making my stomach feel queasy. If Jenna had used IV drugs for recreation, it was a huge surprise to me. It meant that Jeff probably had done the same, and that was hard to swallow; he just didn't seem to need that sort of thing. But maybe I was way too naïve.

By six o'clock I'd finished everything, including getting a hematology consult for Jenna and was making my way to Stephen's office, where we'd agreed to meet. My depression was worsening with every step, not having a clue about how to get through the conversation without breaking down into worthless tears. Self-pity seemed undeserved, though, when I thought about what people like Jenna, or even Dru, were going through. My own life was no longer a major priority. That's just the way it was.

I knocked on his hallway door and thought I heard him say it was unlocked, so I walked in. He was sitting at his desk, his back to me, staring at his computer monitor. I walked around to the front of his desk and sat, waiting for him to look at me and dreading the look, terrified of what he might read from my face—and tried to reassure myself that he was only a man and couldn't read thoughts, thank God. I'd been a fool, I thought, not to just write him a note saying it was over.

He finally looked up at me, and his eyes looked like the shine was gone. His mouth took the form of a wry half-smile.

"What's happened, Claudia?"

I shook my head. "Stephen—I just can't tell you. At least not right now. Maybe sometime." Words were coming out very slowly because thoughts were taking so long to be generated.

"Are you in trouble? You need to tell me if you're in trouble."

"No." I knew he could sense the lie. "I have some major problems I need to work out, and I just can't see you or anyone until I get them resolved. That's all, and I can't tell you anymore. Sorry."

"What kind of problems? Health, legal, family, what?"

"I don't want you involved. Don't call me, please."

"Are you depressed?"

"My news hasn't been good lately, but I'm not seriously depressed, not the way you're worried about. I can handle it."

His face hardened.

"I wouldn't think of calling *anyone* who was obviously not interested." He sat back, biting a pencil in his hand. He hadn't given me much of an argument, and that was a real downer. I wondered if he'd cared very much in the first place, then suddenly felt stupid, wanting to get out of the office and run down the hall. Instead, I asked a question, fighting to keep any expression off of my face.

"I just need to ask you something, if you wouldn't mind."

His eyebrows rose, signaling a go-ahead look. I couldn't think of how to word the question.

"You've never heard anything unusual about my father or other staff working here—back when he was here—have you?"

"What do you mean by *unusual?*"

"Well—trouble of any kind?"

"No—but he'd been long gone when I arrived."

"Who would know? Are any faculty left from then? The '80s?"

"Not that I know of offhand. When I first moved here, I met the retired department head. His name is James Renfrew; his picture's in the hallway. Is this important? I suppose there *are* a few staff still working that might have known your father at the time. If I run into any, I'll let you know."

I didn't want him asking any questions on my behalf.

"Just page me if you think of anyone who was around then."

I got up, anxious to get out. He stayed in his chair. I opened the hall door and turned back to say thanks. He got up and grabbed my arm.

"Claudia, don't be stupid," he said. "Let me know if you need help."

I nodded, and then walked quickly down the hall.

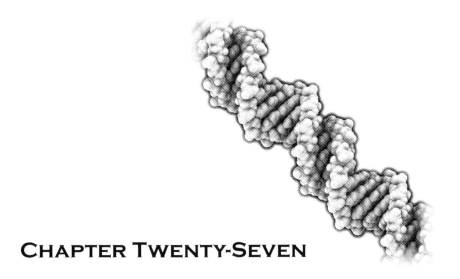

Chapter Twenty-Seven

WHEN I WALKED INTO THE house, the unmistakable smell of cigar smoke nearly knocked me over. Apparently Dru had found my dad's old stash of cigars in his office, and I regretted not having tossed them.

"Dru, you're going to set the fire alarm off with those old things," I said as I walked into the room. I was going to nag her more, but she looked almost relaxed, sitting on the floor in her bare feet with her smoke and piles of papers and folders around her. I decided to bear it. Besides, I needed someone in my life. She offered me a light, but I went for a cold beer instead.

"You look down," she said.

"I've had better days."

"How's that girl doing? Jeff's girlfriend."

"No good. Worse today. Turns out she may have used some IV drugs, but the tox screen didn't show much of anything. They think she may have something called purpura fulminans."

"Purple *what?*"

"Purpura. It's an unusual disease—very bad. The small blood vessels in the skin get plugged by clots, cutting off the blood supply. The skin turns dark, and large areas just—die off. Sometimes it's triggered by an infection, sometimes by a faulty coagulation system, sometimes even by some drugs.

Jenna's fingers and toes aren't getting any blood circulation, and right now they don't look too good."

She made a face, and I wanted a subject change. "How'd you do today? Did you get everything out of the safe?"

"Yeah. I can't believe you never really went through it."

"I got the wills out when I needed them—and the gun later. I didn't feel much like looking at anything else."

She pulled a cardboard box toward her and stuck her arm into it.

"Well, we have a little bit of jewelry." She pulled out a tiny pair of diamond studs in a little red box, an antique diamond-studded art deco watch, and an old men's pocket watch made of different shades of gold with a horse on the cover. They looked vaguely familiar, but I'd forgotten about them. My mother mostly wore bigger costume jewelry.

"Then we have some nice coins that could come in handy some day— Krugerrands and Canadian Maple Leafs." She held up several small plastic pouches of coins. "Real," she said. "Nothing much else except some keys— any idea what they open?"

I shook my head. They didn't look like house or car keys.

"The rest is their wills, which you don't need anymore, and some old checkbooks and transaction registers. Nothing helpful."

"Anything else in the stacks and boxes?"

"Well, cuz, a lot of this means zilch to me. I have trouble pronouncing the words, let alone know what they mean when it comes to his books and papers. I did run across this in a pile of his stuff."

She handed me a pamphlet from the university's college of biological sciences dated 1985. I thumbed through it, going to the description of the genetics department that included pictures and lists of the faculty. There was old Dr. Renfrew, the department head, looking the same as in the hallway. My father looked very young, with loads of dark hair and no mustache. The department wasn't large, and there were three faculty I didn't recognize, including a woman and a man with the same last name— married I guessed. My eyes stuck to the last picture, a middle-aged man with light-colored eyes and blond, wavy hair wearing round glasses that gave the face intelligence; it was serious but handsome and looked familiar, but I couldn't really place where I'd seen it. His name was Dr. Samuel Kral, and it didn't sound familiar.

I sat and waded through the papers and files that Dru hadn't found relevant, just to make sure nothing of interest was there, but found nothing helpful—no references or notes by my father regarding Kral or any other faculty. Two hours later I was worn out, and Dru and I dined on popcorn for dinner.

"You know, cuz," she said, "if there *is* someone who wants to hurt you and me so much, and if your dad knew him—or her—I wonder why your dad didn't warn you or something. You know?"

I shook my head, wondering the same thing.

"Maybe he just didn't realize it," was all I could think to say, knowing where she was going next.

"So do you think the car crash was really an accident?"

My mind was going back—not wanting to go there.

"The weather was bad that night, raining hard with slippery roads. You know how bad they get after it's been dry for a long time. They slid off the road." I shrugged. "I never heard anyone mention anything suspicious about it."

"But you didn't really investigate it at all, did you?"

"The police report sounded right to me. I did wonder if they'd been drinking and arguing again—like they'd done before. I just wanted to get past it. Besides, I had no reason to suspect anything unusual."

"Sorry to bring it up. It's just that all this—crap—has made me wonder."

We went upstairs, and I fell into my own bed after a long, hot bath. Dru had the TV on down the hall, and I fell asleep, thinking about why a car skidded off the road.

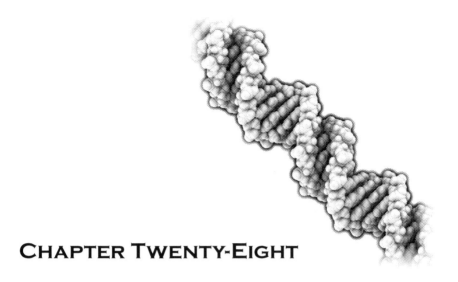

CHAPTER TWENTY-EIGHT

IT'S THE MUSIC THAT DRAWS me down the stairway. I hug the banister instinctively, ducking down behind it for cover, my hands clasping onto one vertical bar after another, my knees bent almost painfully. I have to hoist my nightshirt up to prevent tripping over it.

It's a waltz—Strauss, I think—and I congratulate myself for remembering my lessons. Now I'm staring at her, standing there in the living room looking gorgeous in a long green dress with a deep V neckline. There's a ring on her right hand with a huge white pearl on it, a symbol, she'd said, of her one beautiful child. A man is standing close, his hands on her shoulders, now slowly moving down her arms, now drawing something from the pocket of his expensive dinner jacket. The object is delicately placed around her neck with slow, gliding movements, now in front, then twisted behind her beautiful neck. It shines on her, matching the gloss of his hair, both golden in hue. She stares at him, seeing nothing else, even though I make a tiny tap on the railing to smile at her and get one back. He moves in front of her now, and I can't see where his hands go—they're moving down the front of her dress, and his head bends down to kiss something I can't see. His left hand comes up, wrapping around her neck and encircling it—but it's impossibly long. It stretches and stretches until it's not an arm anymore. It's a long black thing that coils and coils around her, then around them both, growing huge, and they scream in agony, bonded together *by a horror. I clutch the bars and cry, trying to shake them open like a prison door . . .*

My eyes opened, and I let my breath out with the relief that comes when bad dreams end, but I wondered if something seen and long forgotten had triggered it. I sat up, feeling sweaty and thirsty, and turned the small lamp on to get some water. I brought it back to the bed and froze, my eyes transfixed on the pillow. A long black snake showed its head from underneath; then the body slowly made its way across the whiteness, oscillating rhythmically, flicking its tongue in and out. Dru's name came screaming out of my mouth; then I screamed it again, losing all sense of self-control. I ran to the door, opened it and yelled again.

Dru came out of her room slowly, a gun in her hand, and I signaled her toward my bed, pointing to the pillow where it still moved. She looked at me quizzically. I pointed to the ugly thing and jumped back, warning her not to touch it as her hand shot out toward it. She kept moving though, until her hand clamped around it, around nothing. I stared at her, blinking my eyes until the snake became blurry, a series of small black dots, and finally disappeared.

She sat on the edge of the bed, her feet wet from the spilled water. I picked up the glass and wiped the floor.

"Cuz," she said, shaking her head, "we've got to hold ourselves together."

"I can't believe I did that—saw that. Nothing like that's ever happened to me before. Damn, it looked real."

"Well, at least you didn't shoot it. I'll stay here until you fall asleep and make sure you don't cry 'snake' again."

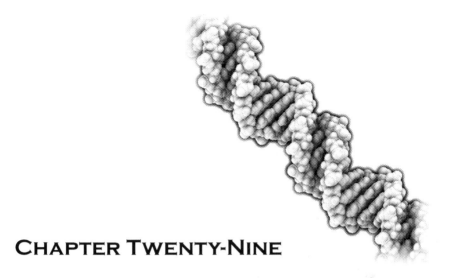

CHAPTER TWENTY-NINE

FIRST THING ON THURSDAY MORNING, I ditched my purse and stopped by the ICU to check on Jenna; I had a really bad feeling about her that made my previous night's ordeal seem trivial and ridiculous. While looking up her records and reading, a nurse sitting next to me at the station just shook her head in a hopeless gesture.

"What a shame," she lamented. "The girl's just rotting away."

The skin biopsy showed thrombosis (clots) in the capillaries of the skin with resulting hemorrhage and swelling, findings they concluded were consistent with purpura fulminans. Her bleeding problem was worsening, as her coagulation system was pathologically turned on and out of control. The black and blue ecchymotic areas of skin were darkening and expanding, and the very distal areas of the feet and hands were showing signs of cell death or necrosis. Her doctors were trying plasma exchange therapy, heparin, steroids, antibiotics, virtually anything that might help, but some of the dead areas would likely need surgical debridement, possibly amputation. The worst areas were her toes and part of her left arm near the antecubital fossa (inner elbow). It was a nightmare beyond any horror story. They were still postulating some kind of weird drug reaction; it had been reported with a few drugs in past case reports. There was still no evidence for an infectious cause.

I dreaded it, but I walked slightly into her room to take a quick look. Her face and arms were swollen and distorted, and, thank God, she was sleeping. Huge black splotches were apparent on her face and left arm. I walked out, unable to look anymore, thinking of my last time in a hospital as a patient. But what I'd had was nothing like Jenna's disease; mine had been a transient, though frightening, bleeding disorder that had resolved pretty quickly. It seemed she was just one very unlucky woman.

I worked furiously through the morning and got Luis to cover things for an hour while I drove over to Dr. Katy's office for a quick lunch she'd ordered in for the two of us after I'd called her earlier. She was sitting behind her desk looking expectant, knowing I was there for a reason.

I dug right in.

"Katy—I need to ask you a few questions about my dad."

She raised her eyebrows. "Ask."

"Did he have—well, was there anyone you know of who really didn't like him, maybe even hated him?"

"Why? Is something going on? Tell me, Claudia."

"No, not really. Nothing much. I just ran across some old papers that made me wonder about it." I hoped my lying was improving with practice.

"What kind of papers?"

She was making me work for my info. "Just some notes that got me wondering, that's all. He had a little notebook I'd never really read before. It didn't mention any names." Another lie.

"Well, he had a falling out—a rather big falling out—with another doctor in the department." She hesitated. "You know, we were both at the university back then, in the 1980s."

"You were pretty good friends," I said.

"Yes." The way she said it again made me think they'd been pretty close . . .

"I'm glad." I don't know why I said it, but it felt good.

"The doctor's name was Samuel Kral, and he was a specialist in reproductive genetics with an MD and PhD, I think. A tall, blond, good-looking man from Europe, thick accent—but the few times I saw him, he struck me as a strange duck. He and your father worked together for a while, collaborated on a few papers, I think, until the collaboration blew up for some reason. I sensed there was some jealousy of your father on

Kral's part. Anyway, there were all kinds of rumors floating around, and one day Kral left, and I never heard anything more about him."

"Did he leave or was he fired?"

"He just left, as far as I know, but it was right in the middle of the academic year. I thought it was a little strange."

"So—did he socialize with my parents much, do you know?" I wasn't sure where I was going with this, but my recent dream came to mind.

She stiffened slightly at the question. "Well, they all knew one another. I met him at a few parties your parents were at. Supposedly he had a wife, but I never saw her anywhere socially or otherwise; then I heard a rumor she had died. I vaguely remember she had some kind of medical problem, but I never really heard what it was."

"Do you know if he had kids?"

She shook her head. I decided I might as well plow ahead.

"Do you think he could have had some kind of relationship with my mother?"

She stopped eating and thought for a minute.

"Claudia, I'm not sure. Certainly they knew each other, and once I saw him talking with her for quite some time at a party, obviously taken with her, but a lot of men were. Ultimately, though, your mother and father decided to stick things out, as far as I know, and Kral disappeared from the scene."

"You never heard where he went or if my father had any contact with him after that?"

"Your father never talked about him; I don't think he wanted to. Kral wasn't exactly your typical south Texas conversation material. What's this really about, anyway? You're not telling me everything."

"Nothing serious—don't worry about it. But—I'd rather you didn't mention to anyone that I asked about him."

She looked at me hard, then shook her head. "Claudia, you're as stubborn and enigmatic as your father, and I *am* worried. You know you can confide in me if you're in trouble. I'll be absolutely discreet."

"I'll let you know," I said, going out the door, but she looked concerned.

When I got to my car, I gave Dru a call. Loud opera was blaring in the background.

"I didn't know you liked that music," I said.

"I don't, but I figure if I play it real loud it might sound better, and I'll learn something. Expand my musical horizons. Hold on, I'll turn it down."

"Dru, get on the Internet and see if you can find out anything more about Dr. Kral. Dr. Katy says he and my father had a falling out about something. Also, see if you can find any correspondence Dad had with any attorneys, especially around the '80s."

"Will do. And bring food. Barbecue. I like the big sausages."

"Right."

The afternoon turned into a long one, with two new admits and a conference late in the afternoon. By the time I got home with the barbecue, it was almost eight-thirty. Dru gulped it down with some beer, not saying much until she sat back and groaned.

"Was that good for you? That was sure good for me, cuz."

"It was—orgasmagenic, as an old prof used to say." I filled her in on most of what Dr. Katy had said, including her inference that my mother and Kral may have known each other pretty well. She didn't comment on what I'd said.

"What'd you find out? Anything?"

She gave a funny small grin, and we took our beers to the office. She sat at the desk, and I took a spot on the floor with the piles of files and papers around me. Dru was starting to look almost normal in the dim light, much of the swelling having resolved and only a few black and blue spots remaining.

"OK, cuz, let's start with the buzzards—I mean lawyers. There isn't a whole lot that I found. Your family's will lists Jim Abrams as the attorney. I guess you probably know him, right?"

"Yeah. A nice enough old guy. He helped me arrange a few things after the accident, but I haven't talked to him since. I guess I could call him tomorrow and see if he knows anything about legal work problems my dad might have had."

"The only other thing I found was this letter to your dad from a law firm representing the university. It looks like it was crumpled up, then unfolded for some reason. It's dated in 1987, signed by Mr. Radke from Radke, Marlborough, Roland and James, LLC." She handed it to me. "It doesn't say much—just that they're scheduling a meeting with him in their offices, maybe at his request from what I can tell. Here's the two phone numbers of the law firms." She handed me the numbers.

"Now—on to Dr. Samuel Kral. There isn't a whole lot to be found on him, at least not where I checked. I found a few references to some papers he'd written back in the '80s, and I printed out the short list for you."

I looked at the list, and nothing seemed particularly interesting—a few boring-sounding papers on reproductive genetics in mice.

"I couldn't find any evidence that he died. Then I ran across an old bio that listed him as born in Prague, where he got his MD and PhD, and I found the same picture that was on the old faculty list."

"So he was Czech."

"Check. But get this. I was looking for some relatives or information about him in the Czech Republic and in Slovakia, and Kral is the name of a village in Slovakia. Also some well-known Czechs have that name, and it's the name of a hotel in a town I couldn't start to pronounce. Then I looked in the Wictionary for the hell of it, and guess what Kral means?"

"Slither on your belly like a snake?"

"Cuz, Kral in Czech means *king*."

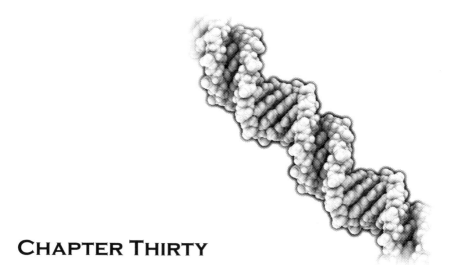

CHAPTER THIRTY

ON FRIDAY MORNING, I GOT paged to Still's office. As I walked in, Linda signaled me over to her desk. Behind her I could just see Still sitting at his desk, engaged in what looked like a stressful phone call. He looked up and saw me, then got up and shut the door. Linda shook her head.

"It seems no news is good news these days."

"Something bad?" I ventured.

"Can't discuss it, really. But Dr. Still wanted me to tell you we're getting you some more help. The service has gotten busy, and we're pulling a fellow from one of the labs for the time being. Dr. Jennings. She said she'd be glad to help."

Julie. Could my life get any more complicated, I wondered. I thanked her and walked over to our office, where Jeff's desk was showing signs of the new interloper. A pink sweater was draped over the back of his chair, and a few charts were stacked in the center. The room smelled of Hypnotic Poison, or whatever perfume she was wearing that day. I sat down at my desk, a wave of nausea suddenly overcoming me. I wanted to run away somewhere and start all over. My cell phone rang, and it was Stephen, making me feel even worse.

"I've been worried about you. How are things?"

"Oh—all right. Still trying to help out Dru."

Long pause.

"Claudia, I did find out that Dr. Renfrew is still alive. He's apparently in his 90s and in a nursing home here, the Oaklands Home. I could drive you there some time if you'd like."

"Thanks, Stephen, I really appreciate it. I'll let you know." So I left the door open, even though I knew I shouldn't have. I sat there trying to pull myself together by reading my e-mail, when Julie walked in, and the aroma got stronger.

"Hey, darlin', you look like tragedy has bestruck you. Cheer up. I'm here to help. No more easy lab life for a while."

I wasn't sure if it was my imagination, but I thought she looked thinner. She sat down and pulled a package of diet cookies out of a drawer.

"I'm about to gag on these things, but so far they're working. How you doing? Have not heard another word about Jeffrey lately. Can you believe what's going on with Jenna? They're taking her for some debriding today, but I think two of her toes are goners."

The good thing about talking to Julie is you never need to say much. I shook my head.

"Rumor has it they found some morphine at her place. Hard to believe—she and Jeff into drugs and all."

"They still don't know what triggered the reaction, do they?"

"Not really. She had some Ketorolac too, and that's been reported to cause this kind of reaction. Absolutely no infection so far and no signs of trauma. Weird."

"Time for rounds," I said.

The day seemed unending, but things finally got wrapped up at six-thirty. A white van stayed behind me most of the way home, and I half wondered about it in my fried state of mind, but it turned off before I did. Dru was definitely looking better and was getting cabin fever, pacing the kitchen floor and puffing as I walked in the door. I took a swig of the beer she was drinking, and we sat at the kitchen table.

"Chance finally called," she said.

"And?"

"And he sounded—I don't know—not so good. He was talking fast and soft. Said he was trying to take care of things but it might take a little more time. He has some important information to retrieve. He says to stay put and don't talk to anyone and don't try to call him."

"Oh, great."

"Cuz, I'm really worried about him—not to mention us. We need to do something more. Find out more. We can't just sit here."

"OK, Dru. Let's calm down and think this over. What do we know? Jer tried to kill you and said he was after me too. Jer and Chance are related—brothers, maybe? Both had the last name of King; both wore the snake helix. Jer had big-time snake tattoos. Chance had a snaky dick—well, I'm not sure *what* that was, but the experience was venomous. This sounds like some stupid horror movie."

I took another swig to clear my brain.

"Jer said something to you about venom being the king, right?"

"He said that venom is king, and he wouldn't betray a great scientist."

"Well, I feel almost certain Kral is the scientist, don't you? He may well have changed his name to King, and Jer and Chance are probably relatives, maybe his kids. If he and my father had a major falling out, he could be behind all this. I'll try to talk to those attorneys and Dr. Renfrew, the old retired department head, early next week."

She shook her head. "We need to do more, and fast. Jer has a ranch near Devine, with a small ranch house on it. I was there several times. Never saw anyone else there. I want to go back and see what we can find."

"Like *what?*"

"I'm not sure. Maybe we can find out where this so-called scientist lives. We'll go tomorrow."

"I've got to work in the morning."

"We'll go later in the evening, take your Explorer. I'll get some things together. Oh—and I need your credit card for some supplies."

I handed it to her, not liking the idea. "My funds aren't limitless," I said.

She ignored the remark. "Have you got high boots?"

"Cowboy boots? Yeah, why? Who doesn't?"

"We'll be walking through some wooded areas, probably. You know, it's a *ranch*. And we won't be driving big-as-life right up to the front door."

"OK, I get it. So what's in the woods? What animals?"

"The usual, cuz. Deer, hogs, coyotes, bobcats, snakes . . ."

"Snakes? Did you see snakes there? What is it with them and snakes? The snake helix, snake tattoos, snaky-looking dicks. Did Jeremy keep snakes?"

"Calm down. I didn't see a single snake there—except for Jeremy. We probably won't run across a single snake. Just a precaution. Have you got some flashlights?"

"Under the kitchen sink."

"Where's that gun of yours, cuz? Let me see if you know how to use it."

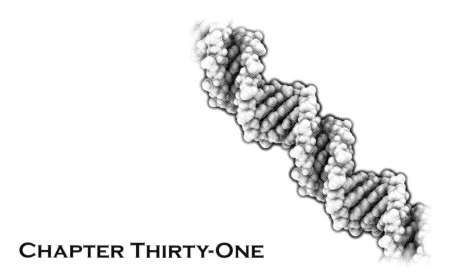

Chapter Thirty-One

DRU WENT OVER THE BASICS of using my Beretta like she was an expert, flicking it around and making me nervous. I decided to stand behind her and watch. Then we put together some supplies in the kitchen: flashlights, our boots, some mace she found in a kitchen drawer, and an old cane from the hall closet. It wasn't making me happy. Later we celebrated Friday night with a nice little spaghetti dinner and got into a serious debate about the virtues of clockwise vs. counterclockwise rotation of the noodles around a fork.

I struggled to get myself up on Saturday morning, wanting desperately to just hug my sheets all day. I forced myself to get going, and later that morning ran into Julie in our office. She walked in looking somber and plunked down into her chair.

"Damn, Jenna's really bad," she said, searching for something in a drawer and then pulling out a broken cookie. She stuffed a piece in her mouth and garbled what sounded like "I don't think she's going to make it."

A rock fell into my stomach at the thought of her decaying body.

"Worse?" I asked.

She nodded. "Sometimes those reactions just can't be stopped once they get started." She was quiet for a while, then swallowed and looked up at me.

"I saw Palmer at happy hour at Charlie's last night."

"Really?" I tried to sound unconcerned. He didn't seem like the Charlie's happy hour type.

"Yeah. It was pretty funny, really. He was sitting with a group of us, and in walks this tall, slinky redhead in a short skirt and boots, like some prowling ex-Dallas Cowboys cheerleader. He seems like such a cool guy, but I swear his face got red. Anyway, they got up and went outside, but I got up and peeked out there, where they were having one juicy argument in the parking lot. I guess she took off, because he came back and sat down for a while longer." She started twisting a tendril of hair around her finger, a habit she had. "At any rate, I got a chance to talk to him for a while, and he said transferring to his lab probably wouldn't be a problem." She looked at me, waiting for a reaction, obviously.

"Great," I said, and meant it. I still didn't see Julie as a threat, and the point was really moot. There was no way I wanted to involve Stephen in my problems.

She leaned her head to the side and looked at me. "You seeing him?"

"It's not really working out right now," I said as I got up to leave, with my eyes threatening to mist up. "Good luck."

At home, Dru was bouncing off the walls, putting things in the Explorer, checking the tires, checking the weather and the news and throwing clothes on and off. I wondered if she'd taken something I should worry about. After throwing a pizza in the oven, I made her sit down and eat with me.

"So," I said, "just where is this ranch we're driving to?"

"As I said, cuz, it's near Devine, about an hour away, and no, it's not the King Ranch, at least not the King Ranch you've heard about that's huge and famous."

"I figured that."

"This place has no signs—just a fence and a metal gate at the entrance—well, and a 'no trespassing' sign."

"So, Dru, just what do you think we'll accomplish doing this?"

She sighed, like I was a foolish child asking questions with obvious answers.

"We're going to try and find a connection to *Kral* or maybe his *location*. It should be safe for now—no one but Chance and us know Jer is dead yet, and I never saw any visitors when I was there."

I didn't feel convinced that no one would be looking for Jer, but we fidgeted around until after six, then finished putting things in the car. I glanced around nervously as we pulled out of the garage, but it was starting to get dark, and there were no apparent interested onlookers—and no bikes, unfortunately. We drove down I-35 south mostly in silence while the sun finally vanished. It wasn't like Dru to keep the radio off—but then we'd both morphed into different people.

Forty-five minutes later we were at the intersection with Highway 173 near Devine. To our right, several cars and trucks were parked in the lot of a very mature looking wood-frame restaurant, with the name "Double R—home of good country cookin'" painted over the front door. Dru took a couple of quick turns, and we were on a dirt road. I could make out some ranch entrances to our left, and after about ten minutes Dru turned onto a narrow dirt road without a gate and drove down about a quarter mile. Dense mesquite trees bordered the sides of the road, but she found a small clearing on one side, and we parked.

"We're here?" I asked, puzzled by our surroundings.

"We're near," she said, turning off the car lights and speaking softly in a tone that made me want to grab the keys and drive home. She thinks she's some fucking Nancy Dru, I thought, irritated with myself for going along with her.

"Cell phones off," she said, shutting hers down and sticking it into her button-down shirt pocket. I did the same while she grabbed her backpack and the flashlights. Traveling a little lighter, I had only a small pack at my waist containing mainly the Beretta and a few Band-Aids in case I shot myself. We got out and started backtracking to the main road, then walked in the ditch, ducking down when a rare car drove by, until we reached the next ranch entrance, a small dirt road with an old padlocked gate entrance and a weathered fence running off on either side. The gate was only about six feet high, and Dru climbed over it as if she'd done it many times.

"Don't worry, it only carries a mild current," she whispered, jumping down the last two feet.

I followed her over and rushed to catch up as she headed up the road, sticking to the side and trying to avoid overhanging branches. Twenty minutes later we stopped and hung behind a tree. A small one-story wood house stood in a clearing in front of us, with a rough carport to the left of the building. A truck was under the carport; the house was dark.

"OK, we're going in," she announced.

I could see her pupils shining in the dark. She almost sounded excited.

"Dru." I pulled on her arm. "What do we do if someone shows up while we're in there?"

"Then we go to Plan B, cuz."

"And what's that?"

"Not to worry. We won't need it." She actually grinned. "And if we do, just follow me."

"Right. Is that Jeremy's truck?"

"Yeah. Not sure if it runs, though."

She left the tree, and I followed her toward the house, our feet crunching on the dirt front yard. The front entrance was an old aluminum storm door in front of a worn-looking wooden door, with a few wooden stairs leading up to it and a small overhang protecting it a little. Old Christmas icicle lights dangled from the overhang. Dru stopped and looked at me.

"Gloves," she said.

From a pocket, I pulled out a glob of four pairs of latex gloves, and we put them on, double-gloving for a dirty operation. I just shook my head at myself. Dru walked up and tried the front door, but wasn't surprised to find it locked. She flicked her head, signaling me to follow her around to the back. Two windows about three feet off the ground faced the back wooded area. Dru walked to the first one we came to, played around with the old screen on it and finally got it off and put it behind a bush. She took off her backpack and dug out a small crowbar, then stuck the end under the old, rotting window bottom and pried open the window a crack. When she got her fingers under the bottom, the window opened easily, making a rough sound that made me look around nervously. Dru dropped her backpack inside and climbed in, making it look easy; then she helped me in.

Our flashlights showed a small bedroom with a rumpled bed. A small wooden crate served as a side table, and a lamp sat on it. They were about the only things I could make out in the room. The floors were wood planks that squeaked as we moved around.

"Stay here while I take a quick look around," she said, and then was gone before I could answer. I looked back at the open window, torn between leaving it open and closing it. I walked back and closed it nearly to the bottom, then stood still for a long two minutes, the thought *we are amateurs* echoing through my head. Then she was back, talking in a normal voice.

"OK, just look for any helpful info you can find—use your brain— you'll know it if you see it." She grabbed my arm and took us down a short hallway. "This is the living room."

She zipped her light over a room with a couch, two rockers, and an old TV on a stand in front of them. I glimpsed a rock fireplace on one wall.

"We'll leave the lights off. This is the small kitchen," she said, steering me a few feet further. "Garbage is under the sink. Check it out. I'll start with the two bedrooms then do the pantry. Oh, there's a hallway bathroom if you get to it before me. That's about all there is. There's no phone lines; if you find a cell phone, keep it."

She disappeared, and I walked into the living room, hoping Dru would be done before I had to do the garbage. The fireplace had nothing of interest in it that had been burned recently, and a sloppy stack of newspapers and a few porno magazines were by the side of the couch, along with a bunch of empty beer bottles all standing up in rough rows, emitting the foul smell of old beer. I didn't really want to, but I took the cushions off the couch, finding only dust, dirt, and sixteen cents. Gingerly, I stuck my hands down the cracks, coming up with a button and a condom that was all folded and stuck to itself. A light under the furniture revealed only some trophy-sized roaches and some popcorn.

I went to the kitchen, going through the cupboards and drawers, not finding much of interest. A drawer full of papers was mostly receipts and a few bills. Finally left with the garbage under the sink, I found the can full to the brim—just my luck. I picked it up and put it next to the sink, throwing the trash in there as I picked through it, finding only disgusting remnants of ugly old food along with empty beer bottles and used paper plates. Finally, I threw it all back in and looked around for more to do. I walked toward the hall bathroom, where Dru had the door closed with the light on. I slid in, closing the door behind me.

"Anything interesting?" I asked her.

"Just a big disgusting turd that didn't go down," she answered, looking into the toilet bowl at the monster clinging to the side. I tried not to look. "I guess big turds make big turds," she added.

"There's a drawer in the kitchen full of bills and receipts. I didn't really look at everything in there." And I wanted to get out of that bathroom.

She switched off the light and we headed to the kitchen. I pointed out the drawer, and she loaded the contents into her backpack. "There might be something interesting here, cuz. Oh, and look. Here's a checkbook."

"Should we . . ."

She interrupted my question with a quick "Shut up." The reason was obvious. Car lights were coming up the road toward the house. My heart thudded. She closed the drawer and pulled me down to a low walk, and we waddled our way to the bedroom where we'd entered.

"Turn your light off."

The place was dark, and I crouched in bewilderment, wondering if there really was a Plan B. Then, with a soft groan, Dru was lifting something, and I heard the sounds of something happening on the wood floor. Dru was half-kneeling there and pointing her light at a hole. The bed was angled on her back, obviously an old Murphy that would fold into the wall.

"Get down there. Fast."

Her light was shining on the hole, and I could dimly make out a rough ladder leading down into blackness. Sliding in feet first, I felt my way down five steep rungs onto a dirt floor. A backpack came down after me, nicking my right ear and scaring the shit out of me. Dru was starting to come down, and the bed hit the floor with a thud that I was sure the whole county could hear. She moved something over the hole and joined me at the bottom, turning off her light and finding me with her hand in my face. She put her hands on my shoulders, and we played statue, barely breathing.

Eventually, we heard a rattle I guessed was coming from the front door, a shout, and then nothing. Five minutes later, we both jumped at the sound of a loud bang that could have been a gunshot, followed by a banging of wood and heavy footsteps, first going in one direction then eventually heading toward us, along with a low male voice that said what must have been "Jeremy?" Some slivers of light slid in through cracks above us as the light switch in the bedroom was flicked on, and we held our breaths, our foreheads touching and slick.

"Jeremy, where the fuck are you?" the voice said. It sounded a little raspy. The agonizing seconds ticked by, the footsteps walking heavily around the room, pausing, then eventually leaving, and the light shards disappeared. We could still hear the steps checking things out, pausing now and then, and finally stopping. The toilet flushed, and I thought I heart him say "shit." Eventually another noise became evident—the TV was on. I could feel Dru shaking her head in the dark.

After a minute, she knelt down on the dirt and flicked on her light, leaving it on the floor. She sat down, her back against a wall and hands tucked between her knees and signaled me to join her. I chose to squat as long as I could stand it, not wanting to sit down. After turning my light on, I skimmed the beam low along the floor. The room was a small cellar that looked no more than about twelve by twelve feet, the walls formed by cement blocks. Old open wood shelves lined the walls, with the exception of what looked like a half-sized refrigerator or freezer in the middle on one side. I realized it was making a very soft humming sound that would likely be hard to hear from above.

Feeling a little braver, I moved the light up and around the room a little higher. The shelves were filthy. The ones on my left held jars of pigment, what I figured was tattoo paraphernalia, some ammunition boxes, and two small glass aquariums or terrariums that looked empty. On the shelves to my right I could make out more pigment jars and a box of small empty vials with black screw caps. The far wall was mostly clear, with a couple of hooks on it, one holding a worn sheepskin jacket with a torn sleeve and what looked like leather chaps.

I turned the light toward Dru. She was leaning against the wall, her eyes closed. After a few seconds she opened them and lifted her head, making a quiet sign with her finger against her mouth. Then she surprised me by getting on her knees and crawling toward the appliance on the opposite wall. I grabbed her by the back of her belt, but she turned her head and shook it at me, mouthing "It's OK."

My ears were tingling, waiting for her to make a mistake and a noise audible to the man above. She lay on her side on the floor and opened the door to what was a small freezer sitting on a rough wood platform about six inches above the floor. I slowly edged closer to grab my own view of the contents. On the lower shelves were some bags of white powder piled on each other, looking like a common illegal substance. Dru was pointing at the bags, but I was more interested in the two upper shelves that held a thermometer and several test tube racks filled with small vials containing what looked like a powdery or crystalline material. Some contained frozen liquid. I pushed Dru's head out of the way to get a better look at the vials that were neatly labeled with printed labels. I could read the ones facing me, making out C. *Atrox*, C. *Adamanteus*, C-911.2, C-911.3, C. *Horridus* and several more. I looked at Dru, who gave me a quizzical look back, and shut the door painfully slowly. The motor immediately started humming again.

We stayed on the floor like that for at least an hour, until the sound of the TV ended and the heavy footsteps seemed to leave the house. I thought I heard a car or truck starting up. We waited ten minutes more; then Dru started back up the wood ladder.

"I think we're clear, cuz," she declared, moving some boards at the top, then pushing hard to raise the bed that hit the wall with a soft thud. I started to go up, handing her the backpack. Then I turned back, moving to the freezer and opening it again.

"Hang on a sec," I said in a loud whisper, still afraid of making noise. I grabbed the racks, looking for some tubes that had the same labels, hoping they wouldn't be missed, then grabbed four with names and four with numbers, taking off my outer left glove and sticking them in there and then into my shirt pocket. I went up the ladder.

"Good idea," she said, "if we can find out what they are."

She rearranged the boards over the hole and pulled down the Murphy bed. I was frazzled.

"Dru, let's get the hell out of here."

"Just one more thing," she said. She pulled a power cord for a computer out of the backpack. "This goes with something, but I didn't find it here, did you?"

"No, but who knows where it could be."

"We'll see," she said, heading toward the front door and examining the broken lock that had been shot out. "We could go this way, but let's go the way we came in."

We left through the window, with Dru shutting it hard and replacing the screen. She walked over to the parked truck instead of to the road and shined her light into the interior. Grinning, she pulled a large set of keys from her pocket.

"I found these," she said, holding them in my face.

A Toyota key opened the truck, and a minute later she emerged from it with a black laptop and stuck it into her pack. A huge clap of thunder roared overhead, and we started our walk back to the car, then began running as the rain poured on us.

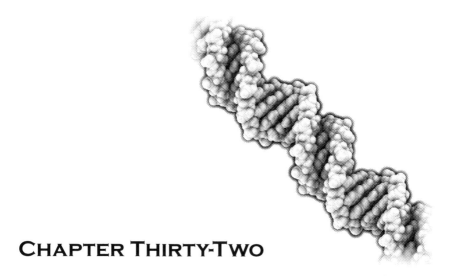

CHAPTER THIRTY-TWO

BY THE TIME WE GOT back to the car, we were drenched, and I was shaking with cold—or a combination of cold and recent fear, I wasn't sure which. It took Dru several back-and-forths to get the car turned around on the narrow, muddy road, and I only felt some tension let up when we were finally out and driving down the interstate. Dru was quiet and intently watching the road. I found a towel on the floor of the backseat and tried to wring out my hair. Dru switched on the radio, and we sat without talking for a good half an hour.

Finally, she leaned back, relaxing a little, and glanced at me. "Cuz, I'm famished."

"Oh my God."

"Well, I am. Can't help it. All that walking, climbing, shaking, running and lifting a Murphy bed—even though it didn't weigh that much—I need a fix from Joe's. I'm taking us to Joe's. We deserve it after all that."

"I'm not sure it's a good idea. I feel safer at home. Not to mention we're a major mess. Do you really want to walk in there looking like two drowned rats? I assume you're talking about Joe Picci's?"

Dru had been there before, I knew, with my family and probably with hers, but I hadn't realized she was a fan of the restaurant.

"Yeah, Picci's. They don't close until eleven tonight, and we can walk in the side door and sit in the back. No one will even notice us. We should get there around quarter-till."

"Yeah, he'll be thrilled."

But there was no dissuading her, and twenty-five minutes later we pulled into the parking lot of Joe Picci's. We tried to clean off our boots a little with the towel, but I could hear mine squeaking as we walked in the side door and found a booth at the back of the restaurant near the kitchen. I was facing the restaurant's main dining room and could make out Joe's younger son Frank minding the bar. He was the first to spot us, or me, and he gave me what might have been a smile and the finger sign that means "just a second." At least I *thought* it was his index finger.

Dru gave me a questioning look, wanting to know what I was looking at.

"It's Frank, coming this way. The good-looking, nice one who'll probably still be nice to two ugly women with soggy hair who are dressed like homeless people and dateless on a Saturday night."

Frank walked over, greeting us with a big hug like we were family or something—just like Joe would. He sat down by Dru, and we chatted a minute, with Dru giving him a beaming smile I hoped would divert his attention from our wardrobes. Frank was tall and well built with curly dark hair and a face I always thought looked mischievous, but in a more mature way now. His older brother, Joe Jr., was shorter and had a big belly, but he was easier to talk with. We ordered spaghetti and meatballs with Chianti, and Frank disappeared into the back. A server walked by, and I asked for a big Styrofoam cup of ice with a lid, along with our water. Very few people were left in the place.

A minute later we got the wine and water. When no one was around, I pulled the glove containing the vials out of my bag and stuck it in the cup of ice.

"Please don't let me forget this," I said, looking at Dru.

"So what is it? Drugs?"

"Not exactly. Look at the labels on these. They're names of animal species. Maybe spiders. Or snakes. Dru, this might be lyophilized snake venom."

"Ly what?" She took the cup, peering at a visible vial in the glove.

"Freeze-dried. Freeze-dried snake venoms; it's a way to preserve them. They have enzymes that can degenerate."

"C. *Horridus*," she read. "Doesn't sound good. More snake stuff," she said, looking at me.

"Yeah, more snakes. There were some empty terrariums in the cellar, but you never saw any snakes or terrariums there?"

"No. But I hadn't actually been down in that cellar before. I saw Jer go down a few times to get coke or some supplies, but that's all. He called it his secret vault that he built himself. I knew it was there, and it was Plan B—for basement."

I took back the cup, putting on the lid.

"Some of them were names, some numbers. Don't know what the numbers mean. I'll look up the names tomorrow."

"How can we find out what it is?"

"I'm pondering that. I can't exactly broadcast that I have a nice collection of possible snake venoms. We need to talk to Chance. By the way, did you run across anything besides the computer? Did you find a cell phone, or did he have one on him?"

"I only have that stack of papers we took and the key ring. If he had a phone on him, Chance might have taken it. We *do* need to talk to him—or find him."

"Dru, *this* little deal scared the shit out of me. And who *was* that in the house? Any ideas?"

"I don't know. Maybe a friend, a ranch worker, a neighbor, who knows?"

"Well, it was someone who wasn't afraid to shoot out the lock on the front door. I'd say he probably knew Jer pretty well."

"Are you thinking *Kral*? Cuz, if you are, our visitor doesn't seem to fit the profile."

"Who knows *what* Kral's like now? He may not have a persona anything like the staid professor of genetics he used to be."

"Maybe he wasn't so staid back then, either."

We were interrupted by the sound of the double doors to the kitchen opening behind us, and the older Joe came out carrying two huge plates of pasta. He gave us a big grin as he put the plates down.

"For my two favorite ladies," he said, and then I saw him taking note of our physical state, and his grin ratcheted down a slight notch.

"You two been playing cowboy out in this kind of weather?"

I couldn't think of what to say, so I looked at Dru for an answer.

"Oh, Joe, we went to a friend's ranch and got rained on. And the food was rotten—so here we are."

"Well, eat up." He strolled to the bar and chatted with Frank for a minute, then was back to refill our wine glasses.

"Wine's on the house," he said. "You girls need it."

Dru attacked her plate, and to my surprise, I started scarfing mine down too; what else was there to enjoy at that point, I thought. When we finished, Joe brought out two slices of cream cake and sat with us for a minute.

"You two be careful driving home now. How's those fine boys of yours, by the way?" He was looking at Dru.

"Oh. Just great," she said, slightly choking on her cake.

"Well, bring 'um by sometime. And this one's on me."

We left around midnight with the cup of ice in my hand and got home feeling exhausted and damp. Before putting the vials in the freezer, I wrote down the ones with names, including *C. Atrox*, *C. Adamanteus and C. Horridus*. Five others had numbers on the vials. I took a hot shower to warm up but couldn't go to sleep without looking up the names on the Internet and wasn't surprised to find they represented three species of pit vipers or rattlesnakes of the genus *Crotalus*, hence the names, *Crotalus Atrox* or western diamondback, *Crotalus Adamanteus* or eastern diamondback, and *Crotalus Horridus* or timber rattlesnake. Surprisingly, *C. Horridus*, found in the Northeast US, was described as having a high venom yield but a mild disposition. The eastern diamondback had really long fangs and was not as nice, with its venom having high hemorrhagic activity. The western diamondback had loads of venom and a tendency to be very aggressive when wound up.

That seemed enough to confirm the tubes contained pit viper venoms, but I wondered about the numbered tubes. Could they be altered venoms, combinations of venoms, some kind of purified by-products or maybe even hybrid venoms? Reading on, it sounded as though some species, if related closely enough, could be hybridized. But we hadn't seen any snakes around the ranch, so the origin of the venoms was a puzzle. They could have been bought, I figured, but the labels didn't look terribly professional; they didn't suggest labels from a commercial laboratory, but that didn't rule out a commercial source.

Dru walked into the study before going upstairs, and I showed her what I'd found.

"Venoms," she said, half asleep. She had the backpack in her hand and was turning to go upstairs. "So where are the fucking snakes?"

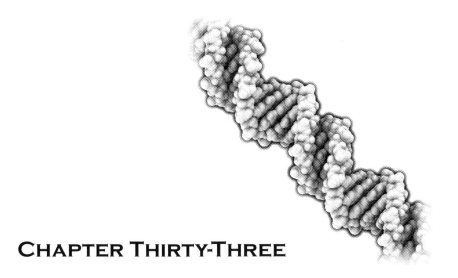

CHAPTER THIRTY-THREE

I FINALLY GOT IN BED but couldn't shut my brain down, even though I wanted sleep desperately. Finally giving up, I got up and went downstairs, got some water and then poured a thin layer of scotch in a glass, hoping that would knock me out. I wandered into the study and sat in the familiar chair at the desk and stared at the shelves, only a small lamp on the desk giving off a little light. My hands were folded on my lap, and I felt like a nun saying a rosary without thinking, the automatic words rolling through my brain and meaning nothing as the beads were pulled slowly between thumb and index finger. I finally got up and walked to the shelves, pulled out his book again and flipped to the page with the sticky note. The chapter was on chemical mutagens, and the page was filled with diagrams of chemical compounds with names like acridines, alkylating agents and nitrous acid, compounds that apparently wreak havoc with DNA, causing chromosome breaks, base mis-pairings and numerous other catastrophes.

The letter "M" was capitalized and on the sticky note, with the word "modification" underneath. I couldn't think of anything it might indicate; it might have been a research idea or a reference to one of his projects. Maybe it was totally unimportant, but the note seemed to have meant something to him, and I couldn't help feeling it was a message to me.

Thinking about messages, the letters from the football schedule came to mind again, and I went to the kitchen to retrieve my purse. I pulled out the football schedule, looking at the letters AGATTCC once more. Unlikely though it seemed, it could represent numbers on phone keys, 2428822. Using the desk phone, I blocked my number and called the phone number I'd found on Jeff's desk. When the voice told me to enter my sequence, I pressed the letters and waited, not really expecting anything but holding my breath nonetheless.

"Welcome, player number 77," the voice said. You have 30,287 points. A payoff schedule will be available as previously instructed."

So my hunch had been right. I'd need to make a phone call. By then, I was finally getting groggy. I wandered into the kitchen and saw the new set of keys on the table—a large, heavy ring with all shapes and sizes on it—and I wondered why Tats had needed so many. After putting them in a drawer, I went to bed.

Sunday morning we slept late, and I found Dru downstairs around noon. She made a big omelet, and I spent the afternoon going through mail and paying bills while Dru looked at Jer's computer.

"Loads of porno sites," she said.

"Are you surprised?"

"Well, he had me. So, yeah, I'm a little surprised."

"Right."

She came in an hour later.

"Well, I got into his e-mail. He had some from what sounds like a tattoo artist guy named Hog. Anyway, he visited tattoo supply websites and ordered some supplies. But there *is* an interesting e-mail. Well, maybe interesting. It's about a snake delivery on February seventeenth and a scheduled second delivery date of April twenty-fifth. The e-mail is from a Raymond Webb, and it sounds like the deliveries are from Jer to this guy. I don't know the name—Jer never mentioned him. So far I can't find Webb's name in the local directory or Googling. I didn't get much of anything else. I'm going to look through the papers you got out of that kitchen drawer."

She went upstairs and got the backpack, bringing it down and unloading a pile of crinkled and dirty papers on the desk. I thought I could smell stale French fries. She started making piles, spelling out to me what was in each. Household bills, receipts for the tattoo trade, including needles, gloves, disinfectants. A small receipt was really crinkled into a mess, but she opened it and squinted, trying to read the print.

"Bingo," she said. "It's a gas receipt from the seventeenth. He got gas in Laredo, cuz. I'm on it like flies on shit."

"Right."

She disappeared for half an hour; then she came back in with a bottle of beer. For each of us.

"A toast to tracking down Mr. Raymond Webb. Here's his address in Laredo.

We need to find out more about this guy. He could be a link to Kral and maybe to Chance. We need to go to Laredo—tomorrow."

"I can't go tomorrow. You know I need to work. I can't just call in."

"Cuz, I know Chance is in trouble. I just know it. Don't ask me how. You need to get some time off or I'll just go by myself."

"Now hold on, Dru. You can't go running down there by yourself, and you need to calm down. Chance is a big boy. For all we know, he's gone off somewhere, and we'll never hear from him again. Give me a day or two."

"You're wrong about him, cuz. He's not like that."

"And you've known him how long?"

"I can read him, Claudia, believe me." She was starting to get testy.

"All right, all right. It's only been four or five days since he called, so let me go to work tomorrow and figure something out. He said things were under control, whatever that meant."

"A few days ago you were all for getting more information right away."

I had no idea what I'd do and spent the night dreading the next morning.

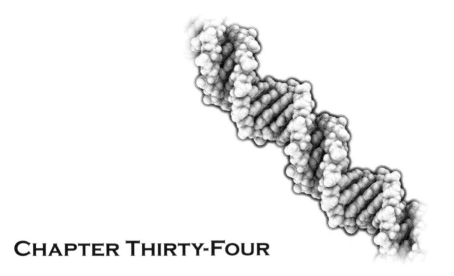

Chapter Thirty-Four

I WAS DOING PATIENT ROUNDS with Luis on Monday morning, feeling another hole forming in the bottom of my stomach. He was talking, and I had to force myself to listen, twice not noticing he was asking me a question. I used a blazing headache as an excuse. Thoughts weren't coalescing in my brain.

I called Detective Garcia as soon as I had a chance, explaining the number I'd entered as a sequence and relaying the phone message I'd received in response. His reaction was disappointing, to say the least, and he didn't seem impressed by my information.

"Thank you, Dr. Ranelli," was his cool reply. "We've pretty much tracked down the information we need from that telephone number, but we sincerely appreciate the call."

That was it. So much for my investigative abilities.

I briefly saw Julie on the ward later that day, and she gave me a cryptic signal that I thought meant we should talk in our office. I wondered if word was spreading that I was a total space cadet. She was sitting at her desk an hour later.

"Hey, you stay too long at the watering hole last night?" She almost looked pleased.

"I look that bad, huh?"

"More unhappy than anything. But those bags under your eyes don't help much. Are those scratches on your neck? I hope you had fun getting those."

Running my fingers over the skin, I felt some fine scratches I hadn't even noticed and gave a small laugh.

"Not really. Just doing a little yard work; I'm not particularly good at it."

I sat down. She had more info for me, obviously bubbling to the surface, anxious to get out of her mouth.

"Jenna's dead. Died this morning. Got septic this weekend and went fast. Autopsy's going on right now downstairs."

"Not at the ME's?"

"Apparently it doesn't sound like a medical examiner's case, and they didn't take it. Still seems like probably an unusual drug reaction. Very weird, though. Scary."

I really wasn't surprised at the news. The times were not good.

"And more bad news, really." She hesitated.

"What?" I wondered if maybe some news of my imminent arrest was making the rounds, maybe for failing to report a killing.

"A body's been found near Blanco."

"Jeff?" Who else would it be?

"They don't know for sure yet. It's badly burned. DNA pending. They still haven't located next of kin, though, as far as I've heard."

"I wonder what the hell he could have been doing over there?"

"Don't have any idea. I'll keep you posted on what I can find. It hasn't made the news yet."

"You sure hear a lot."

"My family has con-nections, honey. Comes in handy sometimes."

I decided to skip the Monday conference (again) and went down to the morgue to pay my last respects to Jenna, having no intention of going to a funeral. It was a small, sub-optimally ventilated room in the basement, and I had to call on a speakerphone outside the door. I put on the obligatory paper wardrobe from boxes containing gowns, hats, masks and booties sitting on a nearby shelf. The assistant, whom I'd met before, let me in, and the pathologist was in the middle of bread-loafing the liver, nearly getting his masked nose into each slice as he peered closely, his knife making uniform cuts through the organ. He saw my nametag and department, looking up as I walked in. I knew the familiar smell and forced myself to ignore it.

"What a mess," he said to me. "Her extremities are necrosing off. *Were.* A hell of a way to go."

I just stared at the huge mess Jenna's body had become. What wasn't decaying was mainly covered by huge dark splotches, her skin sloughing off in some places. An infection of the dead tissue was adding to the foul smell.

"So you guys were calling it adult purpura fulminans, cause unknown?" he asked.

"Well, I wasn't treating her, but I sort of knew her—a little. She presented with DIC. Bad, no apparent cause. Negative cultures. I'm sure you read all that. Skin biopsy showing thrombosis consistent with that diagnosis. Apparently it was out of control. There's been some speculation about a possible drug reaction, but nothing definite as far as I know. I imagine the attending will be down to see this."

"Sounds like the subject of a future grand rounds to me. I found some GI bleeding, adrenal and renal hemorrhage, pulmonary congestion."

He picked up a lung and cut through it, removing a two-inch segment. Then he gave it a good squeeze for my benefit, and bloody fluid foamed out, dripping all over his already-bloody glove. He gave a shrug. "Like I said, she's a mess."

"Yeah. That's life."

I went back upstairs and out one of the sets of hospital doors on a side that bordered a small, slightly worn-looking park. It was a bright, sunny day in the high seventies, and I took off my white coat and walked across the street. I sat on a bench and waited for the conference to end. My cell rang, and I hesitated in answering, seeing Stephen Palmer on the ID.

"Claudia, it's Stephen."

"I know." I knew the emotionless tone of my speech would worry him, but there was nothing to be done about it.

He paused, then finally said, "Claudia, I spoke with Dr. Renfrew over the weekend—at the nursing home. His mind isn't entirely what it was, I'm sure, but I believe what he told me is likely true."

I wasn't happy with that, and it added to my worries.

"Stephen," I said, trying not to sound too worried or irritated, "I really didn't want you out asking things about my father. I thought we agreed you wouldn't."

"Claudia, I've only spoken with *him*, and I doubt he'll remember the conversation for more than a few minutes. Do you or do you not want to hear what he had to say?"

"I do. Want to hear about it."

He gave a sigh I could just hear.

"He seemed to say that your father and a Dr. Kral had a major falling out. It sounded as though Kral was a geneticist on the faculty at the same time, supposedly a brilliant man. Your father apparently told Renfrew at one point that he was concerned about the nature of Kral's studies, even implying some of them might be with data obtained outside of approved research protocols, but Renfrew claims he never saw any evidence of that. Kral thoroughly denied those allegations, but the antagonism between the two was evident, with your father seemingly maintaining that Kral should lose his staff appointment. Renfrew thought maybe your father was jealous of Kral, but when Kral left the staff suddenly with no warning and no forwarding information, Renfrew changed his mind. Still, Renfrew maintains he never found any evidence in Kral's lab or in any of his papers that his research was questionable. He seems to vaguely remember some letters of inquiry he received about Kral after he left, but Renfrew has no recollection of whom they were from. It sounds as though your father dropped the subject after Kral left. It's all pretty interesting, if you don't mind my saying. I'm looking up some of Kral's published research articles, but he wasn't terribly prolific. I'd like to talk with you," he threw in at the end.

I thought I was ready for that, but I wasn't. I could barely speak.

"Stephen, I just can't talk right now. I wish I could. Right now I'm going to talk with Still—I'm going to ask for a leave of absence if he'll give me one. Otherwise I'm just quitting the fellowship."

"Claudia, what the hell's going on?"

"I'm really sorry. I'll talk to you tomorrow."

I turned off my cell, having made a decision without really consulting myself, but it felt like the only option. Later, back at my office, I called Still's secretary and told her I needed to speak to him right away—an emergency situation. At four-thirty I was sitting across from him.

"Doctor, is there something we can help you with? This is an awfully bad time to lose another physician on your service."

Still was giving me the guilt trip, and I was afraid I'd cave in.

"Sorry," I said, feeling lame about the whole thing, including my lack of a clear reason. "I really need to do this. It's a major family problem."

He gave me a questioning look, and I figured he probably knew there was hardly any family left.

"How long?"

I hadn't thought it out clearly, but I said, "Six months max. Maybe less."

"Can you give me a few days to regroup the staff?"

"Sure." I couldn't desert him immediately.

"By the way, Claudia," he started, and I froze, wondering what question he'd be bringing up. "Do you happen to know anything—unusual—about Dr. Dunn—Jeff Dunn?" He had a troubled, quizzical look on his face. What did *unusual* mean, I wondered. Probably being dead was unusual, but he may not have been privy to Julie's rumors.

"Not really. He seemed—seems—pretty normal. A good doctor, nice guy. Why?"

"Well, obviously we're fearing the worst. And no one's found any next of kin at this point."

I didn't know what to say. "I liked Jeff. He seemed like a pretty normal guy to me. I think he mentioned a father, but it was probably a short remark. I don't remember him mentioning any specific family he was in contact with recently. Have you heard anything more?"

"No. We're waiting for the police to figure things out."

I figured he knew more than he was going to tell me, but I wanted to be out of that office ASAP.

Linda was sitting at her desk when I left. She looked up at me and shook her head.

"This department's going to hell," she said. "Thank God you're around, or Still would have a heart attack." I walked out quickly, before he could have one.

When I got home, Dru was chain smoking at the kitchen table, fumbling around with her cell phone. Four empty beer bottles, a Coke can and a bottle of rum were on the table.

"Have some friends over for drinks, Dru?"

She looked up, giving me a wicked smile. "I don't remember." She shook her head. "No Chance again. We need to check out the guy in Laredo."

I sat down. "Dru, I got a leave of absence from work today. I just need to give them a couple of days to get re-staffed. We could go on Thursday—late morning probably. We'll still get there by daylight."

"Every day we wait could mean something. Maybe something bad we might be able to prevent."

"We don't have any reason to believe he's in trouble. He said it's under control."

"I have this bad feeling."

"That's because you drank at least four beers and half a bottle of rum. We'll go Thursday. Why don't you go and get some rest?"

She got up to go upstairs.

"There's something rotten in Laredo, cuz."

I cleaned up the mess, ate something and caught the news. There was no mention of a burned body found near Blanco, and I was too tired to check the news online. Depressed, I went into Dru's bathroom and pilfered an Ambien. All I could think about was the suspension of my career as a doctor (maybe the end of it?) and about Kral, the seeming origin of all my problems. The mad professor. The ultimate meanie. A modern-day Moriarty, I thought. M . . . M is for Moriarty? Maybe. Dad had read most of Sherlock Holmes to me when I was small, and I ate it up. "Are there really people like Moriarty?" I'd asked him one time. I don't remember if he answered.

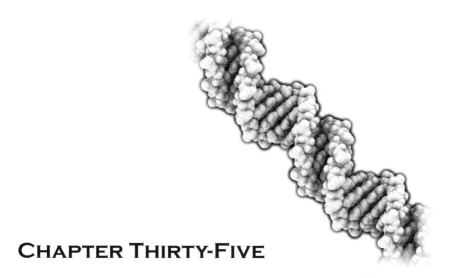

Chapter Thirty-Five

I WALKED AROUND WORK IN a daze on Tuesday and Wednesday, fearing questions about why I was leaving, not looking at anyone longer than necessary. Julie was one of the first I told, since she'd be bearing some of the brunt of my decision.

"You're kidding," she said, putting her hands on her newly shrunken hips. She almost seemed sorry for me. "There's got to be more to this than a troubled cousin who's staying with you."

"It's a lot of things that struck at once. Things are still—unwinding. I'll tell you about it sometime."

Right, I thought.

"I'm really sorry to leave you like this," I added.

"I'll bet some of the staff can help me out, sugar," she said, smiling, and we both knew she meant a certain molecular geneticist. And that was my next problem. I couldn't face seeing him and had decided to take a cowardly approach, which embarrassed the hell out of me. It took twenty minutes for me to write the note, ten for me to walk over and slip it under his hallway door with his name and "CONFIDENTIAL" on the envelope, and five minutes to get to my car before the real slobbering started. It was almost seven, and I figured he wouldn't find it until Wednesday morning.

Dru was gone when I got home, no sign of her in the house and her car gone from the garage. I had a sinking feeling for her and for me and didn't need to be alone at that point—couldn't be. I called her cell, but only voice mail answered.

"Damn it, Dru, call me right away," was my message.

Sitting down at the kitchen table, I saw a small note propped on a beer bottle that was loosely closed with an old cork.

"Cuz—Be home late. Don't worry. D"

I immediately started to worry and drank the warm beer. Ten minutes later, totally groggy, I wondered if she'd slipped something into it. Now I'm pretty sure she did. I collapsed on the couch and didn't move until the sounds of the garage door opening and the kitchen door slamming shut woke me. It was ten-thirty or so. After grabbing a beer from the fridge, she came in and nearly sat on my feet. She was wearing jeans, engineers' boots, a scruffy brown leather jacket and a knit cap pulled down low over most of her head. And she looked excited.

"You went to Laredo." I shook my head at her. "What happened?"

She took a long drink, pulled off the hat and rested her head on the couch back.

"It was a long day, cuz."

She sat up and looked at me.

"I sat in my car near Webb's house for at least three hours. He finally showed up, stayed inside for a good hour, and then I followed him."

"Oh God."

"You said it. Then he made stops at Home Depot, a liquor store and a FedEx office. Finally I followed him for a couple of miles to a warehouse area, but I didn't dare follow any further. I could see the building he went to. I brought these."

She pulled a small pair of binoculars from her jacket pocket.

"I saw a black truck parked by his. It had something like *RayVen Industries* printed on the side. Interesting, huh? I'm definitely going back to find out more about RayVen Industries."

She took another long swig and sat back, giving me an I-told-you-so look.

"You're not going without me this time, Dru. It can wait until Thursday."

She nodded. I suspected she would have preferred some company.

"Thursday it is. Just get the hell back here early enough."

"So what about Webb? What does he look like?"

"I didn't get a chance to get close. I just saw him pull up in the driveway and park in the garage. He wore a cowboy hat—black. I'd say middle-aged, probably dark hair, tight butt, no glasses, spit out the window a few times. He looked pretty well built when I glimpsed him getting out of his truck by the warehouse."

"How do you plan on finding out more? We can't just go strolling in there."

"Hopefully, we can just ask a few questions. We'll see. I'm planning it out. Trust me. And tomorrow I'll see what I can find out from here. Maybe they have a website."

I was too groggy to ask much more, except for one thing.

"Did you add something to that beer?"

"Of course not." She got up to go upstairs.

"Don't ever do that again. It's dangerous!" I yelled as she ran up.

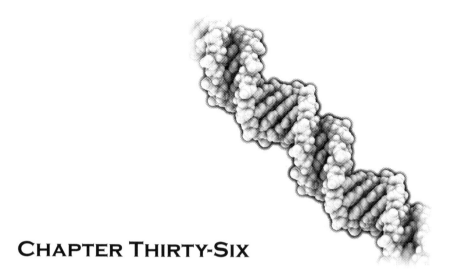

Chapter Thirty-Six

WEDNESDAY WAS MY LAST FULL day to get much of anything done, and most of it was spent going over last minute information about patients and projects with Luis and Julie. Another resident was scheduled to show up on Thursday, but they'd have their hands full. Any spare thoughts were on Stephen, wondering when he'd found my note, half expecting him to call, disappointed when he hadn't by the end of the day. But that was for the better.

I found Dru asleep in her room at home, her laptop on the bed with her. The day was damp and chilly, and I put a log in the living room fireplace. When she came down, we sat in front of it, dunking toast in hot coffee.

"So, what did you find on RayVen Industries—anything?"

"It's interesting, cuz. I got directed to a website, but the address in Laredo doesn't sound right—not the address of the warehouse he went to—and it's advertised as a glass company, like windows, mirrors, tabletops, and aquariums and terrariums. They call the store Ray Glass. Clever, huh?"

"Yeah, clever, but not what I was thinking."

"You were thinking what I was thinking. Jer's e-mail mentioned a snake delivery. I thought *Ven* in *RayVen* stood for venom—as in snake venom."

We sat in silence for a while, listening to the wind pick up and knock a tree limb against the window. Finally she said, "Maybe glass is only part of the story—part of the business. Maybe something is in their terrariums."

Vaguely I heard a car door shut, and a minute later we jumped when the front doorbell rang. I looked at Dru, but she shook her head. The blinds and drapes were closed, but the large wood front door had a peephole. Dru ran up to take a look, obviously hoping Chance had shown up, and made a racket as she tripped and almost fell on the rug and rattled a picture on the entryway wall. She turned back to me.

"It's some *guy*," she whispered.

I moved her out of the way to take a look. Even with no porch light on I could see Stephen, looking chilly in a long wool coat with the collar up.

"Who is he?" She was grabbing my shoulder.

"A friend from work." I didn't want to open the door, but he had to know I was there after all that racket.

Dru looked at me. "More than a friend," she said. She shook her head. "Might as well open it. Just get rid of him fast."

Opening the door, I wondered how bad I looked. Bad was probably a good thing, under the circumstances.

"Dr. Palmer. What a surprise. Come out of the cold." My mouth was dry.

"Is it any warmer in here?" he asked, walking in. He had a knack for being a smart aleck. He walked into the living room, and Dru hovered behind me. He glanced at her, and I remembered my manners.

"Dr. Palmer, this is my cousin Dru. She's staying with me for a while."

If he was surprised to see a young woman in leggings and a Lethal Threat Flying Skull shirt with a long braid and cowboy boots, he didn't show it. They said their hellos, and it was awkward for a few seconds, until Dru said she had things to take care of upstairs and trotted up and out of sight, closing her bedroom door with a helpful thud. I was at a loss. We sat down on opposite ends of the sofa, the fire going and making my face feel hot.

"I thought I deserved more than a note," he said, looking as good as usual, sitting in his coat with his hands in his pockets, looking at the fire. I had on a big long sweater that covered my hands and had a big cowl collar that I could bury my face into if I wanted to sink down and get lost.

"You're right. You did. It was easier for *me*—and, really, I didn't know if you'd even care that much."

"You don't think much of yourself, do you?"

I didn't know what to say to that.

"Stephen, normally I'm a pretty self-confident person. I'm proud of my parents, what I've done, how I've lived. I'll fight for people I care about. But this isn't a—normal time for me. And I absolutely don't want you involved in my problems. I know you'd feel the same if you were in my place, so I hope you can respect that." I was trying to sound firm but heard my voice crack and waver. It hurt to swallow.

"Does this have anything to do with your father and that Dr. Kral that Renfrew mentioned? Or are you in some other kind of trouble? I don't like the sound of what you're telling me."

"No. It's just personal. Dr. Kral's dead. I was just wondering about my father; I wondered if anything was bothering him when he—they—died."

Lying was starting to get easier.

"How do you know Kral's dead?"

"I just spoke with somebody who knew him—pretty well."

"So you're worrying about your father's state of mind when he died? Why worry about that now? Why let it ruin your life?"

I sighed, trying to think of what to say—then deciding to go for some mental imbalance, embarrassing though it was.

"Stephen, sometimes some of us just can't cope with the past—or the present, for that matter. I need a break from reality. Don't waste your time worrying about me."

Oh that hurt and sounded so stupid. Slushy. Mushy.

He exhaled deeply and looked at me, shaking his head.

"Claudia, I don't understand a word of what you're telling me."

He got up and moved next to me on the sofa, sitting down close and grabbing me by the shoulders, drawing my face close to his. His eyes looked moist and clear, and I knew I shouldn't look at them—and was, in fact, on the brink of letting go, but another pair of eyes I remembered from a picture stopped me, and I panicked, needing a quick end to the situation.

"Dru!" I screamed at the top of my voice. "Dru!" I yelled again as my vocal cords stung from the volume.

I heard the thud of boots coming rapidly down the stairs—and then she was hugging me, running her hand through my hair. I clung to her like a life raft and cried like a two-year-old.

"Get her some help," Stephen said.

And the front door closed.

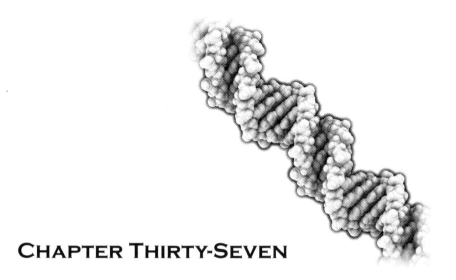

Chapter Thirty-Seven

I GOT UP THE NEXT morning feeling exhausted and extremely embarrassed, deciding a definitely tougher stance was absolutely necessary for survival. I'd have a very difficult time ever looking Stephen in the eyes again and would probably avoid it if at all possible.

Dru was up early too, and we collided in the kitchen as she was backing away from a smoking toaster.

"I thought I told you I preferred no smoking in the house."

"Very funny, cuz. If you'd leave the little dial where I set it, I wouldn't be burning the house down." Her eyes lingered on mine—mine still a little reddish and puffy. "You feeling better?"

"Mucho better. No more crying. I'm done with that. I *did* get rid of him in a hurry, though, didn't I?"

"Yeah. Too bad. He looked hot."

I gave her a dirty look.

"Sorry. Some day maybe you can try to convince him you're really sane. Right now, we'd best get going. Long drive ahead."

I drove to the office for the last time and stared at my books and desk contents, deciding what to take and what to leave there. Leaving the books, I got most of my desk items in a box. My white coat I left hanging on a hook, lost among several others. I left the box on the desk and stopped at

Still's office. Luckily Linda wasn't at her desk, and Still's door was open, so I poked my head in. I wasn't the only one looking a little tired; his usually animated face was looking not-so-sparkly. We said our mutually non-ebullient hellos, and I stayed in the doorway.

"Dr. Ranelli, we have the service covered for now, but I would sure appreciate it if you could return soon. Your family has an excellent reputation around this institution, and you'll be missed. Keep in touch."

I promised to do that, but wondered how he'd feel if he'd known what I'd been up to lately. I stopped to get my box and left a note for Julie, thanking her and wishing her luck, the latter of which I didn't really mean.

At home, there was a strange vehicle in the garage that wasn't Dru's. I walked in, afraid we had an unexpected visitor, hoping it might be Chance. It was neither. Dru was in the kitchen with her backpack and a grocery bag on the table, putting some drinks in a cooler.

"Where's your car?" I asked.

"Rented one, cuz. I think it's better to use something different once in a while. Go change so we can get moving."

I wasn't sure that was going to be much help, but I ran upstairs and got my jeans and boots on and stuck the Beretta in my little bag again, then tucked it under the seat of the small tan Toyota pickup as we got started.

"You have a plan, I assume, Sherlock?"

"Yeah. Sort of. I want to go back to that warehouse and see if we can find out something. This could be a dead end; I don't know. Something tells me it's worth a try."

We drove over the flat, dry landscape for three hours, the scenery displaying shades of brown and bright yellow tones due to the lack of rain. A few oil rigs looked like small rockets about to launch. Dru had a map, and we exited to the west of the city onto Mines Road into a definitely warehouse-looking area. She eventually made two right turns, and we were looking at a small paved road heading toward at least three good-sized buildings that didn't have much in the way of identifying signage, as far as I could tell.

"Dru, this doesn't look like a glass dealership to me," I said.

"This apparently is warehousing. The retail shop is near downtown, according to the address. But this is where Webb came."

There was a metal gate onto the property, but it was open, and there seemed to be a distinct lack of activity around the place. Dru pulled off to the side of the street we were on and shut off the motor. She reached behind her for her backpack and unzipped it, then pulled out a black wig and spent ten minutes getting it on with my help. Next, her hoodie came off, and she unzipped her tight sweater underneath enough to show some cleavage. Some dark lipstick the color of de-oxygenated lips and some big ear hoops completed the picture.

"Really," I said. "What's your story line?"

"I'm looking for my cousin Juan."

"You don't have a cousin Juan."

"Yeah, but there's bound to be one here."

She drove the truck into the driveway and parked it in an inconspicuous spot next to an enclosed larger truck that partially hid us from view.

"You stay here and stay low," she said. "I don't see Webb's car. He drives a white Cadillac Escalade. The glass business must be good here. Hopefully I won't be long."

She disappeared in her tight jeans and cowboy boots, and I sat there listening and watching, hoping no one would find me. An irritating thirty minutes later I heard a male and female voice approaching in my direction, the conversation in rapid Spanish, and I cracked the window. Dru had been raised speaking partial English, partial Spanish and had no problems navigating with the latter. I, on the other hand, knew a bare minimum and could only pick out a few words they spoke. They had come out from behind the first warehouse, and I caught a glimpse of a handsome guy with a short black ponytail and muscles proudly displayed in a short-sleeved T-shirt. They walked behind the truck next to me, and the conversation went on for a few minutes before they walked to the front and climbed into the truck. I ducked. When I looked again, they were driving down the road toward the farthest warehouse. They disappeared around a corner.

I suddenly felt exposed without the big truck around. I listened for sounds of approaching voices or vehicles. A few minutes later, there were faint sounds of two guys talking, then laughing, and I caught a whiff of cigarette smoke. About fifteen minutes after that, I heard a car coming pretty rapidly up the driveway, then skirt far to my left and stop. The car door slammed, and I waited for the sound of approaching footsteps and a voice asking me what the hell I was doing there.

But the footsteps didn't approach, and when I got the nerve to peek out, no one was in sight—but the sounds of some voices shouting were coming from somewhere nearby. Unfortunately, a white Escalade was parked directly in front of the warehouse entrance. I was stuck, trying to figure out what to do, knowing I really didn't want to talk to Webb. My instinct told me to get the truck out of there, and that's what I did. Dru had left the keys in the ignition, and I drove it back out of the gate as inconspicuously as you can drive a truck down a road and then parked on the street, trying to use a few bushes as camouflage. Wouldn't you know, about two minutes later the automatic gate closed. I sat on the street worried sick about Dru, until finally the enclosed truck came back toward the first warehouse and stopped by the side of it. It stayed there for a few minutes; then Dru jumped out the passenger door and looked around, obviously noting the absence of me and the truck. Finally she noticed me on the street and gave a small wave, then disappeared back into the truck, and it started heading toward the gate and the street. The gate opened, and the truck pulled up in front of mine. Dru jumped out, joined me, and we drove off.

"Webb showed up," I said. "I didn't want to get stuck inside the gate."

"Good thinking, cuz," she said, looking back.

"Was that Juan?"

"Actually, that was Daniel."

I was half listening, trying to concentrate on what was around me, and after a few blocks, I noticed a white vehicle behind us. I slightly panicked at the thought it might be an Escalade. It was too far behind to tell, but by the time we were back onto I-35 it was nowhere that I could see, and I started to relax.

"So what happened back there?"

"Well, I saw him working in the back, loading some boxes or whatever, and he told me it was a warehouse not open to the public—but we got to chatting about all kinds of shit, and eventually I asked him what they stored. At first he said it was just glass and glass products, glass cutting equipment, terrariums and the like, so I glommed onto the terrarium comment and said something about animals people put in terrariums, including snakes, like I was really interested in snakes or something. And he bit."

She looked at me with a half smile.

"And that's when you drove off to the other building?"

"Yeah. He said that's where the snakes were kept and I could see it if I didn't tell a soul. I said I wouldn't, of course, and we went into the building."

"I probably shouldn't have let you go alone."

"I had my gun, and I wasn't particularly worried about him—he seemed OK—nice, actually. We went in through an unloading area with all kinds of boxes and junk piled up in it, and I asked him where they got the snakes and what they did with them. He said they come in from different places, mostly in Texas, but the really interesting ones are brought in by a guy from Devine who's an expert at breeding. The description is Jeremy."

"Was," I corrected.

"Yeah. He was pretty vague about what they did with them, but he mumbled something about a lab that collects the venom and makes things from it; I didn't really understand what he meant. Maybe they make antivenoms?"

"Venins," I corrected. "Antivenins."

Actually, I found out later that Dru was right. Although antivenin was the original terminology, in 1981 the World Health Organization decided that the correct terminology in English would be "antivenom."

"Venoms, venins, whatever. I don't know if the lab is nearby or what. Oh—and I asked him who owns the warehouse, but he didn't want to go there—said he'd be in trouble just for showing me this place. Then he showed me a few snakes in one of the rooms, but he said the rest of the place was off limits. Anyway, we shot the bull for a while longer, and I promised I'd give him a call—said I was visiting my dad in Laredo."

She looked straight ahead with a somber expression, and I figured that more than conversation had probably taken place in that warehouse. But she didn't want to go there, and neither did I.

We started the long drive back at six o'clock and got held up in a long line at the border patrol station.

"Take that wig and lipstick off," I told Dru. "They'll think—well, just take it off."

She did, wiping off the lipstick with her arm.

"We missed something at Devine," she said. "Obviously there's something going on there that we missed. We need to go back."

"Dru, we're going in circles, and we may never accomplish anything."

"I think it's worth checking out. We should probably just go straight there."

"It's too late. It'll be after ten, and we won't know where we're going. Let's go home and see if we can find the ranch on a satellite map. Maybe we can see where the road goes and if there are other buildings on the property. We don't even know how big that ranch is."

"OK. We go tomorrow. But so far we've found out a little more each time we've checked around, and Chance still hasn't called. I can't just sit and wait."

I couldn't either, but I wished to hell it didn't involve a bunch of snakes.

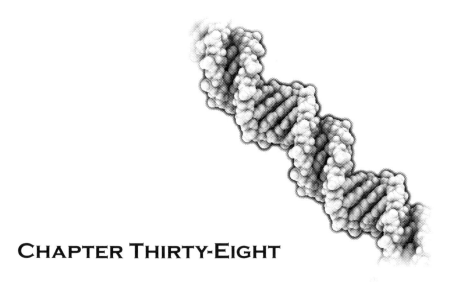

CHAPTER THIRTY-EIGHT

DESPITE HER EXPRESSED DESIRE TO get back to Devine in a hurry, Dru slept late on Friday. I suspected that her friend Ambien had something to do with it. At any rate, we both decided it might be better to rest up during the day and get there later when fewer or no people might be around. We checked out an online satellite map, but the area was confusing. The ranch was off a small road that wasn't labeled on the maps we saw, and the road might have been put in after the air photos were taken. We finally found an area that could have been the one—a large ranch with a small building about the right distance from the road. The small road on the property wound past the house and further into the densely-treed property, then split into two roads, each heading toward the far corners of the ranch. There didn't seem to be much else there, but on the road going to the east was a rooftop of a somewhat obscured building. By our rough measurements, it looked to be about a mile from the house.

We waited until eight o'clock that night to leave, putting on our boots and dressing for some possibly rough walking. The weather had gotten warm during the day but it was chilly at night, and it didn't get dark until after seven since the daylight saving time change. Making the drive south once more, we used the small rental truck and again parked on the narrow road next to the ranch entrance. With our jackets wrapped around our waists, we retraced our previous route. This time we were a little more brave, walking on the road until we got near to the house, then sticking to the side of the road until we were sure no one was there.

The house was dark, and Jer's truck was where we'd seen it last, no sign of it having been moved. A quick peek at the front door showed the lock hadn't been fixed since it was shot out. The road skirted to the right of the house and was rough gravel. It crunched as we walked along behind the beam from Dru's flashlight. She kept the pace to a pretty fast walk, but the road wound around a tank, then down a hill and back up again, turning the mile into a longer trek. Forty minutes later the road ran alongside a tall wire perimeter fence. Dru shined her light up to the top of it.

"High," she said. "Barbed wire on top."

We could see a large building inside, one story and probably concrete.

"How the hell are we going to get in there, Dru?"

She shook her head, and we walked on, then stopped suddenly and dove to the wooded side of the road. We could hear voices not far ahead. Two men were talking, and we could make out bits of their conversation that became more obscured when the wind picked up.

". . . finish the perimeter check."

". . . she'll never know. Keep mine cold. And tell Sonia I'm coming."

". . . gonna get paid?"

"See you in twenty . . . close up."

The voices trailed away.

"Sounds like they're leaving," Dru said. "Let's find the entrance."

We stuck to the side of the road, and about fifty feet further along we spotted the gate. It was just as tall as the rest of the fencing.

"Stay here a second," she said. Crouching low, she ran up to the gate. I could just make out a DANGER sign on it. She came back and knelt beside me.

"*Shit*. Shit, shit, shit—It only opens with a remote control."

I'd been thinking the same thing, slapping myself for a lack of common sense or foresight. We both knew what we'd forgotten to do. She looked at me.

"Well, maybe not shit yet; maybe just a stinking fart."

"Did you see one in there?" I asked her.

"I didn't notice. We were in kind of a hurry. I've got to go back there. You stay and watch. Got your phone on vibrate?"

"Everything's vibrating."

"Is there reception here?"

I looked at my phone. "One or two bars. Wish I were in one."

"Let me know if anything's headed my way," she said, giving me a tap on the back and heading back toward the house.

I stayed crouched behind some bushes across from the gate until my knees started throbbing, and I finally put them on the ground. The temperature was cooling down rapidly, and I slipped the jacket and some driving gloves on, but I still felt shaky. Five minutes later the gate opened, and an SUV came out, heading back toward the house. A light came on over the gate as it opened and shut. I flattened to the ground as the headlights came directly at me before turning. Rising back up, I caught enough of a glimpse that suggested no passenger was in the car. I pulled out my phone.

"Dru, SUV coming back in your direction. No passenger as far as I can tell."

"Got it," she said, like it was no big deal. "Viper One over and out."

I guessed I was Viper Two. I decided Viper Two was not in the best location, being right smack in front of the lights of an outgoing vehicle, so I moved over to the left of the gate. A few minutes later, some bushes behind me started making swishing noises, and I became transfixed staring toward them, wondering what sort of hellish creature might emerge. About twenty minutes later, a huge black pickup drove to the gate and went out. I caught a glimpse of a guy in a black cowboy hat. I looked up toward the light again, looking for a camera. None there, but I wasn't positive. I called Dru once more.

"Dru. Second vehicle coming your way. Big black monster truck that ate Chicago. What's happening?"

"OK so far. The first car's gone. I'm almost at the house. I'll let you know soon."

"The place is dark," I said. "Probably everyone's gone."

"Stay put, cuz. Viper One out."

I did, even as the temperature kept falling. I took off a glove and sat playing blackjack on my cell phone as a distraction. Half an hour later, a pickup came toward the gate, and I recognized the dark vehicle as Jeremy's. Dru was driving and pulled up in front of the gate and rolled down the window. I came out of the bushes.

"I found a remote opener behind the visor. Let's hope it works. Jump in, cuz."

I ran around the truck and got in, feeling uncomfortable in his vehicle. Dru had the opener in her hand and pushed the button. The gate hesitated, then opened, and we drove through as the light beamed down on us, showing a small road winding to and around the building. We followed the road, and I turned around, watching the gate close behind us as we made our way around the rectangular building made of cement blocks—a building apparently without windows. We passed a bank of air conditioning units on the side and parked in the back. On the back end of the building there was a metal door to the left and a closed, wide loading door to the right.

"I had a hell of a time getting this thing to start," she said, giving the truck door a kick as we got out. She pulled out the big key ring she'd taken from the house.

"One of these should fit, with any luck."

"I wonder if there's an alarm system."

"Probably nothing that would alert the police, I'm thinking. Something tells me Jer would not want the police called to this place. Let's try the back door," she said, walking to the gray metal door with a key lock and an intercom to the left of it. The second key she tried opened it, and she led the way in, both of us with our flashlights on.

I held my breath and waited for an alarm to sound, but nothing happened—no beeps, no nothing. We scanned the walls, but no alarm system was obvious. It didn't comfort me much. We scanned the room with our lights. It was humming with the low-level sound of appliances, apparently freezers and refrigerators. Piles of boxes were at the far end, along with a sink that was nearly obscured. The floor felt gritty.

Straight ahead was a dark hallway, which we headed down single-file, Dru in front. She flashed at a closed door to our right that had Clean Room stenciled on it. It was locked, and she waved us forward with her light. The hallway split into left and right corridors, and I followed her to the left. Several yards down the corridor was a heavy door to our right; this one was stenciled with Restricted Entry.

Dru raised her eyebrows and tilted her head to the side, giving me a sign that she wanted to check it out. This door was also locked with a keyed lock; to the right was a card reader. Since no card key was on her ring, she tried the key ring again and found a match next to the back door key. She pulled the door open slowly, flashed her light around the room, and then snapped on a light switch to her left. The room wasn't large but it was full of boxes and implements. A line of storage cupboards with a countertop lined one wall. Another wall had a large area of wall hooks holding tongs, poles, long and hooked implements, coats, a shovel, and things I didn't recognize. I spotted some masks and bags in open boxes and a box full of dirty towels. A first aid kit hung on part of a wall. A side-by-side refrigerator/freezer hummed directly to our right. Piles of more boxes were to our far right all along the wall. Straight-ahead was another metal door, this one stenciled "Danger, Hot Room, Authorized Personnel Only."

Dru started to pull it open, and I shook my head. She ignored me and pulled it open, which took some work because the lower door edge appeared to have a rubber shield, eliminating any crack at the bottom. This room felt large, and the cement floor again made the gritty sound beneath our feet. We swept our lights, and the shine of glass flashed back from everywhere. I didn't really want to know, but I swept my light over a bank of switches by the door, and Dru flicked them on, one by one. Fluorescent lights on the ceiling blinked on, and terrariums came into view. Many terrariums, stacks and stacks of them, all seemingly containing snakes, some housing around four or five, but I wasn't counting and didn't want to look for too long. We walked around, taking in the setup. Dru came over to me.

"Cuz, is this legal?"

I shook my head. "I have no idea."

It looked like most of the units had temperature and humidity recorders, and a sticker on the upper front of each unit classified its contents. I recognized some species names, often Crotalus. The stickers also had the number and sex of the snakes inside, and each sticker had a series of numbers and data obviously of importance to the keepers. Written charts with recordings of feedings, sheddings, defecation, and whatever else they did hung from each stack of units. I picked a chart up, and Dru looked over my shoulder.

"God," she said, "they even want to know when a snake takes a shit?"

A very large terrarium was somewhat isolated and to the side of the entrance. Peering inside, I could make out some nice climbing branches, some rocks and plastic-looking plants and a water bowl, all in a bed of wood chips. I couldn't see a snake in that one, and a large padlock was hanging from the open lid. We tiptoed to the far end of the room, afraid of arousing the populace, toward another closed heavy door stenciled with Hibernation Room. We cracked open the door and entered the chilly room, snapping on the lights and seeing more terrariums and a wall of refrigeration. Something thumped against the glass of one container, and we both jumped and then laughed nervously when nothing more happened.

The room looked like a dead end, so we cut the lights and left through the larger room, returning back to where the hallway split; and then we headed down the other hall. A small room to our right had an Office sign on the door, which was slightly open. We went inside and turned on the light. The room was a mess, with papers and boxes scattered everywhere, file drawers open, and a computer sitting on a filthy desk. An inner door in the small room was made of solid metal and locked with a large, sturdy padlock. Dru looked at the bottom.

"Turn off the light, cuz."

I knew what she was looking at; I'd seen it too. I switched off the office light. A crack of light could just be seen at the bottom of the metal door. Dru yanked on the padlock, but it didn't budge, of course.

"Is someone in there? Hello."

No answer. We both had our ears to the door, but it was dead quiet. Getting down, I peeked under but couldn't see anything except a few inches of floor. Dru pulled out the key ring again.

"Well, if the snake that ate Chicago is in there, it'll probably eat us too, cuz."

I couldn't argue the point. She tried the keys, but our luck with locks had run out; nothing opened it.

Dru yelled another hello, and I cringed at the loud sound that echoed down the hall. Then we heard a loud thunk and a scraping noise coming closer to the door. The light coming through the crack dimmed to almost nothing. A voice on the other side whispered something.

"Ape—the desk."

Dru and I looked at each other.

"Chance? Is that you?" she said loudly.

We waited several seconds; then she asked again. I could sense movement on the other side. Seconds later something slid under the door, and Dru grabbed it. I recognized the bloody object in her hand—a silver chain with a coiled snake and helix.

"The desk," came across louder this time. "Key's taped under it."

"Hold on and we'll look," Dru yelled. She ran and flipped the light back on. I pulled the chair away from the front and got on my back under the desk with my flashlight. I saw nothing. Dru started feeling under the bottoms of the sides, then under the side drawers.

"Dru, open the middle drawer."

It was tight, but she finally tugged it open, and I got a mouthful of sawdust. A piece of gray duct tape was stuck tightly under the desk bottom, and I yanked it off. A key clattered to the floor. Dru grabbed it and, after fumbling for a while, finally got the door open. Chance literally fell into the room. We managed to lift his upper body off the floor and prop him against the wall. He was a mess—obviously weak and lethargic—and his mouth, shirt and hands were bloody. And the smell was bad.

"Chance, are you hurt?" Dru asked, helping him lift his head. She looked at me for help. "Is he hurt?"

After quickly looking him over, I opened his shirt, checking him over as best I could. There were no slashes, unusual holes or palpable abnormal cracks. There were, however, some large ecchymoses, or black-and-blue marks, on his skin. I pulled his lips away from his gums; they were swollen and bleeding. From the look of his shirt, I guessed he had vomited blood he'd swallowed. His skin felt hot and damp.

"He's sick, Dru. He's really sick, and we need to get him to a hospital ASAP."

She nodded, her eyes getting steamy.

"Dru, have you got anything to drink in your backpack?"

"Yeah. It's in the truck. Be right back."

She sprinted out. I found a small bathroom down the hall and tried to clean off Chance's face with a cool towel. Dru came back with two

Cokes, and he seemed to revive a little after getting some liquid down. Ten minutes later he seemed more alert and looked around.

"Chance, we need to get you to a hospital," I said. "Should we call 911?"

"No," he said, grabbing my arm. "We need to get Tony."

"Who's Tony?" Dru and I asked simultaneously.

Chance got up slowly, sliding his back up the wall for support then managing to get on his feet, leaning on the wall slightly. He shook his head to clear some obvious dizziness. I gave him the Coke bottle.

"Drink some more before you start moving."

He did and then slowly started walking to the hallway, while fumbling in his pants pocket. He brought out a key and opened a door leading to the same small room with the implements and supplies, knocking away some boxes to reach the other side. Then he went into the big snake room, grabbing some kind of long hook and a bag before entering.

We followed him to the big terrarium, where he looked at the empty enclosure, and I could see the rush of blood to his face. Flinging the hook into the front glass in a sudden furious gesture, he broke the glass, and red froth splattered from his mouth. He looked desperately around the big room, peering into the tanks, furiously pulling down front lids and crashing more with his hook. Dru ran to him, trying to stop the violence, but he pushed her away. I heard the sound of rattles coming from all directions, and I could hardly breath.

He went into the hibernation room, and we stood together listening to the sounds of his rampage. Finally she followed him in there, and I waited for her to retrieve him, suddenly feeling an overpowering urgency to get out. I thought I heard some heavy steps coming toward the room, and suddenly a loud male voice yelled, "Mr. King? Jeremy? You in here? Where you been, man?"

He was definitely headed in my direction. I ran into the hibernation room, closing the door. Quickly glancing around, I realized the room was empty.

"Dru," I whispered. There was no answer, and a huge hot wave flashed through me. Could they—would they—have actually left me, and it seemed the obvious answer had to be yes. I flipped off the light and started groping my way to a far corner. It was also obvious that there had to be another way out of the room. Suddenly I regretted having turned the light off, but either way it would have been too late. The guy was in the room, flipping the light on before I'd gotten very far. I turned, and we stared. He was tall and big and was holding a shotgun.

"Who the *fuck* are you, and what have you done to this place? You better talk fast."

"Jer—Jeremy sent me. I'm a friend. He sent me to check on the place."

It wasn't much, but I said it fast, figuring my chances of leaving the place were likely minimal.

"Now why would he send . . ."

His words were interrupted by the sound of lights and power going out. Everything went dark, and the humming of equipment and air just stopped.

"*Now* what the fuck."

"I didn't do *that*," I said.

We both turned at the sound of some movement in the big room next to us.

"Don't move," he said, apparently to me, as he turned back the way he'd come. I really couldn't see enough to do anything. I grabbed the light out of my pocket and edged toward the big room.

The next minutes were a blur of movements, sounds and contacts that couldn't be sorted with accuracy. I thought I heard someone say "you!" then the sound of a huge gunshot blasted in my ears and reverberated through the building. Glass shattered, rattles rattled from everywhere. I tried to shine a light on the action, and it looked like Chance and the big guy were fighting it out on the floor, but Chance seemed far too weak to do much.

Then a whole stack of terrariums toppled over, making a huge crashing sound as glass broke and spattered. I stepped forward, then felt something like a thick rope under my foot and hopped away from it as fast as I could. Dru came in the door with a flashlight and her gun but dropped her light when the guy started toward her. It looked like he grabbed her foot before she could even lift her gun, and she went down, crashing her head against the front glass of a terrarium, then crumpling to the floor.

I pulled out my gun, trying to turn off the safety, but I figured he probably had one too, and I didn't want to flash my light around and show him where I was. I heard a groan coming from Chance, who was apparently still on the floor. The big guy was walking around, probably looking for me and getting closer. I had my gun ready, as I crouched in what I thought was a far corner.

"Fuck," I heard him say, as a rattle went off, and it sounded like he backed up in another direction, probably heading back toward the entrance door, and I was shaking, not daring to move. The door apparently opened and closed, but that was followed immediately by a fury of grunting sounds, thuds and finally some dragging noises. Eventually the sounds faded into the next room, and I was left alone with Dru and Chance, as far as I could tell.

"Don't move," a voice said. "I'll get the lights."

Slow, shuffling steps left the room, and I remained frozen, wondering if I really wanted to see what was nearby. My light looked small in the big room. Something slapped me on the shoulder, then fell to the floor, and I took several steps nearer the center of the room, stifling a scream. Rattles again, but I could see no animals immediately around my feet.

A minute later the lights and power blinked and whirred on. Dru was on the floor near the entrance by the big terrarium, moving slowly, her hand going to a bloody spot on her scalp. She touched it and jerked her hand away in pain. Several snakes—black, brown, gray, white—separated us, and I was trying to figure a way to weave my way over to her. I had my gun, but I wondered if I could even hit one. The big guy's shotgun would have been a much better weapon, but it was nowhere in sight.

Then Chance was standing in the doorway, not looking strong but managing to prop himself upright. His face was bloody again, and his right hand left a bloody mark on the doorframe.

"Stay where you are," he said, looking down at Dru, then over at me and at the scattered animals on the floor. There were more loose ones hanging out of shattered front lids and on top of lower shelves and storage units. He had a long-handled hook in his hand and limped into the room, hooking a snake that was making its way toward Dru, grabbing it behind the head in a swift, deft motion and flinging it into a unit. He repeated the action until the floor was relatively clear, and I watched in fascination at the fearless way he handled the animals, flinging them as if they were stuffed toys. Apparently he saw the look on my face.

"I'm immune," he said. "At least to *most* of these."

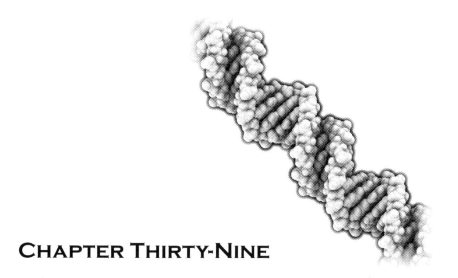

CHAPTER THIRTY-NINE

THE SNAKES BETWEEN US HAD been removed, and I let my breath out, suddenly aware I hadn't expelled any air for a while. But Chance was looking at me with an alarmed expression on his face, and I suddenly became aware of movement to the right of my face. One of the white snakes was perched for a bite, and I thought it was a done deed as it approached me. The snake hook came hurtling through the air, whizzing by my eyes, and the movement stopped. I ran to the other side of the room, clutching the spot that should have been bitten but wasn't.

Chance signaled me for some help, and we dragged Dru from the room and took her back to the office, placing her in the chair. We'd seen no one else around. She could sit up, and I took a look at her head. A good-sized triangular shard of glass was embedded in her scalp. I pulled it out, and Chance, kneeling on the floor, too weak to stand, put some pressure on it with a wad of paper. I found a piece of ice in a freezer, along with numerous neatly packaged frozen mice. We replaced the paper with some ice in a towel, and Dru seemed to be regaining some function.

"Let's get out of here," Chance said.

Dru nodded.

After managing to get out the back door, we saw the big black truck I'd seen earlier now parked next to Jeremy's. I packed Dru and Chance in the back of Jeremy's truck and took the big key ring from Dru. Chance was starting to look pale, and new blood was coming from his nose.

"We're going to a hospital," I said.

There was no answer, no argument as I drove to the entrance gate. The gate was on the ground on the inside of the perimeter, apparently smashed down by a large vehicle that had come in. What looked to be a large, light-colored truck with a front grill guard had just gone through and was stopped on the road. I strained but couldn't see the driver. Then it headed down the road and disappeared around a bend. I stopped to watch it leave and gave a long sigh, resting my forehead on the steering wheel. Then I drove over the fallen gate and down the road to the ranch entrance, where we found that gate unlocked and open. I took us straight to our rental truck, and we reloaded ourselves into it, leaving Jeremy's truck there. Thirty minutes later we stopped outside the emergency room of a small private hospital on the south side of town. I ran in to find some help.

Twenty minutes later they were each in a cubicle, and I had no idea what either of them was saying, if anything. I told the triage nurse Dru was my cousin and the guy was a friend of hers that I didn't know, but that Dru apparently had gotten hurt, and he seemed very ill. I said I'd found them that way and thought Dru had fallen trying to help him. Then I sat and waited until there'd probably been enough time to get a CBC, or complete blood count, ordered and run on Chance.

After about an hour of sitting, I tried to fix my disheveled appearance a little, then ran up to the lab. It wasn't huge and it was staffed minimally at night, as I'd expected. Winding my way around to the hematology area, I found a lab tech who was looking at blood smears. I pulled out my medical ID from the university hospital and flashed it.

"Hi, I'm Dr. Ranelli from University Hospital. I'm a hematology fellow. You have a CBC and smear here on a friend of my cousin. They're both in the ER. Her name's Dru Salinas. His name's Chance, or something like that."

He showed me the CBC printouts. Chance was still a "John Doe." Dru's numbers looked good. Chance's were a disaster. His white count was very high, and his hemoglobin and platelets were both at low levels, especially the platelets, explaining the severe bruising and bleeding. I sat down at the microscope and looked at his smear. Myeloid blasts were in his blood, with a few telltale Auer rods inside some of them, making a diagnosis of acute myeloid leukemia obvious. After returning to the ER, I sat for a while, thinking, but not making a lot of progress. I finally decided to talk to the ER doctor seeing Chance. Dru had gotten her head stitched up and came out to wait with me, looking much better, albeit with a big bandage.

"It's numb," she said, patting her head. "How's Chance?"

I didn't know what to say, so the truth would have to do.

"Dru, he's got acute leukemia—blood cancer. That's why he's so bruised and bleeding."

Her face went really white.

"How do you know?"

"I went up to the lab and looked at his blood counts and blood smear. It's definitely acute myeloid leukemia. He needs big-time chemotherapy right away."

"Can they do it here? Now?"

"Probably not here, but they can stabilize him and stop the bleeding for now. He needs to be seen by an oncologist—like what I do. I'm going to talk to the ER doctor right now. Sit here and rest a while."

She had stood up, wanting to see him, and I gently pushed her back down.

The ER doctor on duty turned out to be a Dr. Bruce Ramirez, a nice guy in what I guessed to be his early fifties, with receding red hair and a pronounced hard blink that made my eyes hurt. I introduced myself, after the desk clerk had led me to a small room off the reception area where he was sitting and staring at some x-rays on the wall. I explained that Chance was a friend of my cousin, the woman he'd just stitched up. I flashed my hospital ID again.

"You've undoubtedly seen his CBC," I said. "I ran up and looked at his blood smear. He's definitely got acute myeloid leukemia. Can you get him some red cells and platelets tonight?"

"He just got a single-donor platelet unit. Red cells are going in as we speak. I ordered two red cell units and another platelet pack. He'll need to be transferred for therapy, I assume. Maybe to your place?"

I wasn't sure and shook my head. We were in a smaller hospital affiliated with a larger downtown facility that could treat leukemics, but

I had the feeling Chance had no insurance, and the county hospital might be his destination.

"His left antecubital fossa is really scarred up for some reason." He raised his eyebrows with a questioning look.

"I have no idea. Can I see him for a second?"

He led me to Chance's cubicle, and I walked through the closed curtains.

"I'll be nearby," Bruce said. "Got a lady who just came in with acute pulmonary edema. Busy night."

Chance was lying quietly with his eyes closed. Red cells were going in through an IV in his right antecubital vein. I walked over to his left side, gently turning his arm so I could see the inner aspect of his elbow. It looked as though two old parallel scars were in the area, large and ugly enough to make you choose the other arm for an IV site.

He opened his eyes, looking down at my hand on his arm.

"An old battle wound." He smiled slightly.

"How you feeling?"

"Better by the second."

"Chance . . ." I needed to tell him what I'd seen and wanted to do it while Dru wasn't around.

"I know," he said, looking at me calmly. "I've got leukemia."

The guy was one surprise after another.

"I saw it. In the lab. Acute myeloid leukemia with very low platelets. Chance, you need chemotherapy right away."

He was quiet, but had a wry look on his face.

"Claudia, you're going to find this hard to believe, especially being in your profession, but what I need right now is to get some blood and get out of here. There's something I need to do, and I'll need some help from you, but believe me, it's the only way for me in the long run—if there *is* a long run for me. I'll explain more later, but I'm leaving here tonight."

My head felt hot with exasperation.

"Chance, you're kidding me. Chemo is your only hope right now."

He shook his head, expressing his own exasperation.

"*Out. Tonight.* And please be calm so Dru doesn't get too upset. I said I'll explain." He was emphatic. I felt sick.

"You'll finish the rest of the transfusions, right?"

He nodded.

"Rest up," I said. "Dru and I'll get some coffee."

He took my hand and gave it a small squeeze, and I felt a strange wave of warmth mixed with something like fear spreading up my arm and through me. I suddenly wanted it to last longer, but I knew Dru would be waiting, so I left.

She was pacing the floor in the waiting room. She came to an abrupt halt when I walked in.

"He's looking a lot better," I quickly reassured her. "The rest of the blood needs to get transfused. Let's get some coffee."

We found some incredibly bitter tasting stuff in a vending machine down the hall, and some powdery so-called creamer wouldn't even dissolve in it. I got her to sit for a while.

"He won't stay and get treated," I said.

She jerked her head up, looking at me with the same incredulous look I'd given Chance.

"What the fu . . . Why not?"

I just shook my head. "He says there's something he's absolutely got to do."

"Yeah. That's just what he said the last time he disappeared—and look how far *that* got him."

"I know, I know. But he's insisting. Says he'll explain it, and he said something about needing our help. I guess he's coming home with us?"

I raised my eyebrows with the last question.

"I guess so, cuz. There's plenty of room in the master bed."

It was almost seven in the morning by the time we got out of the ER, and I promised Bruce I'd see that Chance got his therapy soon, although a shard of guilt stabbed through me as I said it. Chance's color was back to normal, and he walked out of the ER with only a little assistance from us. We bought him three candy bars, which he devoured in a minute.

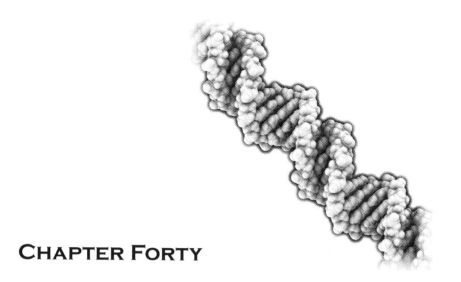

CHAPTER FORTY

WE GOT HOME IN THE morning, exhausted and dirty, none of us knowing what to do first. At the kitchen table, we sat and drank a gallon of orange juice. Then we all took showers and met again in the kitchen, where Dru talked me into making a big batch of pancakes. It was obvious she and I were too high-strung to sleep, but I was worried about Chance, and he agreed to get some rest upstairs after breakfast.

Dru got him settled in her bed, then joined me at the table for a while longer, where she drank a beer and put her feet on another chair. Even with the bandage on her head, she looked much better in a fuzzy white robe with her hair pulled back.

"Well, that was some wild ride, cuz."

"Yup. Wild." That was an understatement.

We were silent for a minute.

"Somebody saved our asses."

"I know."

"I wonder who it was."

"That I don't know."

More silence as she sipped her beer. A burp came up unexpectedly, and we both laughed.

"I don't know," I continued, "but I'm wondering . . ."

"I think we're wondering in the same direction, cuz. He and your dad were good buds, right? And he seemed concerned about us—like he cared or something."

"Yeah—but he had no idea what we were involved with. I just don't think he knew enough about what we were doing to follow us or have us followed. And it wasn't Joe who tackled that big guy—at least not by himself."

"But he could have with the help of Frank or Joe Jr., or both. I wonder what happened to the big guy?"

I shook my head. "Maybe they hauled him off?"

"Maybe we're better off not knowing," she said, but I knew I'd try to find out eventually, and she probably would too.

"That was some snake farm, or whatever the hell you call it," she said.

"It looked like they were doing some high-powered breeding there. I guess we found the source of those dried venoms in Jeremy's freezer. They must be breeding different species for their venoms. The white ones must be albinos."

"That sounds like something more scientific than Jer could handle by himself," she mused. "I'd bet Kral's behind it. The old guy."

"But handling things from where?"

She shook her head. "That Tony thing was sure weird. Tony the snake, I guess."

"I assume so. Maybe a really big snake, judging by the size of that terrarium."

"Chance has a few questions to answer," she said, getting up slowly and stiffly, and heading for the stairs. "I'll see you in a few hours. Get some sleep, cuz. And thanks for the pancakes."

I still didn't feel like sleeping, so I washed the dishes and plowed through the mail piled by the front door under the mail slot. More bills to pay. Dru had made substantial use of my credit card, and I was wondering how much financial damage the whole mess would cause. My eyes were beginning to hurt. I made my way upstairs and crashed onto the bed.

A few jumbled thoughts were running through my brain. Tony—a snake named Tony. Strange name for a snake. The name made me think of my father. Everyone called him Anthony or Antonio. Everyone except Joe Picci, who always called him Tony.

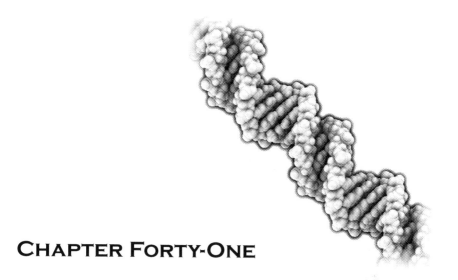

CHAPTER FORTY-ONE

SEVERAL HOURS LATER I AWOKE to a sunny St. Patrick's Day, not feeling particularly lucky. I took a long shower again, moving slowly, feeling sluggish. I opened the bedroom door, smelling coffee and hearing voices downstairs. I went down and found Dru and Chance back at the kitchen table, she pouring coffee and he sitting back and looking clean and much better. He wore a blue long-sleeved shirt I recognized as one my father had worn, and his white hair stood out against the deep blue background. I could make out glimpses of the silver chain once again hanging from his neck.

"So how are you two doing?" I asked, trying to sound optimistic as I got my coffee and joined them. I sat next to Chance, since Dru had taken her usual two chairs, one for her feet. They looked at each other across the table, Dru giving him what seemed like an exasperated look.

"He still won't agree to chemo," Dru said. "Does my face look blue to you?"

"Only the usual black-and-blue," I said.

She gave me a dirty look.

Chance gave a sigh. "This is hard to explain," he said.

"Give it a try," Dru prodded.

"What's going to cure my leukemia is a drug—a reversal drug that I need to get from my father—and I think that at this point he'll give it to me."

"Reversal of *what?* I don't understand this," Dru said, shaking her head.

But I thought I knew the direction in which he was headed.

"I have a genetic mutation that can cause cancer," he said slowly, looking at her, then at me. "It can cause all kinds of cancers, but in my case, I've got acute leukemia. My father is a skilled scientist and geneticist. When he learned I had this, he spent nearly every minute of his life looking for a drug that could counteract the effects of the mutation—a compound that could restore the normal function of the protein that the normal gene produces to fight off cancers. The mutated gene that I have doesn't make a functional protein, so I can't fight off this disease. He found a compound that restores the protein's normal function. That's about as simple as I can make it," he said, looking at Dru.

"You're kidding me," I said, astonished at his claim of a reversal drug. "Scientists have been doing research for years for that kind of drug—one that doesn't have deleterious side effects and works to fight the cancers by restoring the protein's normal function. Why wouldn't he come out and share this kind of discovery with the whole world? He'd be unbelievably famous and would be helping tons of people." It was too big to comprehend.

Chance gave a wry, half-grin. "Right. Only you don't *know* the man. You don't know the methods he used to get those results, to test the drug—and you don't *want* to know. Maybe he'll find a way to let the world know he's got it, but it won't be through the usual channels, I guarantee it. And besides, it might not work in people who have different variants of this mutation."

"So you've taken it?" I asked. "When? What is it?" My heart was galloping at the last question.

"I've taken it since I was about fifteen, even before he knew exactly how it would work. He tested more than one compound on me, but this is the one he settled on after some more studies. He gave it to me about once a month, and I never got sick, never got any tumors, nothing. I didn't even understand what was going on until I was older and started nosing around. Still, it wasn't until I was in college that I really had some understanding of the situation. He never told me what it is. I should have kept some, but he always insisted on injecting it himself."

"Has anyone else in your family had cancers at relatively young ages?" I asked, knowing that the TP53 mutation could be inherited, causing numerous different kinds of tumors in young people.

He gave that wry half-smile again. "My mother died of cancer." It sounded like that wasn't a good subject for him, and I left it at that.

"So," I said, "do you really have PhDs in biochemistry and genetics?"

He looked flushed for a second. "I have a BS and PhD in zoology with a minor in genetics. That's it. And I did spend some time working in a genetics lab in Houston. I've read a lot, learned a lot from *him*."

"So what happened?" Dru asked, sitting up. "Where's the drug you were taking? Why were you locked in that room?"

"We had a falling out, to put it nicely." He looked at me. "I didn't agree with things he wanted me to do. Jer played along—always. I didn't. It had been over six months since my last dose, and I guess he thought I'd tell him everything—about where Jeremy was, you—everything."

He paused, finishing the last of his coffee. "When I didn't, he had Rolf lock me in that room—until I came around," he said. I'd already been feeling a little sick, but it got worse fast, especially over the last week. Amazing," he said, shaking his head.

"So you think he'll change his mind *now*?" Dru sounded skeptical.

He shrugged. "My bet is he will. I think he'll give it to me when he learns what I've got."

"Are you going to tell him about Jeremy? He was your brother, right?"

"I guess I'll tell him that I killed Jer in self-defense. You two won't even have been there. The two of us fought. He's a half-brother, by the way—different mother—she died too. He knows Jeremy goes berserk on drugs sometimes and gets violent."

"Who *is* your father?" I had to ask. "Have I met him?"

Chance was silent, looking down at his hands. He finally looked up and said "Believe me, you don't need or want to know. It's best if you don't. Let me take care of this—please."

Dru was having none of that again.

"Is his name *Kral*, by any chance?" Dru asked.

"His name is *King*," Chance said, looking hard at her, then at me.

"Kral means King in Czech," Drew said. "Is he Czech, maybe?"

Chance ignored that. "He's a dangerous man, and you both need to remember that. Let me handle this."

"Chance," I asked, "how in the world can you handle anything when you have acute leukemia? You don't even know how long it would take to convince him. And where is he, anyway?"

"That's where I'll need a little help from you," he said softly, looking at me. "Can you keep those blasts at bay for a little while without giving me the big guns? Just buy me some time?"

I put my head in my hands.

"Maybe just a little Ara-C?" he went on. "Sub-Q."

Dru was looking at me. I wondered how he knew about the drug.

"I'll see what I can do," I finally said, dreading the idea that he might die while I was giving him suboptimal doses of what he needed. It was only a small part of the treatment he needed.

"It's the only thing I'll do," he said with finality.

"Great. Thanks." I was feeling sick again.

Dru gave a sigh, a worried look on her face. "What was that place he had you locked in, anyway? They breed snakes there?"

Chance hesitated, and then answered. "Yeah, obviously snakes are bred there. Poisonous snakes, or 'hot' snakes as some people say. It was Jer's deal, mainly, but obviously he had my father's heavy guidance. Jer didn't know a gene from a bean—but he made money selling snakes and venom to various customers, some legal, some probably questionable. Don't ask me. Hybrid hot snakes and their venoms were a hobby with my father, the geneticist. He did studies for years on the effects of venoms, some at the university, some on his own or in some other labs. He didn't tell me much. But Jer and I grew up around those snakes, and they were like pets to us."

"Ugh," Dru said, and I echoed her sentiment.

"They're part of nature, and some are extraordinary animals. My *father* is the twisted creature here."

"You said you were immune," I said. "What did you mean?"

He sighed. "My genius of a father immunized us to most of the venoms of the species he handled. Weird, I know, but he did it. I'm not sure if he immunized himself, though—he thinks he can handle those things."

"I didn't know you could do that," I said, somewhat incredulous. "It's got to be really dangerous."

"He gave us tiny doses when we were young, then gradually increased the dose. Jer had a bad reaction to a dose, but my dad got him through it. This went on for months, years. Then we just got booster shots periodically."

"Did it work?" I asked, fascinated by the pure nerve of the man, jeopardizing the lives of his own sons.

"Jer was bitten a few times and survived without major problems. We had antivenom around too, of course."

"How about you?" Dru questioned, looking intently at him.

A strange, blank look came over his face. He finally said "Yeah, me too—but I survived."

We were quiet for a while, and Dru got us coffee refills. When she sat down, she asked, "So who's Tony? You sure got wound up when you saw that cage was empty."

Chance looked uncomfortable. "Yeah, that was stupid of me. I wasn't exactly in a normal state of mind at that point. Tony is an old rattler hybrid—unique really. There may never be another like him, and there are no exact progeny. I wanted to take him with me, but he was obviously gone. My guess is that my father has him. I'll find out soon enough. What I'd like to know is who rescued us."

Dru and I looked at each other, not knowing what to say. She looked for a second like she was going to say something, but I gave her what I hoped was a "don't say anything" look, and she just shook her head, indicating she had no idea. I shrugged my shoulders. I didn't want to bring up Joe Picci or his sons when it was pure conjecture on our part.

Chance looked at us. "Well, I'd really like to know if you two come up with any ideas, because I have no idea. It couldn't have been easy to dispense with Rolf so quickly, and I'd like to know what happened to him."

"So would I," I said. Dru was silent, then looked at me.

"Cuz, if you're going to get him that medicine, don't you think we'd better get moving with it?"

I tried once more. "Chance, you really need to get high-dose chemotherapy for this disease. I'm afraid this low-dose medicine isn't going to hold you for very long, and you could hemorrhage or get a serious infection. *Please* let me get you the right treatment."

He just shook his head. "I'll do it with or without the low dose med, but I need to get to him soon. High dose chemo would incapacitate me for too long, and I need to get that reversal drug. End of story."

I left them sitting at the table, while I was trying to figure out where to start.

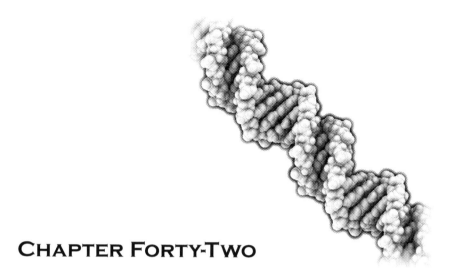

CHAPTER FORTY-TWO

MY BODY STARTED DOING THINGS, while my mind was rebelling. I didn't deserve to be put in this position, I kept thinking, until finally forcing my mind to shut up. I spent a few minutes checking pharmacies online, finding a reasonably nearby one that handled cytarabine, the generic name of the drug that Chance had mentioned. It was possible that low doses might keep the leukemia under some degree of control for a while. I called in prescriptions for the cytarabine, along with some antibiotics and an antifungal drug, and then added some epinephrine in case of a drug reaction.

I went back to the kitchen to tell them I was leaving. They were still at the table, and Dru's eyes looked red.

"I'm going to get some medical supplies and drugs," I said, heading toward the door.

"Wait a sec," Chance said, standing and putting his hand in his pocket. He grabbed his wallet and pulled out five hundred dollar bills. "I *do* have access to money. Remember that I can pay my bills."

I was surprised to see the wallet, which he'd apparently still had while locked up in that office room. He insisted, so I took the cash.

The pharmacy was about a twenty-minute drive away, not too far from the hospital, but I decided to take a small detour on the way. It was around three in the afternoon, and the restaurant didn't open until five on Saturdays. I drove to the back parking lot, then all the way to the end of it where there was a loading entrance into the restaurant. A large white truck was parked close to the entrance, its back end visible to me. Frank Picci was washing it off with a hose and wiping off the tires. The lot was nearly empty, and he spotted me immediately, so I gave him a small wave and parked the car, wondering what in the world I'd say. I got out slowly and walked toward him. He stopped the sprayer, letting it fall to the pavement.

He gave me a smile, but his eyes didn't look as happy as his mouth did.

"Damn mud really sticks to these tires."

I gave a weak smile. "Yeah," I said. "Like pizza dough under your fingernails."

He laughed. "Got that too. Goes with the business."

I felt awkward. He looked casual in a pair of jeans and a short-sleeved polo shirt, a nice shade of purple. I saw no visible bruises as I got closer. Then I glanced at the truck. He saw me looking. It certainly could have been the truck I'd seen, as far as I could tell. I wondered if the front was damaged. Or if a body was in the back seat.

"How've you been? You and your cousin? Up to any mischief these days?"

I wasn't sure where he was going with that. "Uh, a little. Whatever we can get away with. How about you?"

"I try to stay out of trouble—it's not always easy, though." He paused, bending down to wipe off a tire rim. "Hear about the fire by Devine last night?"

Well, bingo. That answered my question, as he knew it would. "No. A *big* fire?"

"Well, not relatively, I suppose. On a ranch outside of town. Gutted the place, I guess."

"A house?"

"No. Some kind of warehouse or something. A solid concrete building."

The conversation was making my head spin. Why weren't we just talking about it instead of pretending we hadn't been there? But I wasn't going to be the one to change the format.

"Anyone hurt?" I ventured.

"The guard thinks the owner's son could have died in the fire. Haven't heard if any bodies were found—human, that is."

"How's the guard—have you heard?" My heart was thumping, hoping the Chicago machine hadn't been at work.

He looked up at me and smiled. "Apparently the guard's fine. I guess he called the owner and gave him the bad news, then decided to go look for employment somewhere else. I heard he didn't really like the climate."

"Really." I felt relieved and decided to believe him. "Any idea who the owner is? Or the son?"

"Haven't heard. They sound like people I'd avoid. I wouldn't take any chances." He moved over to the other side of the van, bending down to work on the other tire. He looked over at me again. "By the way, Dad wants to talk to you. He's not here right now, but give him a call soon, okay? He worries."

I nodded, suddenly wanting to get on with what needed doing.

"Have a great day, Frank," I said, backing away towards my car. "And thanks for all the great—hospitality—the other night."

I jumped in my car, anxious to get away, not anxious to talk to Joe Picci, who suddenly seemed like a scolding parent. But it needed to be done. I thought maybe I could get Dru to do it, but then, how much could we say?

I drove away thinking about all the questions I should have asked and didn't. I should have just come out and asked why they were following Dru and me. It didn't seem as though we'd given them any reason to do that, although Joe *had* seemed concerned about us the night we stopped to eat there. Had my father asked Joe to keep an eye on me? Had he been worried about his life being cut short? What did Joe Picci know? Obviously, I needed to talk with him.

My thoughts strayed to Chance. I wondered how he had access to money, although at his age, he certainly could have some. He'd said it in a way that had made me think he had a lot of it. His father *had* to be Kral. Why wouldn't he just admit it? Chance probably knew why his father wanted to hurt Dru and me, especially me. And why were he and Tats wearing those necklaces? Was it just the family's snake fetish?

I just about hit a curb driving along the road, forcing me to jerk my mind back to driving. I pulled into a McDonald's parking lot and made a phone call. It took me ten minutes of pleading, but I got what was needed, then headed for the hospital. My ID card still worked to get me in the parking ramp, and I went inside to my old office. Few, if any, physician staff would be around at that time on a Saturday. The door was locked, but I still had my key. I went in and closed the door. I sat in my old chair and closed my eyes for a minute. Fifteen minutes later Julie walked in.

"Honey, this better be good. It's Saturday, and I'm fixin' to go out and party tonight, so tell me what's so damned important."

She sat down, swirling her chair to face me. She was in jeans and a red T-shirt, but her white coat was thrown on over them. And she looked like she'd dropped another five pounds.

I explained to her that I had a friend staying with me and that he had acute myeloid leukemia but was refusing conventional therapy or hospitalization, then told her what I planned on doing regarding the low-dose drug therapy. Obviously, I didn't mention anything about the reversal drug Chance had said he needed or about his genetic mutation. Of course she thought I'd lost my mind.

"This is crazy," she said. "Does the guy have a death wish?"

"I'm still hoping to convince him to come in for high dose therapy," I said, looking distraught, I'm sure. "This is all he'll let me do for now."

"Who *is* this guy? Is *he* the reason you left the fellowship?" I think she had a hopeful look on her face.

"Well, yes," I said, swallowing hard. I wondered if she'd run and tell Stephen, or even his tech, Emily. "I do care about him a lot." I swiped at a few surprising tears that were edging out, not quite sure why they were falling. "I'll get the meds."

"You need a few supplies?" she asked astutely.

"I could use a few of the basics—and some CBC tubes—and a green top."

She looked at me with skepticism, and I could read her thoughts.

"Julie—I just might need a CBC or two. I know you can get that done. And maybe some genetics on the blood—your big chance to talk to Dr. Palmer again. I promise this won't be for very long."

"No, he'll probably *die*." She shook her head and got up. "I'll be right back, crazy lady."

A few minutes later she was back, carrying a large, red biohazard bag that she handed over to me.

"Careful, it's got breakables."

I peered inside at blood collection tubes, syringes, needles, gauze, sterile gloves, tourniquets and a few other essentials.

"I stuck a thermometer in there too, in case you don't have one. Sorry, no extra pressure cuffs. And I know nothing about this. I don't make a habit of taking things home from this place."

"Neither do I, Jules. But my dad donated a nice chunk of money to this place. Not a huge amount, but way more than this cost." I looked up at her. "And I really appreciate this."

"Yeah. You kinda owe me," she said. "Good luck. Stay in touch."

I left, hugging the red bag folded up in my arms.

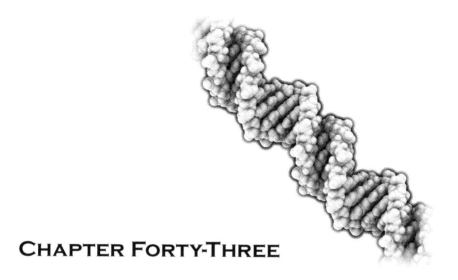

CHAPTER FORTY-THREE

I STOPPED AT THE PHARMACY to pick up the meds, then headed back home, feeling as though I needed some antidepressants for myself but not really wanting to take any. A clear head was a necessity, if that was even possible. It was starting to get dark by the time I pulled into the garage. I noticed Dru's car was back and the rental truck nowhere in sight. The downstairs lights were off, and I flicked some on, dumping everything on the kitchen table, refrigerating the meds that needed it.

Music was playing upstairs. It sounded like classical guitar, and the sound was soothing. Heading upstairs, I leaned on the stair rail, making my way there slowly, trying to concentrate on the music, not making any noise. As I neared the top, I could see the door to my mother's bedroom was partially open. A bedside lamp dimly illuminated the room, and I halted a few steps from the top of the stairs. I turned around to see into the room and caught a glimpse of Chance lying on the bed. I could see him from the waist up, and something was happening that aroused my curiosity. I sat on a step near the top, too tired to even think about what I was doing.

Dru was obviously in the bed with him, and I caught glimpses of her knees and hands as she straddled above him. His shirt was already off, his skin deadly pale against the white sheet. Dru's arms went up and were silhouetted on the wall as she apparently pulled her sweater off, then her bra in a slow, smooth motion. I could almost make out the blinking of his long, pale eyelashes, as he looked up at her, not saying a word or moving of his own volition. Her arms reached down and around his waist, pulling his shorts off, and he raised his hips slightly to accommodate her. I saw glimpses of her head, a white bandage on the back of it, her long hair falling over her face, slightly touching him as she moved. Then her hands were moving slowly on him, back and forth, back and forth on the organ, but I couldn't see them.

"My God," she said.

I could barely hear Chance groan. His eyes were on the ceiling, then his hands moved down toward her. His arms moved further, and she groaned. His head came up slightly, his right arm lifted, and she gave a loud groan. His head went back down, and she was thrusting on top of him, her hair bouncing, the bed creaking. His head rocked from side to side, but he didn't see me. I was transfixed, feeling myself getting moist, a desperate feeling pulsing in my groin. They went on and on interminably, the groans getting louder. I felt myself rocking too, until she screamed, and I put my fist in my mouth. Then she fell on his chest, and they clutched at one another and wound to the side, entwined like two sna . . .

I didn't move, waiting for any further sounds coming from the room. There were some faint whispers; then Dru got up. I quietly made my way downstairs and turned out the lights. In the living room, the last of a recent fire was simmering, and sitting on the sofa, I used my sweater sleeve to swipe some tears I hadn't realized had been shed. The house was quiet. The music had finished, and the upstairs door made a soft thud as it was closed all the way. I threw a log on the fire and found an old knitted throw on a nearby chair. Lying down, I stared at the flames until my eyes burned and I couldn't keep them open any longer.

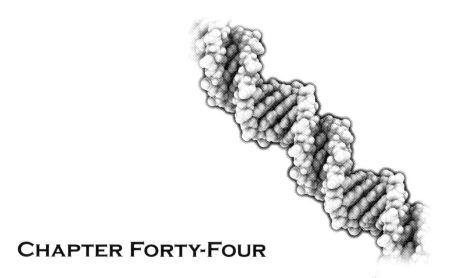

CHAPTER FORTY-FOUR

ON SUNDAY MORNING I WOKE up with the sun and with a sore neck and moist armpits from sweating in my sleep. I drank some orange juice and went up to my room to shower and change. The door to the master was still closed, and no sounds came from behind it. Downstairs an hour later, Dru was at the kitchen table, drinking a beer and smoking. Her hands had the tiniest of tremors.

"You OK?" I asked.

"About as good as can be expected. Considering—and all." Her voice trailed off.

Apparently the sexual ecstasy had worn off, and I figured she was back down to earth, mainly worried about Chance.

"You've really got it for that guy, don't you?"

She looked at me and pursed her lips. "Yeah, you could say that."

We were quiet for a while, and I made some coffee.

"You going to give him that medicine soon?"

"Yeah, this morning. Let me know when he's ready. I need to draw some blood, too."

A few minutes later she left me to drink my coffee and trotted up the stairway. I could hear dim voices upstairs, then some water running. Half an hour later she was back downstairs.

"Well, cuz, he looks pretty good. Says he's ready for you." She shrugged her shoulders.

"Be there in a minute."

I got the dose of cytarabine ready and found a serving tray to put most of my supplies on, then trotted upstairs to play doctor, nurse and medical quack. Chance was sitting on the bed, propped up with two pillows behind him and his hands behind his head, looking relaxed. His eyes looked clear and alert, his white hair clean and whispy. He had a white T-shirt on, and a sheet covered the rest of him.

I put my tray down and sat on the side of the bed, then took his temperature.

"Great. Ninety-eight six."

Dru let out a sigh. I grabbed a syringe and four blood tubes, then prepped his right forearm for a blood-draw and was about to tie the tourniquet. I looked over, and Dru was looking a little pale. She stood up.

"You know what, cuz? I think I'll go put some gas in the Explorer. Keys are downstairs?"

"Check my bureau," I said. It was hard to believe this would make Dru queasy, but she obviously was. She walked out, leaving us alone. Chance's arm had carelessly fallen across my leg, and I finished prepping it, acutely aware of the feeling of its presence. A feeling of unbidden warmth started to spread through me. I could feel his stare, and I tried not to return it, but I looked at him despite myself. There was a desperation—no, a pleading—in his eyes that I wanted to ignore but couldn't. Then he had that wry half-smile on his face again.

I gave him the subcutaneous injection and put down the syringe, then drew the four tubes of blood and put them on the tray, releasing the tourniquet and pressing gauze onto the phlebotomy site.

"I'm a mess, Claudia," he said in a soft voice, his other arm still propped behind his head, his eyes half closed. He had that ethereal look again, the one I remembered under the clock at the hotel in San Francisco, and that night was returning in a vapor from under the door, seeping through the room. There was a hot spot on my leg from the touch of his arm.

"I'm sorry, Claudia. I really didn't want to hurt you." His voice was barely a whisper.

The words bounced inside my brain. I was trying to sort them.

"What did you *do?*" I asked.

"My father forced me—well, I was willing. I thought I could do it."

"Do *what?*"

"He had Jer give me a bad venom, but I didn't use it the way he wanted. I diluted it—a lot. I couldn't give it undiluted the way he wanted—it was too dangerous."

He let out a long sigh.

"Go on," I said, my throat contracting.

"I put something in your wine at the restaurant—and you passed out for a while in the hotel room."

"I figured that."

"I had a syringe with the diluted venom in it and a long needle. He gave me a metal trumpet—a guiding device for long needles that's used to give local anesthetics in the vagina during deliveries. I guess I cut myself with the needle trying to manipulate the thing. I'm sorry—I just blindly put it inside you, and when it felt like the guide was in, I pushed the needle through it and emptied the syringe."

I couldn't speak for a minute. My whole head was in flames, but really, it was what I'd suspected, wasn't it?

"Venom—what kind of venom?" I wasn't even sure what I was asking.

"I'm not sure. Jer gave it to me." Even *he* seemed dissatisfied with his answer. "Some kind of pit viper venom he got from my father."

I felt dizzy.

"So you gave me a venom—and I had a bad reaction. The pain, the bleeding . . ."

"Yes, but I couldn't go through with it. When I saw what happened, even though I really diluted it, I just couldn't let the reaction go on."

"Remember that nerdy hospital resident? The guy in San Francisco with the round glasses and spiky hair?"

I did. One of the many people I'd said very little to.

"Yeah."

"Well—I gave him enough money to give you a couple of doses of antivenom, just to make sure you didn't have a huge reaction, and he watched you to make sure you didn't have an allergic reaction to the antivenom. You were too out of it to remember. He told me they almost did a hysterectomy."

"Lucky me." I couldn't understand the venom thing. "What the hell is the deal with your father and venoms, anyway?"

He let out a prolonged exhale. "Like I said, he was fascinated by viperids and their venoms. The complexities of the venoms, their compositions, their toxic effects. At first he was fascinated by the prospect of their medicinal value—then later he turned toward the toxic effects—and eventually the genetic effects."

"Genetic effects—that's a new one." My heart was starting to flutter.

"Then he produced Tony, our miracle hybrid."

"The snake you were looking for."

"Yeah—Tony was the culmination of all his studies. He did experiments with Tony's venom on mice, and they got cancers. He was ecstatic. My mother got two cancers and died. I think he gave her the venom." He shook his head and raised his eyebrows, looking at me. "I guess, but who knows?"

I looked at him, not having a clue about what to say. "I've never heard of venoms inducing genetic changes."

"No—and you *won't* read about it. Sure, there are some papers mentioning venoms inducing destabilization of DNA in lymphocytes *in vitro*, but this stuff that I'm talking about isn't published."

"So what *are* you talking about? Specifically."

"You won't believe this, but here goes." He looked at me for a second, seeming to scan my eyes. "I *am* a genetic mess. It wasn't so bad to start with. Obviously you can guess that I was born with a form of albinism, a relatively mild form it turns out. Luckily, my vision's been pretty good—some forms of the disease have a big problem with that—and I'm starting to get a little pigment in my skin, which is good. More than I had when I was really young."

He glanced at his forearms, and he rubbed one. I noticed some light freckling on the lower arms. "The sun bothers me a little, but I don't get out into it very much."

"And the other mutation?" I asked.

"I've got one that leads to cancer—and I wasn't born with it."

I was beginning to put the picture together, and it was grotesque. I waited for him to go on.

"When I was fourteen, Jer decided to play a little trick on me one summer." The half-smile re-appeared. "He put Tony in my bed."

"Oh God," was all I could say.

He brought up his left arm, showing me the large scars on the inner elbow.

"Tony bit hard right there," he said, nodding toward the scars. "I literally had to pry him off, and it bled like crazy. He bit right into the vein. But Dad took care of me right away, and the reaction wasn't too bad, partly because I had some immunity and partly because he had antivenom on hand, and the scar seemed minor compared to what might have happened. He just about killed Jeremy for doing it. He didn't like anyone fooling with his projects, and Tony was off-limits."

He rubbed his forefinger up and down the scars and then looked up at me.

"I didn't think much more about it until about a year later when Dad sat me down one night. He'd always been taking blood samples from us, needing them for this or that experiment or test—we never really knew what to make of it. He worked in a lab, but he rarely mentioned what he was doing."

"A lab where?"

He shook his head, dismissing the question as unimportant or as something not pertinent—or something he didn't want me to know.

"He said I had a bad genetic mutation and that I got it from Tony's bite according to what he could tell. He was doing more work on it, but his experiments with mice seemed to corroborate his suspicions. It was a mutation that permitted cancer cells to survive. Then, before I had a chance to let that sink in, he said that he was also working on something that could reverse the mutation's effects—the drug we were talking about yesterday, the reversal drug."

He sighed, and I could tell he was picturing that night with his father.

"He started to give me injections of a compound, but I had some reactions to it, and then we tried three or four more. I'm not sure how many or what they were, but I was scared to death and went along with it. Eventually he settled on one that he's used for several years. He calls it Anti-TNT—at least around me."

"And you have no idea what it is? Not even a guess?"

He shook his head.

"Oh, I know what people have been working on, but exactly what compound he had I really have no idea. The man's a perverted genius. I'm hoping, now—considering what I've got—that he'll be sane enough to tell me what it is. Or at least give me some to get analyzed."

"But," I said, confused, "think of all the people who could potentially be helped with a successful compound that reverses the effects of the TP53 gene mutation."

His head jerked, and he looked hard at me.

"I never mentioned what the mutation *was*. Are you guessing?"

I'd known that I'd bring it up sooner or later if he didn't mention the mutation specifically. Still, I felt the blood in my face.

"Chance, you left a little DNA sample behind in the hotel room."

He looked ahead, obviously mulling over the events of that night. Then he smiled at me.

"I left them in the room, didn't I? My shorts."

I nodded. "There was a small spot on them."

He shook his head. "Like I said, I stabbed myself with the needle, but I didn't notice that blood got anywhere."

He paused. "And why would you have them tested for a mutation?"

I wasn't sure how to explain it. Had I imagined the snake thing that night?

"Well—when you were standing in that dark hotel room and I was moaning and bleeding on the bed—well—I thought your dick down there," I nodded toward the sheet covering him, "was a snake. Or that you were holding a snake there—or something." I gave a big shrug. "I asked a friend to see if it was human—or not. And he analyzed the TP53 gene— it's been used for species identification."

Chance raised his eyebrows.

"So—this 'he' person found it was human but had a TP53 mutation."

"Well, he said it needed confirmation with sequencing, but, yes, he thought there was a mutation. And I told him *nothing* about where the sample came from—nothing. He knew my father, and he did me a favor."

I didn't want him asking questions about who my friend might be. He was silent for a few seconds.

"I believe you."

Something was welling up that needed an answer.

"Chance. Why in the world does you father hate me—us? Dru and me? I heard he and my father didn't get along, but could it have been *that* bad?"

He pursed his lips, obviously thinking this over.

"He hated your father, I know that much. But I think there's probably more to the story than *I* can tell you. Of course, I never met your father. I was a little kid when my father left the university—or when he was forced out, according to him. All of a sudden, we had to pick up and leave. Jer and I were pretty much in the dark about why, except that some jealous guy he worked with had gotten my father in trouble—accused him of using dangerous research methods, I learned later. Maybe in some human trials."

He shook his head. "I wouldn't put it past him. Years later he told me the man's name and showed me a book by him that my father called a pile of trash. Said his own work would dwarf Ranelli's in importance someday, and said that I could help him let the world know what he'd done—only *I* could put it in a better context—an acceptable format. Lately I've been a real disappointment to him."

I hated to ask, but I did. "So—you don't think he had anything to do with my mother and father's death in a car accident five years ago, do you? Did he mention the accident?"

"I remember that he mentioned the bastard was dead and deserved to be, but I never heard him say anything indicating he had something to do with it. Car accidents weren't his style—not his specialty. He would have found something a lot more—kinky."

Like venom in a needle, I thought.

"So why *me* right now?"

He shrugged his shoulders. "Hated your father—hated you, I guess. He didn't want your family line to continue. That venom should have at least triggered a hysterectomy—if I'd given it as a full dose."

I closed my eyes, feeling the pain and blood again.

"And he's sick right now—physically unwell. Whatever he needs to finish up, I think he sees a need to finish—and that's another reason why I think I can get the reversal drug from him."

"And Dru. Why hurt Dru?"

"Just to hurt you more, especially after you survived San Francisco. Jer wasn't really planning to kill her, I don't think. In fact, I think he got to liking her—but in the end, he had to do whatever our mutual parent wanted done. Jer can't—couldn't—survive on his own, either."

"Was he bitten too?"

"He got a taste of Tony's venom—but I doubt that it was accidental."

I shouldn't have been surprised by what he was saying, but the bizarre story seemed to have no ending. I wondered what else Kral had done to them—or to his wife or wives.

"So where is he now? Where does he live?"

He shook his head again. "Can't tell you right now. It's not safe—really not a good idea for you to know. And maybe there's some selfishness on my part—I can't afford to have things botched right now."

He paused, then went on. "Can you please tell me who helped us get out of the ranch, Claudia? I have a feeling you know."

I hesitated, trying to weigh the implications of telling him.

"I'm still not sure," I said, deciding not to get Picci's name involved in our mess, at least for the moment. But I did decide to mention one thing he might want to know.

"I heard the big building at the ranch burned down after we left."

He grimaced, briefly shutting his eyes.

"I'd hoped to get back there and look for more information—maybe some files he'd left there, check the information in the PC—and see what venom samples were there. Well, there's no time for that now, anyway. I need to get right to him—face to face. I'll probably go tomorrow."

I looked at the blood tubes sitting by the bed.

"Chance, we should check your blood counts first. I have a friend at the hospital who can get these results for me."

"I'll probably go no matter what they show. I can't just sit here."

We were quiet for a second, and I looked down, realizing he was holding my hand. He sat forward a little, then reached around his neck and pulled out the silver chain from under his T-shirt. He loosened the clasp and pulled the necklace away from him. The snake and helix were snapped together, not making a sound.

"Hold on to this for me, will you?" he said softly. I sat there, in silent acceptance. He pulled my hair aside and fastened it around my neck, then let it slide inside my shirt. The metal felt warm from the heat of his skin—either that, or it was generating a heat of its own.

"What does it mean, Chance?"

He gave his head a slight shake.

"It represents a lifetime of questions, of pain—of promise—of regrets."

"Jeremy wore one too."

He nodded.

"Dru has it. In a box."

"I know," he said. "*He* wears one too. It was his reminder to us that we were all bound together. He told us never to lose them."

"Don't you think you should leave it on, then? At least until you see him?"

"I doubt it'll matter at this point." He looked at me for a few seconds.

"Claudia, take it off and put it away for me in a safe place—along with the other one. Think of them as luck for me, if you can bear to think of that."

"Of course I wish you luck," I said, hearing my voice crack and looking down at the sheet. Some shards of bright sunlight were filtering through the window edges and streaking across the bed, and I noticed the translucence of the sheet. I could make out some color underneath. He saw me looking at it, and I could feel heat in my face. The sheet moved just slightly, and I almost jumped—but instead watched with curiosity and with something else—some other feeling.

I couldn't help myself. I placed my fingers on the sheet covering the bulge and moved them up and down the shaft slowly, until I heard him groan and it lifted slightly from his body. Then I stopped and looked at him.

"Go ahead and look, Claudia," he whispered. "You want to look at it—you want to know."

Really, I already knew, but my fingers wrapped around the sheet edge curled at his waist, and I pulled it down slowly, brushing my fingers over the taut organ as I pulled the cloth down past it. His eyes closed, then opened into slits. I looked down and saw my hand curl around the serpent whose colors were red, black, and green . . . Four diamonds ran up the shaft, smooth and clear in the erect position.

"That must have hurt like hell," I said softly.

"Jer's artwork," he said. "But we had some help holding it taut."

I held onto it, its warmth growing in my hand. Slowly I moved my hand up and down, my thumb on the diamonds, not thinking about what I was doing or about any consequences.

"Chance—what did you whisper to me that night? It sounded like something in Latin—some words in Latin?"

He shook his head. "Don't remember. I probably said I hated him."

My hand began moving slightly faster, stroking the thing without knowing why, wanting to lose my thoughts in the act, wanting to torture it to a climax. Dimly in the background I heard a door shut downstairs, and I jerked back to reality. In a minute, I heard Dru's footsteps on the stairway. Chance pulled the sheet over him and rolled onto his side, his back to the doorway. I gathered the blood tubes and turned off the light, just as Dru reached the door.

"Let him rest," I said. "He needs it."

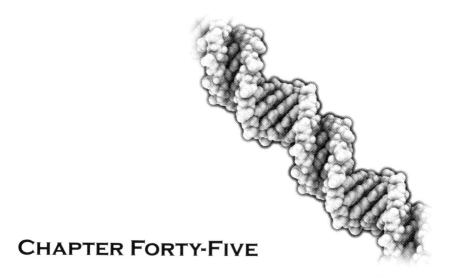

CHAPTER FORTY-FIVE

WE WALKED DOWNSTAIRS SLOWLY AND in silence. My ears felt strangely tight, and I wondered what Dru was thinking. We walked to the kitchen, where she grabbed a beer and we sat.

"Dru," I started. "This is really a dangerous situation for Chance. I'm afraid this low-dose chemo isn't going to be enough to hold him for long."

"Well, cuz, he's convinced his father will give him the reversal drug, and I can't talk him out of trying."

"By the way," I added, "he admitted Kral is his father—no big surprise there. And even if Kral does give him the drug, what's stopping Kral from still hurting *us*?"

She shook her head. "Chance promised me he'd take care of that. Kral won't be a problem."

"How will he manage *that?*"

She shrugged her shoulders. "I guess we'll see."

"When you talk to him, see if you can find out where Kral lives and where Chance grew up. He wouldn't tell me. We need to know that."

She nodded and pulled out a cigarette.

"Dru—I stopped by Picci's restaurant yesterday. Frank was outside washing a big white truck. Joe wasn't around."

She perked up. "The truck we saw at the ranch?"

"It sure looked like it. I didn't get a look at the front, but he essentially admitted he'd been there. He told me the place burned down, apparently right after we left. He said Joe wants to talk to me."

"So you think Joe had Frank follow us because he was worried?"

"I guess so. Probably both of the boys. I didn't know he cared so much—what's *that* all about?" I wondered out loud.

She shook her head. "Don't know, but I'm sure-as-shit glad they *feel* that way."

"By the way, Dru, I didn't tell Chance the Piccis helped us. I think we should keep their names to ourselves for now. And keep Stephen out of it—don't mention his name."

She sat in silence, apparently thinking this over.

"When Chance goes, I'm going with him." She looked at me, waiting for my protestations.

"He probably won't let you go with him. And he probably doesn't want Kral to see you."

"Well then I'm following him."

"That's too dangerous for you."

"Well—then maybe the Piccis will help again." She gulped the rest of her beer; then she looked over at me—at my neck.

"What's that necklace you're wearing?"

My face burned again as I lifted it out and took it off.

"Chance wants us to keep them for him—the one Jer wore, too. Apparently his father had these made for the three of them. Chance says to keep them for luck, but maybe they're worth something."

I looked at the necklace more closely. It could have been made of something more expensive than silver—maybe white gold or platinum. And the eye of the snake had a small jewel in it—a diamond maybe. I shrugged my shoulders.

"If you get Jer's, I'll stick them in the safe and show you how to open it," I said.

Dru got up and ran up the stairs. She was back a few minutes later, Jer's necklace in her palm. We put it on the table next to Chance's.

"Jer's has the same stone for the snake's eye," she said. They looked the same lying on the table. I picked them up, and we walked to the safe in my father's office. I showed her the combination, and we put them on a shelf inside the door.

"I think he's awake," Dru said. "I'm going to see how he's doing."

I sat in my father's chair, picked up the phone and called Julie's cell number.

"Julie, I've got some blood tubes for a CBC and that genetic testing we talked about. Can I drop them off somewhere for you to take care of?"

"Claudia, can you drop them off in the morning? They should be OK until then. I'm obviously not at the hospital right now."

Figuring I could do as much, I let it go at that. I could always redraw the CBC in the morning. The genetic tests wouldn't be started until Monday anyway. Dru came back downstairs and started making some clanging noises in the kitchen, then announced an hour later that hamburgers were ready. She disappeared upstairs with food for the two of them, and I sat in the office chomping mine down and doing some reading online about the TP53 gene mutation.

As I'd expected, there was a ton of information about the TP53 gene, which is responsible for the synthesis of the p53 protein. The protein binds to cellular DNA and prevents cells with damaged or mutated DNA from multiplying and causing tumors. Mutations in the TP53 gene prevent the protein from performing its function, and tumors develop. It was no surprise that the research on TP53 gene mutations was extensive, given that this mutation is present in over fifty percent of cancers. A few people are born with an inherited mutation and develop cancers early in life, a condition known as the Li-Fraumeni syndrome, with which I was somewhat familiar. As far as inducers of the mutation in genetically normal people, tobacco, a few chemicals, UV light, and radiation exposure were listed. Obviously, no snake venoms made the list of inducers, but I did run across some studies of a Crotalus venom producing DNA damage in an experimental setting—the reference Chance had mentioned, I assumed.

Recent research seemed concentrated on finding compounds that restore the normal function of the p53 protein, some of which were described as "small molecules" that restore the normal protein structure. But the research sounded slow and methodical, with some of these compounds associated with significant side effects, some needing simultaneous chemotherapy with traditional chemotherapeutic drugs to be effective.

The fact that Kral would be experimenting on Chance with these hit-and-miss compounds was mind-boggling. I wondered if maybe Kral had simply lied about having such a compound and none existed.

What *was* a fact, though, was that Chance did have acute myeloid leukemia. I looked up the incidence of AML with the TP53 gene mutation. It turned out that the incidence was relatively low. Unfortunately, as I'd suspected, the survival was generally poor.

My stomach was getting knotted again. I shut down the computer, wandered over to the bookshelves and grabbed the big book of Sherlock Holmes stories. I read, trying to get my mind off of things, then fell asleep in the chair. Hours later, I awoke confused, hearing a sound I finally recognized as the doorbell and then some heavy knocking. The sound made my heart lurch, but I walked to the door and took a peek. There was no choice but to let her in.

"Hey, I was out running and then thought I might as well drive by and get those samples." Julie was standing there in bike shorts and a long hoodie, her hair in a ponytail. I glanced down at her hips. She still had some saddlebags, but they really weren't too bad. And I know she hated jogging. She sat on the couch while I got the tubes from the kitchen.

"Here they are, Julie. Get a CBC for sure and genetics on the rest—chromosomes, an AML FISH panel with BCR/ABL, the usual AML molecular prognostic tests—and testing for the TP53 mutation—by sequencing."

FISH is an acronym for fluorescence in situ hybridization, a method of looking for specific genetic mutations that have prognostic and therapeutic significance. Cells from samples such as blood, bone marrow, body fluids or excised tumors are examined under a special microscope after a DNA "probe" for the specific mutation has been added to the sample. It's a sensitive technique, but not as sensitive or specific as molecular genetic testing (sequencing) for the TP53 mutation, especially when only a very small number of mutated cells are present.

"TP53? Claudia, that's not exactly very common in acute leukemia—and it could be done more easily by FISH."

"Julie—just humor me, will you? There might be a family history involving TP53 here." Well, that was true to a point; I didn't want to tell her the history involved kinky snakes.

"Really? How old is this guy?"

"In his twenties," I said. "It's not Li-Fraumeni."

"And I'm supposed to get these genetic tests done *how*? Honey, he's not a hospital patient."

I sighed, not really knowing how to say it. "Take them to Palmer," I said. "Tell him they're from me and these are additional samples from the same patient I had him screen recently. It would be a huge favor and scientifically worth it. I'll explain more later."

"And you think he'll run them based on my saying *that*?"

"Well, you could add it might be a life or death situation. Make my case for me. I know you're dying to. Tell him to look hard at the TP53 gene."

She shook her head, looking exasperated, but not too exasperated to talk with Stephen, I could tell that much. "There's obviously a whole lot you're not telling me about this, but I'll give it a try. By the way, I'd really like to see him." She looked at me hard, then added, "If I'm taking this responsibility, Claudia, I really want to see him." She said the last six words slowly and emphatically, letting them sink in. She knew I needed her.

I ran upstairs and knocked on the bedroom door. I heard Chance tell me to come in, so I opened it. He was half-sitting on the bed, reading something; Dru was asleep next to him.

"Chance, there's someone downstairs who needs to see you—just for a second. It's the doctor I know from work who'll be getting me the lab results we need. I think she just needs to see you're stable."

"You mean she needs to know I'm not croaking yet?"

"Yeah—something like that. Would you mind?"

"Be there in a sec," he said, and I nodded and turned, just as he was whipping the sheet off and sitting up. I walked back down to Julie, wondering what she would think of the diamond-backed dick if she saw it. *Crotalus phallus.*

I returned to Julie, and a minute later Chance trotted down the stairs, looking alert and agile, despite some increased angularity to his face from a little weight loss. I saw the acute look of fascination in Julie's eyes. Chance was someone who always generated a second look, if not a stare. I introduced them, not using his last name.

Julie stared down at the tubes I'd given her. "So I guess I'll just label these as Chance," she said, looking up at him. "I guess that's good enough and probably appropriate." She paused, looking at his eyes. "I suppose you know that you'd be much better off in a doctor's office right now, getting a bone marrow biopsy and treatment for your leukemia."

Chance nodded. "I'll get there soon enough. And I can't tell you how much I—we—appreciate your help."

She looked at us both, mentally pairing us up, I knew.

"And you're not cousins?"

I shook my head. "Dru is my cousin—a girl. She's asleep upstairs." I let her think what she wanted. I couldn't afford not to, since I was the one needing the favors.

She headed toward the door. "I'll give you a call in the morning," she said.

A few seconds later, I heard Dru's footsteps coming down the stairs.

"Who was that?" she asked in a croaky voice.

I looked at Chance and said, "That was the doctor who's helping me. She took the blood tubes for testing."

Dru sat down and looked up at Chance. "Chance says he wants to go tomorrow," she said in a worried voice.

"We really need to get the test results back first." I looked at Chance. "Please, let's at least get the blood counts."

He nodded, and they both went into the kitchen. I sat on the couch, staring at the fireplace, listening to the pop of beer can tabs and the sounds of a search for food in the refrigerator. I had no appetite at all and sat listening to their muted words that I couldn't really hear. I felt like an outsider, waiting helplessly for the climax of a story I should be a part of but wasn't. Finally I went upstairs and lay on my bed, tired of it all. I would just wait and see what happened.

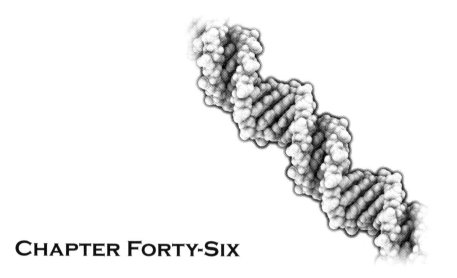

CHAPTER FORTY-SIX

I DON'T REMEMBER WHEN I finally fell asleep, but I didn't even bother to take my clothes off beforehand—only my shoes. I dreamed about looking at my own blood and seeing blasts. I had acute leukemia, and I was crying to my mother. "Are you happy now?" I asked her.

A slamming sound woke me up; then someone was shaking my shoulder.

"Come on, Claudia. Wake up. Chance is sick."

I sat up on the edge of the bed, shaking my head to clear it. It still looked dark outside.

"Come and take a look," she said, grabbing my arm and pulling me toward the door. I stumbled into their bedroom, looking at Chance on the bed. His shirt was off, and his whole upper body was sopping wet with perspiration. His forehead was hot, and his hands were shaking. He looked at me, but I wondered if he was seeing.

I looked at Dru. "We need to get him hospitalized. He's got an infection—sepsis. You'd better just call EMS. I'm afraid he could have a seizure."

He shook his head. "I can make it to the car. Just take me there. Maybe just some antibiotics, and I can be out."

I shook my head at Dru, conveying the absurdity of that thought.

"Let's just get him in the car and take him in," she said. "It'll be just as fast as waiting for EMS."

She threw some clothes on, and we got him into some pants; then we helped him down to the car. He really couldn't stand on his own, but he had enough strength to help us out a little. I drove as fast as I dared to the university hospital ER.

We got some help getting him inside, and when he was situated in a cubicle, I explained Chance's condition to the resident covering the medical area, and she got a CBC and cultures collected and sent to the lab. Dru and I were hovering around the bed after samples had been drawn and an IV with antibiotics had been started. They were about to take him away for x-rays.

"He's definitely not coming home with us tonight, Dru. I'm waiting for the CBC results then I'm probably going to call Julie. He needs chemo *now*."

Her eyes were starting to get damp again. Chance wasn't completely out of it, and he looked at me without protesting what I'd said. He mumbled something that sounded like "I guess it's inevitable."

I decided to make a run to the lab again, not willing to wait for the results to reach the ER. Dru stayed with him while I ran down several hallways to the lab.

The results were as bad as I feared. The white blood cell count was high, with mainly blasts in the blood. His platelets had fallen again, though not as low as they'd been the first time. I ran back to tell the resident the news, though she would obviously check it out for herself. Then I told Dru and Chance.

"The leukemia's worse, I'm afraid. The white count's gone up even more, with mainly blasts in the blood and no normal white cells to fight off an infection. I'm calling Julie."

"When will she get here?" Dru asked.

"Probably around eight. He can get some x-rays done in the meantime."

I spoke with the resident about Julie coming in to get Chance admitted and ready for chemotherapy. He'd need a bone marrow biopsy. Then she could get the samples to Stephen, who could run them on a true inpatient. Chance had managed to sign all the usual hospital documents, though his hand shook terribly as he did it.

When they wheeled him off to radiology, we retreated to the waiting room, drinking the old, bitter coffee sitting on a table. We sat in silence for a long time, but I could tell Dru was thinking hard about something, and her eyes lost the dampness and seemed to harden into some sort of resolve. I was afraid of what she was about to say. Finally, she lifted her chin off of her palm and looked at me.

"Cuz—you know we can't just sit here and wait."

"And just what did you have in mind?" I asked, knowing what would come next.

"We need to go see that asshole Kral. Maybe he'll get that reversal drug for Chance if he knows how sick he is."

"But we don't even know where he is. How're we going to find him?"

"He lives in a house in Laredo. I know where it is."

"And how do you know *that?*" I was wondering what she hadn't been telling me.

"Because I talked to Frank Picci last night."

"And?"

"And he said that they—Joe Jr. and him—had talked to the guard from the Devine place, a guy named Rolf. The one we ran into in the snake house. They asked him who was running the show there—the main man behind it. He gave them Ray Webb's name as someone who knew. Then they followed Webb in Laredo out to Kral's place."

"What happened to Rolf?"

"I think they either paid him off or convinced him to leave. Frank said no one got hurt."

"So Frank Picci knows where Kral lives."

She nodded.

"And did he tell you?"

"Pretty much. But he told me to stay away from the guy. They would help us if Kral made any more threats or tried to hurt us. He said they could take care of him if they really had to."

"Oh, God," I said.

"I told them absolutely not to approach him yet."

"And why would the Piccis do all this for *us?*" I wondered aloud, perplexed at the depth of their willingness to help and to jeopardize themselves.

She shrugged. "I've been wondering the same thing." She paused. "You know, cuz, your dad wasn't the only one who played poker with Joe senior. My dad was in that little club too—for a while, anyway. Maybe something happened with that group—maybe a mafia thing. I don't know. Talk to Joe, maybe he'll tell you. He said he wants to talk to you, didn't he?"

I nodded. "But I really don't think they're mafia. My dad wouldn't have had anything to do with that. I'm sure he wouldn't."

"And obviously, there were things your dad never told you."

That hung in the air for a while, like an acrid smell.

"Well, Dru—did you dad ever say anything about any of this stuff? Kral or mafia or whatever?"

"No," she said, not sounding anxious to discuss her father. "We never talked about shit like that. But when I asked Chance—just now—if that was where Kral lives—where Frank said he lives—he nodded yes. And he didn't object when I said I'm going there."

"Dru, Chance barely knows where he *is*. He probably doesn't even know what you asked him."

"Yes—he did. He told me that Kral goes by the name of a Mr. Samuel."

"Yet another name."

"Yup."

"And what makes you think we can just waltz up to Mr. Samuel and he'll give us the magic potion? First of all, he'll see you're still alive, and he'll want to know where Jeremy is. I assume he set Jeremy up to kill you. And secondly, if *I'm* there, it's like walking into the lion's den. He *hates* me, obviously."

"Whether you come or not, cuz, I'm going. And I'll go armed. And I'm going to get Frank to cover my ass."

I pinched my nose hard between my eyes, squeezing them shut.

"Dru. This isn't the Wild West. This is stupid and dangerous. We should just go to the police." But I knew before I'd finished the sentence it was too late for that. There was a body, Jeremy's, I didn't know the whereabouts of, among a myriad of other things.

"Get real," she said. "We need to get the reversal drug. And it's way too late for that."

"Maybe there's no reversal drug, Dru. Have you thought about *that*? Kral could have made up the whole thing as some bizarre way to keep those boys in line. In fact, the more I think about it, the more preposterous it seems. We don't even know for sure yet if Chance really has the mutation."

"Yeah, well I believe what Chance has said—and I think you do too. I think he's got that mutation—the 53 or whatever it is. He sure as hell has leukemia. And if there's a drug, I'm sure as hell going to get it." Her face was getting red with her rising determination.

"Settle down," I said, but neither of us could really do that. We just got quiet for a while, until I realized it was about seven in the morning, late enough to call Julie. I caught her getting ready for work, and she agreed to stop by the ER first thing.

"Julie's almost on her way."

Dru nodded, still looking resolute. We sat watching the morning news, and I wondered what was going on with the investigation of Jeff's disappearance. I hadn't heard any news recently, but then I really hadn't been listening. A little over an hour later, Julie called my phone.

"Hey Claud, I'm here in the ER, and they say he's in radiology. Are you in the waiting room?"

"Yeah. Don't move. I'll be right there." I signaled to Dru I'd be right back. She started to get up, and I motioned her back down, giving her a signal to stay put.

Julie was at the nursing station looking at the ER notes on Chance. She looked up at me and shook her head. "Looks like we need to go to plan B right away," she said.

"Yeah, blast away, Julie. He finally realizes he can't go any longer without it. Can you take him?"

"Honey, I'll make it happen. And those genetics you wanted? I'll make sure they get done."

I noticed she was looking well put-together that morning. The sweater was a nice shade of blue, tight and a little too low cut for a medical professional. We both knew she'd be talking to Stephen that day.

"He's signed all the admission forms. Take good care of him."

"Don't worry, Claudia. He won't be croaking on *my* watch. I'll be back when they call me." She turned and walked out, and I returned to Dru. We waited around until Chance finally got back from radiology, then spent a few minutes with him in the ER.

"Chance," I said. "Julie's going to take good care of you here and start your chemo. We'll be back to check on you later."

He looked groggy, maybe not comprehending, but he was getting transfused again and seemed stable. His temperature seemed to be dropping a bit. Dru wedged her way in and took his hand, tears starting to slide down her face. I left them alone for a few minutes, and I heard the vague, soft sounds of a conversation through the curtains. When she came out, her face was resolute again.

"Let's get home," she said. "I've got a trip to make."

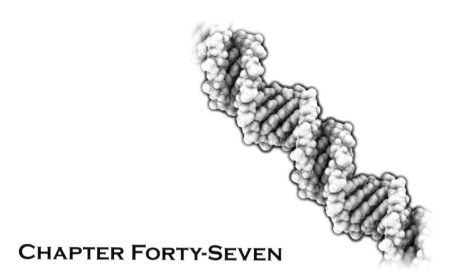

CHAPTER FORTY-SEVEN

WE DROVE HOME IN SILENCE, with Dru staring straight ahead while I tried to concentrate on the road. She was creating tension between us, and I felt as though it was her passive-aggressive way of making me feel guilty, which I did. Guilty for exactly *what* I wasn't sure, but I figured she wanted to do things her way and didn't really want to do them alone. I couldn't blame her. What I could fault her for, though, was letting Chance become the total focus of her life. Suddenly she was more concerned about him than about me or even about herself. She hadn't mentioned her kids in days, and I wondered if she'd even given a single thought to them lately. I decided to bring up the subject.

"Dru, what about your kids? You could get hurt or worse. Aren't you worried about what that would do to them?"

She didn't answer me for a while, just stared out the window frowning. Finally she answered.

"I've thought about that a lot, cuz, and I think maybe they're better off without me. First off, I don't think I'm a good mother—running around with Jer was stupid." She paused for a while. "And I used drugs with him. I didn't tell you the truth about my job. I actually was about to lose it. I tested positive for drugs, and I knew I'd get canned. What kind of a mother does that?"

"Dru, you can change. It's certainly not too late."

"It's too late. They're better off where they are."

"Are they with Martin?" Martin was her ex-husband.

"They're in Minneapolis with his parents right now—but he's nearby. I really don't want to discuss this right now, OK?" Her voice was sounding croaky. I shut up.

She jumped out of the car when we got home and ran up to her room, throwing her clothes off and changing into clean jeans and a shirt. I rinsed off my face and armpits and did the same. I walked into the hall for a second and could hear that she was on the phone, though the conversation was a blur. Fifteen minutes later I heard her come out of the room in her boots. She stood there, waiting to see if I'd come out, I suppose. I tugged my boots on too and came out my door. We looked at each other.

"Got your gun?" she asked. She had her backpack in one hand.

"Yup."

"Cuz, if we leave here now, we'll probably get there around high noon."

I couldn't help but laugh. The whole thing was absurd, but I was going along with it. Who can sit home and read a novel, waiting to see how it ends, when you're a main character in it? That's not to say I wasn't afraid; my stomach was hurting from fear. She went down to the living room and peeked out the front window, then checked her watch.

"Looking for something?" I asked.

"Yeah, a car," she said. "A different car to use. A friend's bringing it over."

I wasn't sure what to make of that.

"Did you talk to Frank Picci again?"

"Yeah. I called him from the hospital." She paused, staring at the road. "He was pissed. Said they wanted to know everything we know about Kral—or Mr. Samuel. Webb called him Samuel. They want to know about Jeremy and Chance. Rolf, the guard mentioned Jeremy and Chance as brothers, and Rolf knew Webb in Laredo as working with them. And Joe Picci wants to know now—today. So you can imagine Frank's reaction when I said I was driving down there today—either alone or with you."

My heart was galloping. It was perfectly reasonable for them to refuse.

"Frank asked me to call him before leaving."

I sat on the couch, waiting for our limo. Ten minutes later, a somewhat battered-looking black SUV pulled into the driveway, and Dru bolted out the kitchen door into the garage. I heard the garage door open and watched as she switched her car for the SUV. I had no idea who the guy was—short, stocky, with dark hair. They talked for a minute, and Dru handed him something that I assumed was cash. She came back in.

"Be right back," she said, running up the stairs again. A few minutes later she was back down, picking up her backpack. I followed her to the SUV and got in.

"Did you talk to Frank?" I asked.

"I told him we had to talk to Kral, Mr. Samuel—alone—but that we could use some backup in case things didn't go well. I told him the guy's real name was probably Samuel Kral. That's all I said."

"What did he say?"

"He said we're on our own."

A pang shot through me, and we drove onto I-35 in silence.

"Where'd you get the SUV?" I asked.

"An old friend from the south side," she said, shrugging her shoulders. "You don't know him."

"Not stolen, I hope."

She gave me an irritated look. "No," she said softly. I wasn't convinced, but decided it was worthless worrying about it.

An hour later we stopped for gas. Dru came out of the restroom, putting her cell phone back in her pocket.

"That was Frank," she said. "He says to wait here for a white van to get behind us—it's them. I told him what we're driving."

"Who's 'them'?"

"Frank and Joe Jr."

"I thought they had a white *truck*."

She shrugged. "I guess they have a white van too. We're the beggars here—I'm not going to interview them about their fleet of vehicles, cuz. And a van can carry a lot of things." She gave me a meaningful glance that I comprehended with some distaste.

We looked around the gas station, but no white vans were in sight. Several minutes later we spotted it, pulled over near the entrance to the station. Dru gave them a small wave, and we got back on the road. Her cell phone rang, and she answered.

"Thanks, Frank," she said, sounding relieved. "We owe you big-time."

I couldn't tell what he said, but Dru laughed. I wondered what could possibly be very funny at that point.

"They know where we're going, and they're going to keep their distance from us."

"It might be better if they lead the way, Dru."

"In front, behind—either way's good for me."

I nodded, my stomach starting to un-knot a bit. Dru had been going about five miles over the speed limit, then slowed it down, putting the car on cruise control. The rest of the trip sped by, as things do when you don't want them to, with the van disappearing and reappearing sporadically in our rear view. As we entered the Laredo metropolitan area, Dru turned east onto highway 20, and the van disappeared again, this time for quite a while before I saw it in the distance. Dru saw me looking.

"Take it easy, cuz. Frank said he'd call me if any problems come up."

"We'd better call him just before we go in, though."

She nodded. After a few miles, she exited to the left, and we drove several blocks into a newer neighborhood that looked to be at least upper-middle class, with homes varying from extra-large to medium in size. More and more empty lots came into view as we drove further. Dru kept checking her cell phone, apparently looking at the directions to the house.

"Is the area gated?" I asked.

"Frank said no. The area's brand new."

I could see that, with the houses getting more and more sparse. We turned onto a smaller road and went about a mile before spotting a big two-story brick house with tall columns in front. The house was apparently just built, with landscaping of the yard obviously not yet finished. It was recessed off the road, and the driveway to the front door was gated. But the gate was wide open and Dru drove in.

"Aren't you going to call Frank first?" I asked quickly, alarmed at her lack of caution.

"Look behind us," she said.

The white van was partially visible on the main road. Dru stopped short of the front door, about halfway down the entrance road, then unbuckled her seat belt.

"You stay here for now," she said.

"What's the point? He'll know we're both here, I'm sure." But then, maybe she did have a point.

"I'll go and see if he's there and if he'll talk to us—scout things out. If you don't hear from me in an hour or if I don't come out"—she shrugged her shoulders—"call Frank, I guess."

"Dru, I think I need to go in there. This didn't start out about you. It was about me."

She shook her head. "Let's start out with me for now. I've got this and this."

She showed me the pistol grip with one hand, and then drew out one of the necklaces with the other, holding it in her palm. "Just in case he needs proof that Chance is with us."

I wondered if that was wise, but who knew? She gave me Frank's number, then got out of the car and walked to the large front door and rang the bell. A minute later I saw one of the double doors open, but I couldn't see who stood inside. Then Dru disappeared. I looked back, comforted that part of the van was still in sight.

The minutes passed agonizingly, and I couldn't concentrate on anything except staring at the front door. There was no apparent activity around the house. Fifteen minutes went by, and I pulled out my phone. I dialed Frank and got no answer, which really rattled me. I dialed twice more and finally left a voice message telling him I was just too worried about Dru to wait any longer. I peeked behind and didn't see the van. Then I jumped out of the car and walked back toward the gate. There wasn't a vehicle in sight, and nausea threatened my stomach contents. I walked toward the front door, my feet feeling leaden, and rang the doorbell. The noise seemed to echo from inside the house, and approaching footsteps followed. I waited.

Finally the door opened. I had no idea who she was—female, maybe forty, tall, ash blonde, with an old Hollywood-style pageboy hairdo, a below-knee knit dress and practical rubber-soled shoes—very attractive. She had about two inches on me, and I stared up at her, not knowing what to say.

"Good afternoon," she said in a pleasant voice that made me wonder if I had dreamed up all the bad things I'd heard about Kral. Or if maybe Jer and Chance were making up a huge mess of a story. "You must be with Miss Salinas. Come in. They're in the office." She smiled.

She took me through a small hallway that led to a large room with a giant fireplace at one end. My boots sounded obnoxiously loud as I walked on travertine marble tile floors. The room was white and cream and empty—no furniture, no nothing. I followed her down another hallway, and we turned left toward some double doors. She knocked, and I heard a rough sound I couldn't decipher. Opening the doors, she led me into what looked like a small library, and this room had some furniture. Two chairs that looked like they belonged in a dining room faced a wood desk that matched some built-in wall shelves—the smell was sawdust.

Dru sat in a chair facing the desk and looked at me when I entered. I couldn't read her face, but it wasn't smiling. Behind the desk sat Kral.

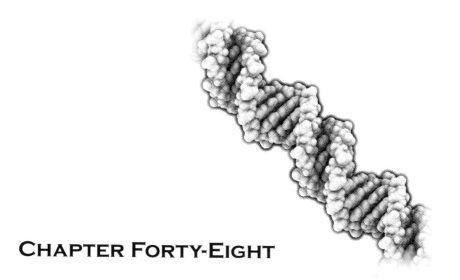

CHAPTER FORTY-EIGHT

I'D WONDERED HOW RECOGNIZABLE KRAL would be if I ever saw him, and I knew him immediately. It was in the eyes, the angular face, the fine longish hair—despite the apparent wasted, ravaged body. It was the remnants of the handsome face I'd seen in the faculty pamphlet, and there was some Chance in it. It was the face in my dream, holding my mother as I peeked from the stairway. The eyes had more blue than Chance's did, despite their milkiness; the hair was a dirty gray, hanging down to his neck in limp, clumped strands and flyaway wisps. As he stood, I saw he wore pinstriped pants held by suspenders with a white shirt that looked stained. Crumpled tissue was clutched in one hand. He didn't offer his hand, which was just as well, I thought. I glanced at his eyes, hoping for some hint of a sane and thoughtful brain. He looked back, apparently studying my face.

"Miss Ranelli, what a pleasant surprise," he said, with a southern European accent that was still obvious. He smiled, showing some very yellow teeth, then sat and nodded to the woman. I looked back at her as she left the room, shutting the door quietly.

"My nurse," he said. "I haven't been feeling totally well lately."

I could hear Dru breathing and some slight gurgling sounds coming from Kral's throat. I glanced over at Dru. She gave her head the slightest of shakes, conveying that things hadn't gone all that well.

"Your cousin has been telling me quite a story, Claudia. May I call you Claudia?"

"Sure." Or call me an idiot for being here.

He bent closer from the other side of the desk, staring hard at my face and squinting. Then he put some little round glasses on to get a better look. I could see part of a silver chain around his neck, and I assumed it was the third necklace Chance had mentioned, but I couldn't see what was hanging from it.

"Yes, the daughter of Antonio and Maria," he said, nodding his head as though it was a great discovery. His voice was thin and high-pitched. "I haven't seen you since you were a small girl. You used to hide from the grown-ups— do you remember that? Probably not," he said, answering his own question. "I see some of each in you, I suppose, though your mother had a much more refined and delicate look about her—but then, she was incomparable in every way. You have a more *coarse* look about you, though not a totally unsatisfactory coarseness. I suppose you might appeal to some men. I've heard your shoulder is quite a mess, though—your mother had *perfect* skin."

Well—there we were, and how do you respond to *that*? I wanted to tell him I'd seen better-looking dead bodies but kept my mouth shut.

"Your cousin here," he said, nodding toward Dru, "says my son Chance is sick, and she thinks that I have a magic potion to cure him." He made a gurgling, laughing sound. "Did you know that lying guard Rolf at Devine called an acquaintance of mine and told him Chance might be *dead*? He said Chance might have died in a fire up there on the ranch."

He stared at both of us. "I wonder who could have put him up to lying like that to me? Who do *you* think?" he said, staring at me.

I shook my head in ignorance.

"And now you both tell me my son is alive and very sick and needs some kind of wonder drug that you think I have?" His voice was getting louder. "What about my *other* son? Do you know where he is too? Do you know where Jeremy is?" he said, staring at me.

I had a huge rope in my throat I had to swallow. "No," I said, shaking my head again. "I don't even *know* Jeremy."

He stared at Dru, and she gave a wooden shake of her head. She obviously wanted a quick subject change, so she asked a question, going in a direction I really wasn't ready to follow.

"We're only trying to help Chance," she said, her eyes getting watery. "Why do you want to hurt us?"

"Hurt you?" he said, clutching his chest like a bad actor. "Why would I want to hurt you?"

I thought I'd better grab the stage from Dru for a minute. "Chance told me what you had him do in San Francisco—with the venom."

His eyes hardened and glistened. He leaned back, looking straight ahead at nothing.

"Such a story. Such complexities are difficult for the average mind to really comprehend. The *science*. Some breakthroughs require finesse, years of plodding experiments. Some just need to be *done*." He looked at me. "Your father didn't understand that. He was too *stupid* to understand the significance of what I did. He was too *stupid* to let me get it done—and he was too *stupid* to really appreciate your mother." He let that sink in for several seconds, and my face was burning.

He went on. "I *vowed* to end his bloodline, but my son let me down."

A question welled up in me, and it all came spilling out. "Did you kill my parents? Did you have anything to do with that accident?"

He looked at me like I was the crazy one.

"Hurt you mother? I *loved* your mother. I loved her like I could love no other woman, child. If anyone was responsible for that crash, it was your father. He was probably arguing with her and drove off the road." He stopped, trying to get his breath.

I looked over at Dru, who gave me a "just shut-up" look. Kral started to wheeze then developed a sudden spell of coughing—a deep, rough coughing fit that brought up a slimy blob of pinkish phlegm that he spat into his hand, then wiped on his pants. When it was over, he laughed.

"This is the supreme irony," he said, shaking his head, half laughing, half coughing. "I discover a wonder drug against human cancers, and I get a cancer that doesn't have the mutation, doesn't respond to the drug." He stood up and looked at us, resting his shaking hand on the desk.

"You think I'm afraid of hell? There is none after this—this is hell. My lungs are rotting. Whatever I do now is all that matters. There are no consequences, no afterlife."

"Then if you have this miracle drug, why not help Chance? Why not help your son?" Dru pleaded, tears running down her face. "Of all people, surely you'd want to help *him*."

Kral stared at her, his face devoid of sympathy.

"You know, child, I'm not sure he's *deserving* of any help." He put his hand on his chin in thought. "And the more I think about it, the more I'm convinced that he deserves nothing from me—nothing. In fact, I believe he may have harmed his own brother. What do you think about that?"

Dru was silent for several seconds, and then said quietly, "I don't believe he could do something like that."

"Then he needs to come here and tell me," Kral said in a firm voice.

"He's too sick," Dru and I echoed at once. Then she reached her hand in her pocket, and I was afraid a gun was coming out. Instead it was the necklace.

She held it out toward him in her palm. "He gave this to us. He trusts us, and he wants us to ask for your help—please."

I closed my eyes, for some reason thinking that hadn't been the best idea. Kral came around the desk and took a close look at the glittering snake-helix in her hand, his eyes nearly squinting shut. He looked at it, then at Dru but said nothing. He opened his eyes; they were as hard as rocks.

"I have other ways to leave my legacy—other than through Chance. Believe me, the world *will* know what I've discovered."

He moved behind us, and we watched, wondering what he was up to. He opened the door and motioned to someone who was obviously standing nearby.

"Rivers, please bring in our other guest, would you?"

He stood at the door, and I looked at Dru.

"Frank didn't answer," I half-whispered, half-mouthed to her. "No van out there."

Her eyes got a little wider. Kral came back into the room, and a few seconds later, a stocky, middle aged guy in coveralls wheeled in a metal cart with a rectangular box on it. The guy seemed nervous, banging the cart against a lamp as he wheeled it near Kral, who was standing near his chair. The box was covered with a cloth. I was getting a sick feeling.

"Thank you," Kral said. "I'll take it from here."

The guy walked out, leaving the door open a crack. Kral gave us a minute to sweat it out before lifting the cloth off the box, which turned out to be a terrarium. Of course. He opened the cover and reached his hand into the container more quickly than we could think about it. Seconds later he had it behind the head and held the rest of the body in his other hand. He placed it on his desk, where it lay, unmoving. Dru and I were holding our breaths. It was a big diamond-back albino. Huge. I could see Dru feeling the handle of her gun, debating whether or not to pull it out. Kral smiled at us.

"This is Tony," he said. "If you don't get excited, he won't."

Dru kept her gun hidden.

"Tony is retired, for the most part," he went on. "He's about twenty, pretty old for his species. Not nearly as lively as he used to be."

Kral looked at me. "Tony is named after your father, of course. After my good friend and colleague Antonio Ranelli, whom I thought should have a *snake* named after him. A special snake." I could see the spittle come from his mouth at his extended pronunciation of the s-words.

He perched on the edge of the desk, his right hand very close to Tony's body, but Kral didn't look worried.

"Tony's venom is very potent—potent indeed. But it's also a very special venom that's quite unkind to one's DNA. Who would have thought so?" he said to me. "Tony is certainly worth another chapter in Antonio's landmark book, don't you think? I can picture it now—'Mechanisms of Mutation Induction, Chapter 13: Tony the Viper Snake.' Certainly it would be the most intriguing chapter in an otherwise quite dull tome. Of course, he would have needed to acknowledge the fact that Tony was the result of my years of work with hybridization."

A second later, he had Tony by the neck again.

"Tony has always had a pretty docile temperament, relatively speaking. Snakes do have personalities, you know—you'd be amazed. Once in a while he does get a little—excited."

I don't know how he did it, but suddenly Tony's mouth opened wide, showing some pretty impressive fangs. Dru and I jumped back in our chairs, though he was still several feet away. Kral laughed again, and this precipitated some coughing. I was afraid he'd drop Tony, but he put the snake down on the desk, where Tony promptly coiled himself up and put his head down.

When Kral had recovered, he said, "I myself am immune to most of these pit viper venoms. But Tony's—I'm not totally sure. The genetic effects, though—that's a different story. One cannot protect oneself from the genetic damage simply by immunizing oneself with diluted venom."

He looked toward the door, where Rivers was standing once more.

"Rivers—the canister, please."

He disappeared down the hall, and Kral sat down. Thankfully, Tony was taking a siesta, but Dru and I couldn't take our eyes off him.

Rivers returned a minute or two later, walking in and carrying something on a wooden tray. It looked like a high-tech ice bucket. He placed it in front of Kral, again looking like he wanted to be somewhere else, careful to keep his distance from Tony. Kral gave him the nod to leave.

"Double check outside," Kral rasped, as Rivers left the room. Then he looked at us with a disgustingly smug expression on his face.

"This, I believe, is what you want, girls. Many a scientist would give his eye teeth for this compound. Yes—it really does exist, and it works—like nothing else. A simple formula, really. It's amazing what a difference a few chemical bonds can make. I would have given the formula to Chance, but alas, soon there'll be no Chance."

He unscrewed the lid from the canister, and a visible waft of cold vapor came out. He tilted the canister to reveal an inner small metallic container covered with frost: then he tilted it back down, and a heavy coughing fit seized him. This one went on for a while, and he started to wheeze heavily, looking hypoxic. I heard Rita say something in the distance, and a few seconds later she walked in with an oxygen tank on wheels. She got it around to Kral, and she was looking even more nervous than Rivers had at the sight of Tony; Kral put the oxygen mask on. Dru looked at me and nodded her head. Rita's back was to us, and Kral was busy trying to breath. She pulled out her gun and stood up, and I did too.

"Don't fucking move," Dru said, pointing her gun at the woman. Mine was pointed at Kral. She glanced back at the door and nodded to me to check the hallway. I took a few steps outside the door, looking around and seeing no one else.

"Watch the snake," she said, as her arm slid toward the canister on the desk, pulling the tray it was on close to our side of the desk. Tony didn't seem to mind, but Kral's eyes were terrifying slits above the mask. Dru grabbed the tray, and we backed out of the room, closing the office doors behind us. Then we headed toward the front door, but before I could open it, it swung open toward me and I got a quick glimpse of Rivers. I felt a sharp, burning prick in my neck. I vaguely recall the sound of something hitting the floor, and that's all I knew.

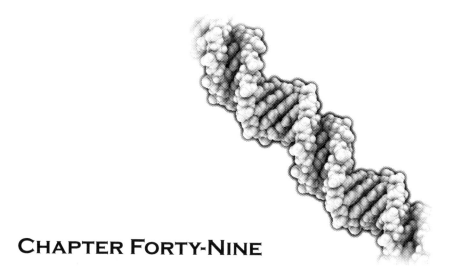

CHAPTER FORTY-NINE

I OPENED MY EYES, FEELING as though I had a massive hangover. I blinked to stay awake and tried to hold my head up. When my eyes began to focus, I finally realized that I was back in Kral's office and Kral was once again behind his desk, looking at my struggle. I tried to wipe my eyes and realized with a panic that my hands were tied to the back of the chair. A glance to my right led to a shooting pain in my neck, and I saw Dru sitting there in the same predicament. She had a gag in her mouth. I moved my own mouth open and shut and realized that mine was still empty. Glancing down, I saw her feet were tied to the chair. I looked down; mine were tied together with what looked like a phone cord.

"Your cousin talks too much," Kral said to me. "She's irritating."

"You can't do this," was all I could think to say, and my voice sounded distant and weak.

"Two armed women come into my house with intent to steal—I believe that I can, Claudia." He paused to let that sink in then went on. "By the way, if you're looking for those friends of yours to save you, those *wop* boys, I'm afraid they've been detained—probably for quite some time." He smiled. "You know, the authorities can be unkind to men suspected of buying and selling arms across the border. Your friends are in a bit of a pickle."

I shook my head, about to deny the accusation.

"It happened back on the highway," he continued, nodding toward the front of the house. "There's more than one white van in Texas."

He got up and walked around the desk toward us, apparently recovered from his hypoxic spell. The oxygen tank was gone; Tony was still on the desk, but he was lying still, back in his terrarium. Kral stopped beside Dru, and she looked up at him, making some grunting sounds. He reached down into her jacket pocket, fumbled for a few seconds then drew out the necklace she had shown him. He opened up his palm, arranged the snake and helix front sides up and clicked them together. He put it close to her face, then grabbed the hair on the top of her head with his left hand and pulled it tight. With his right, he dragged the sharp bottom of the snake's tail deeply along her left cheek, leaving a trail of blood. She tried to squirm away but couldn't move.

"Stop it," I yelled, but it was already done. Then he gave her a huge swat across the face with the back of his hand, and I was afraid her neck was broken.

"Stop," I said again, pleading with him. "Don't take it out on *her.*"

Dru shook her head, tears streaming down. Kral's face was now close to mine, and I could smell the rancidness of him.

He opened his palm, with the blood-smeared necklace in it.

"This necklace belongs to *Jeremiah,*" he said slowly. Dru's head fell forward.

Kral stepped behind us. "Rita," he yelled, opening the door. "Bring me supplies."

I heard a faint voice down the hall, and he left the room, presumably to discuss things with Rita.

"Hang on, Dru," I said, but her head stayed down, and I wasn't sure what I could say at that point. "It's still *me* he's after," was all I could come up with.

A few minutes later Kral came back in, followed by Rita, who once more was wheeling a cart that she pushed next to Kral on his side of the desk.

She glanced at us, then said, "I'm going to lunch now. I'll be back for your next dose," then walked out.

Kral pulled a small vial from his pocket.

"I'm going to reconstitute it to half a mil. We won't need much," he announced.

He unscrewed the lid of the vial, his hands shaking, then put it down. He stuck a small syringe into a vial of what I assumed to be saline and drew some out, then added it to the vial, replaced the cover and mixed the yellowish solution.

Then he picked up another syringe from the cart and walked over to Dru, sticking the contents into Dru's upper arm through her clothes, obviously not concerned about sterile precautions. Dru grunted, shaking her head wildly with helplessness, rattling her chair and shaking out the needle before the injection was totally in. This didn't seem to bother Kral much, who tossed the syringe to the far corner of the room.

"Stop," I yelled again. "*I'm* your problem. Don't do this."

Some large, rough hands grabbed my chin and shoved a rag or a snotty handkerchief in my mouth. I half-gagged on it, struggling to breath through my nose.

Then Kral was in my face again.

"Your cousin is getting sleepy, Claudia. I want to do a demonstration for you—scientist to scientist. An interesting demonstration of the effects of intravenous administration of a snake venom—Tony's toxin, to be specific. You can watch the effects on your cousin. Unfortunately, the show won't last long—this is one of the most potent in the world—the extra-crispy recipe, if you will."

I began sobbing, but Kral seemed not to notice, and it made breathing nearly impossible. I had to fight the panic.

"Untie her right arm," Kral instructed Rivers, who bent down and struggled with the rope. After a minute, he shook his head then headed out the door. Kral sat in silence for a few minutes until Rivers walked in with a kitchen knife.

"There's nothing around here," he complained. He bent down and sliced the ropes holding Dru, who was now out cold, her head rolling around loosely. He grabbed Dru's right arm, pushed up the sleeves of her jacket, and taped the arm, palm side up, to the small arm of the chair, extending Dru's elbow as much as possible. Kral helped him prop up Dru and secure her in the sitting position.

"Move the items from the cart to the front of my desk," Kral instructed.

Rivers grabbed everything, making the transfer. His forehead was dripping sweat, and I tried to catch his eyes, hoping some guilt on his part would surface, but he didn't look at me.

I saw a small needle package, a rubber tourniquet, some tape and a small bag of saline with IV tubing attached. Kral put the tourniquet on Dru's upper arm, and without a skin prep, opened the IV needle and stuck it in Dru's antecubital vein with a surprisingly deft move, considering his shaking hands. He took off the tourniquet, grabbed the IV tubing and attached it, then picked up the saline bag and glanced around the room.

"Grab the lamp," he said to Rivers, nodding at the tall table lamp on his desk. Rivers grabbed it, and Kral hung the bag from the lamp using some tape, then opened the IV line. He put a piece of tape over the needle in Dru's arm and grinned in satisfaction.

"I could have used Tony," he said, "but this is much less obvious than a messy bite, don't you agree?" He paused. "Still, we'll probably have quite a mess to clean up."

He looked at Rivers, who didn't look happy.

"Check the house again," Kral instructed him, and Rivers walked out the door.

Kral picked up a syringe with a needle on it and drew the venom from the vial, letting the bubbles out of it from habit, I guessed.

"We wouldn't want her to die of an air embolism first," he said, giving a croaky laugh.

Holding the syringe and needle in his fingers, Kral squatted next to me.

"Claudia, we've now come to a high point in our lesson on intravenous envenomation. Very few people have had the privilege of observing this phenomenon, and I want you to pay close attention."

I could hardly breath, and I shook my head as hard as I could, trying to plead with my eyes. I wasn't sure *where* his eyes were focused.

"Claudia, this venom contains numerous enzymes that won't be caught up in tissue, as they would with a bite. They'll go straight into the bloodstream, coursing rapidly through her body. Numerous hydrolases, oxidases, pro-coagulants, serine proteases, and phosphodiesterases will lead to tissue destruction, hypotension, swelling, hemorrhage and fasciculations. She may well just asphyxiate."

I stared at his mouth, mesmerized by the alphabet soup of technicals coming from it and dimly aware of snot moving down my upper lip and deep tingling in my hands. My brain felt numb, teetering into the final zone of my life, unable to stop anything, resigned to accept our fate, too late to contemplate our stupidity.

"The snake will kill and break down its prey," he said. He raised a finger in front of my face. "Ah—except for one other unique event that only Tony can trigger. Perhaps you know what that is. Perhaps you know that Crotalid venom can penetrate actively dividing cells. Perhaps you know that it can get into the nucleus, get at the DNA." He paused, obviously enthralled with his discovery. "Perhaps you even know what mutation Tony's venom has caused." He looked hard at my eyes.

"Claudia, I think you *do* understand the significance of all of—this."

He came very close to my face, pushing my hair back behind my left ear.

"You know, you do have your mother's eyes. I wonder . . ."

He shook his head, seemingly to clear it. "First things first." He glanced toward the door, waited several seconds, and then looked at the syringe still in his hand.

"It's time," he said. "Even if there isn't much time, this is the time."

There was a port in the IV line up near the bag of saline, and he stuck the syringe's needle into it, hesitating slightly before pushing the plunger. I shook my head furiously, trying to get his attention, but his thumb began to push the venom into the line. I don't know where any strength came from, but all I could think of doing was to rock my chair sideways, with no luck on the first try. I gave my body the biggest thrust I could, and I felt my chair falling sideways toward Dru's, as I tried to rock my body toward hers, toppling both of our chairs toward the floor and toward Kral.

Dru's chair fell completely on its side and hit the floor with a thud, dragging the lamp and some other things that went crashing down with her. Something sharp hit my forehead, and I tensed—feeling hot, wondering if somehow I'd been bitten by Tony. Blood was dripping down the side of my face. I was stunned, trying to focus my eyes and loosen myself as my chair slipped all the way to the floor. After a few seconds, my mind cleared slightly, and my right hand seemed a little looser. I tried to look toward Dru and thought I saw a slight movement in her hands. On the other side of her, I could make out one of Kral's legs on the floor. I heard him groan, and the leg moved, and I struggled furiously, trying to loosen my hands. He was on his knees, and I saw a very shaky hand grab the top of the desk. Then his head came into view, and he pulled the terrarium toward him. He stood up on very wobbly legs, his hands on the desk to hold himself upright. Then he looked down at me.

"Claudia, Claudia, Claudia, look what you've done. You've stopped the procedure."

His hands were fumbling with Tony's cage, and I thought I heard it opening.

"Shall I let him bite you in the face or bite your cousin? Your choice."

Giving him a few seconds, I tried to jerk my chair closer to the desk, then swung my feet as hard as I could against it. Then I banged it again, and again, and . . .

Kral screamed in a high-pitched voice, then tried to yell for Rivers, but only a thin whine came out. I heard him hit the floor—then some gasping. A minute later, I half saw him stumble behind me and go out the door, slamming it behind him. The rag had come halfway out of my mouth, and I managed to push it the rest of the way out.

"Dru," I said. "Can you hear me? Dru!"

She groaned.

"Don't move," I said.

I thought I heard a small laugh come from her. Then I tried to figure out where Tony was—nowhere that I could see, but my line of site was obviously limited. I was desperately trying to figure a way to get one of us untied, wondering if that kitchen knife was still around, when the office door opened, and my stomach gave a lurch. I braced for the worst, but hands were untying me, cutting through the ropes.

"Claudia, you're OK," the voice said. "Claudia." It was familiar—it was a woman's voice. I wiped my eyes with my shirtsleeves, then looked behind. Dr. Katy gave me a nod and put down a gun. "You've got a piece of something in your forehead," she said, examining it and digging something out of my skin. "A piece of glass. Now help me with your cousin."

My legs were shaky when I stood. I looked around quickly.

"There was a *snake* in here—a huge albino rattler."

She scanned the room quickly, then shook her head.

"Not here now."

"Did you see Kral when you came in?"

She shook her head. "No one in the house so far."

We got Dru's chair back up, and she was all twisted in the ropes. Blood oozed from the IV site where the needle had come out when we toppled over, and she groaned, starting to revive.

"Wait a second," Katy said, then she grabbed her gun and disappeared for a minute, returning with a thin, wet towel in her hand. "I could only find one," she said, ripping it in two and giving me one to put on my forehead. She used the other to wipe Dru's face, and then wound it around her arm to stop the oozing.

"I feel sick," Dru finally croaked, holding her head. She glanced at me. "What happened?"

"Kral got bitten by Tony—then a different posse came," I said, nodding toward Katy.

"Thank God."

Katy took charge.

"What was in that IV?" she asked me.

"Potent rattlesnake venom, or so he said. I think it was."

"Did she get any?"

"I don't think so. It was close."

"Can you drive, Claudia?"

I nodded yes.

"Then get in your car and take 35 a little south and stop at the Medical Center on 59. They have antivenom, I'm pretty sure. Say you were out hiking or something—you can figure it out. Tell them Dru may have been bitten and at least needs observation. Get *going*."

"Katy, Kral may still be around here. He's beyond crazy, and he may still have Tony—the big rattler—with him."

"We'll take care of it," she said, and I wondered who "we" was.

I nodded, starting to steer Dru out of the room and toward the front door. She shook her head wildly, breaking from my arm.

"The reversal drug," she whispered. "It's still here."

I tried to grab her, but she was already heading down the hall. "We need to go."

Katy saw us, and I just shook my head.

"She's looking for a drug—a specific drug that Kral made. I couldn't stop her. She's probably OK if she hasn't had a reaction yet; it should have already happened."

Katy didn't look totally convinced, but we caught up to Dru, and Katy convinced us to sit in the kitchen while she checked the rooms—for Kral and for the canister. She was carrying her gun like she knew what to do with it.

A few minutes later she was back.

"I found Kral," she said. "He can't hurt anyone. And maybe a canister."

Dru stood up on wobbling legs, demanding to see both. We followed Katy to an open wood door at the far end of the main hallway, and I helped Dru get down a curving flight of stairs to a wine cellar.

An ice chest was on the floor at the bottom of the stairs; Kral was slumped over on the floor at the far end of the room, not moving, not looking good.

"Dead?" I asked.

Katy nodded. "He's got a very nasty bite on his right arm. Apparently he was pretty unhealthy to start with, and that tipped him over."

I walked over to him, and Dru followed. His right arm was bitten—bloody and swollen. His mouth dripped frothy fluid that stained his chest, and his face looked blue and bloated. On the floor next to him was a small, broken vial.

"Antivenom," Katy said. "He didn't have time to use it."

Dru turned back, looking at the ice chest on the floor. She opened the lid, and vapor seeped out as she grabbed for the canister.

"Dru," I began, but it was too late.

The cold metal burned her fingers, and the canister crashed to the floor. She looked at me, pleading for help.

Some rags were piled in a corner. I grabbed several of them as protection when opening the container. I looked inside. The inner container had come open, and liquid had spilled out into the outer one. There was still a small amount left in the inner container, so I closed it and put it back into the larger one. I showed it to her.

"Still some there in the original container, Dru. And the stuff that spilled out may still be useful."

I put the canister back in the ice chest and noticed a small vial at the bottom of the chest. I looked at it quickly. It was antivenom, but we had no obvious means to administer it and no way to treat an allergic reaction.

Katy was looking at us with exasperation.

"It's that drug," I said. "We're on our way—and thanks."

I carried the ice chest by the handle, and we made our way upstairs and out the front door.

"Dru, have you got the car keys?" I was suddenly worried that they'd been taken from her. She fished deep in the pocket of her jeans and came out with them. I got her in the car and got us onto the street.

"No hospital," she said, shaking her head wildly.

"Absolutely to a hospital," I said. "Maybe you don't feel anything now, but it might come on all of a sudden if some venom got in you."

"Claudia, I would have felt it by now. You even said so." She started crying. "I won't go in. We need to get back so I can show this to Chance." She gave me a pleading look, hugging the ice chest to her. "I know I'm all right. Just do this!"

She was probably right, but I was worried sick. "Dru, don't do this to me now. We know this place has antivenom. We don't know about any places along the way home. You won't do Chance any good if you croak on me."

"I won't. I'm fine. Let's go see Chance, and Julie can check on me if you want."

So we drove, not taking Dr. Katy's advice. We had some antivenom but no way to administer it. Still, I thought it might come in handy. At any rate, it was probably true that any venom effects would have come on quickly. We cleaned ourselves off with ice and rags, and I had to keep my forehead iced for a while to stop the bleeding. Then I put my bangs over the wound. Dru cleaned her face and hid the cut with her hair and pulled down her shirtsleeves before we went through the border patrol. The cut on her face wasn't seriously deep, but she would have a scar, I thought. I glanced at her frequently the entire drive, but she eventually sat up, looking more alert and determined.

"This isn't enough to cure him, is it?"

"Not if it's not sterile anymore, but some still is. And it should be enough to determine what it is," I said, and she seemed appeased.

It was eight at night by the time we pulled into the hospital. Too late for Julie to still be there, I thought. Chance had been admitted, and we found his room on the oncology ward, where I saw a couple of nurses I knew. Dru and I must have looked like we'd been in a bar brawl, and I chatted with them awkwardly. Chance was asleep, so we sat in his room and stared for a while. Dru had her chance to talk when a lab tech came in and woke him up so she could draw blood. When the tech left, I closed the door, and Dru stood beside him.

"Chance, we got some," she said quietly.

He stared at her, then me. "Oh, my God. What have you two done?"

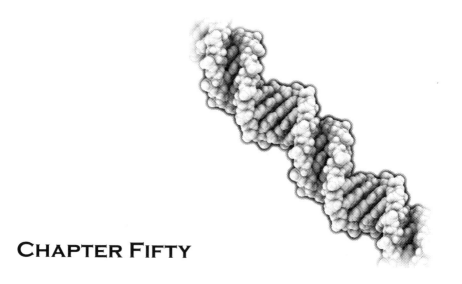

CHAPTER FIFTY

NEITHER OF US KNEW WHAT to say. Finally Dru said, "He tried to kill us. I thought I could convince him to help us—you—if he knew you were sick." She was speaking quickly now, running out of breath. "But he was just crazy. Wouldn't listen. We thought we were goners. He tried to give me venom IV—right into my blood. When Claudia stopped it, he was going to have Tony do it, but Tony bit him and killed him. We found a canister with the drug, but it fell on the floor and spilled. But we saved some."

Chance had a frightened look on his face. "How'd you find him?"

"With the help of some close friends. We trust them," I said. "I trust them with my life—with all our lives. They found us and untied us. And Tony disappeared."

Chance laid his head back, looking confused and exhausted. He looked at Dru, noticing some blood on her cheek. He lifted his arm and pushed back her hair, stroking his finger near the wound. Dru's eyes got moist and tears rolled down. "I'm OK," she said.

I decided we needed to cut things short and discuss the details later.

"Chance, Dru, we need to go and let him get some rest. We need rest too. We'll talk about this later. Chance, I'll put the drug in the freezer, OK?"

He nodded, closing his eyes, and we left with Dru promising to return the next day. It was pretty obvious by that time that Dru was all right as far as any potential venom poisoning was concerned, and she was asleep before we got home.

Exhausted, we went to bed, but we were both up early the next morning, showering and assessing the damages. It looked like she would probably have a scar on her cheek, but it wasn't going to be very obvious; the same applied to the shallow cut on my forehead. I wanted to talk to certain people, like Joe Picci and Dr. Katy, but Dru insisted on going to the hospital. First she called her friend and got the cars exchanged; the poor guy didn't have a clue where we'd taken his.

When we got to Chance's room, I called Julie, who reassured me he was stable and would be getting a line put in for chemotherapy and transfusions. His day was scheduled to be busy, getting him ready for therapy, but Dru insisted on staying around, planting herself firmly in a chair by his bed. Since I had no inclination to sit there all day, I told her I'd pick her up later and left.

Figuring Joe Picci was pretty pissed, I decided to face the music ASAP. I called the restaurant, hoping he'd be there early, and he was. There was a good-sized room in the back of the restaurant that doubled as an office and a poker room, I knew, since I'd been in there with my father, albeit many years before. It was where the poker group met once a month, and I'm sure they got to eat pizza while they were playing.

I got there late in the morning, but the smell of thick marinara was already permeating the place and making me hungry, despite the turbulence in my stomach. I parked in back, and the restaurant door was unlocked. There was no one in sight when I entered. I walked to his office in the back, where the door was open. He was sitting at his desk, which was against the wall, and I went and sat in one of the poker table chairs, turning it to face him. He didn't look happy.

"I just bailed my boys out of the Laredo jail," he said, looking irritated, waiting for a reply.

"Sorry, Joe," I said, shrugging my shoulders. "Dru insisted on going. I couldn't let her go alone, and she got Frank to follow us. I guess Kral had enough connections to get them stopped and arrested."

"What I'm pissed about is that you didn't tell me right away what the fuck was going on. Your father wanted you to trust me. Didn't he tell you that?"

"No, not really. I figured he died too unexpectedly to tell me anything—or didn't realize what Kral might do."

Joe looked surprised. "Well, maybe that's true. I admit I'm surprised he didn't ever tell you I was such a good friend." He thought for a while. "He didn't really mention this guy Kral by name to me, at least not that I remember—just said he was having trouble with another guy at the university—that was way back. But before the accident, he seemed worried about something—said if anything happened to him, would I keep an eye on you. Of course I said I would. I owed him."

"Really? Owed him for what?"

He sat back, looking up at the ceiling, then down at me. "Way back, before you can remember, I was in trouble with some guys in Chicago. Owed 'um big bucks. I was so damned depressed I almost blew my own head off. Your dad bailed me out—saved my ass big time. I still owed him some when he died." He put his head down, shaking it. "I never did tell you. Frank and Joe Jr. think we were just good friends. They don't know nothing about no money, but I knew they could tell something was wrong. I was such an asshole back then."

"So how did you know we were going out to the ranch at Devine?"

"Katy called me. Said she was worried about you, and would I keep a close eye. We started to, then it got reinforced when you and your cousin showed up at the restaurant late that night, sopping wet and looking like two drowned rats. Two nervous rats. You're not good liars."

"Thank God for the help."

"So who's the guy you two rescued? The boys weren't sure what to believe about that."

"Kral's son, Chance."

"Kral's son—are you *nuts?*"

I shook my head, not knowing where to begin. "It's a long story, but he's a good guy. Believe me, it's OK."

I'm not sure he was convinced, but he didn't say anything more about it.

"What happened to the big guy who was at the place?"

"He ain't dead, if that's what you're worried about. He took off. Don't worry about it." He looked like he was picturing an unpleasant thought. "Frank says the place was full of snakes."

"Rattlesnakes," I said.

"Oh, Jeez, I hate 'um. Thank God I wasn't there."

"So how did Katy end up at Kral's house yesterday?"

"From what I know, Frank called her and told her what was going on, and she decided to follow everyone else. Lucky she did. That Katy's quite a character—tougher than most men I know. Did she help you out?"

He had a look on his face that made me think he knew exactly what had happened at Kral's house.

"I think you know the answer to that, Joe. It was a mess."

"Well," he said, relaxing back in his chair again, "she knows how to help clean up a mess. Just ask her."

"I will. Will Frank and Joe Jr. be OK?"

"They're on their way home. Everything's under control. Go back to living a normal life, Claudia. And someday I want to hear the whole story. From *you*."

"Sure," I said, getting up to leave. I'd have to be mighty drunk, I thought.

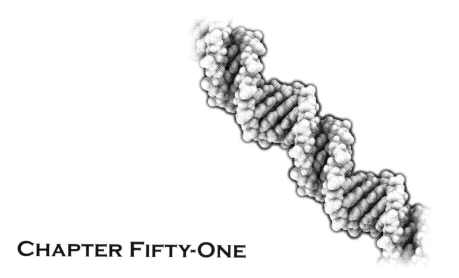

CHAPTER FIFTY-ONE

CHANCE GOT BETTER OVER THE next several days, his fever remitting after antibiotic therapy. Julie began the intensive chemotherapy that would kill off the blasts in his bone marrow, and he tolerated it pretty well. She called me early one day, and I drove in with Dru and stopped on the ward to talk with her in my old office. She had some results on Chance's genetic studies.

"Hey, Claude," she greeted me. "Ready to come back yet? I've got some lab research to do, and I'm getting tired of this patient care stuff."

"Not quite—but pretty soon, probably."

"What's with this 'probably' thing?"

"I'll be back, Julie. What have you got for me?"

"Routine cytogenetics are normal so far."

"And?"

"And results are looking positive for a TP53 gene mutation. FISH studies for the other mutations are negative."

My heart gave a lurch. Even after what Chance and Kral had said, even after what Stephen had suspected from the small sample I'd given him to analyze, I was still hoping that the mutation wasn't there—wasn't a factor in the whole mess. But there it was, and there was no way around it.

I spent a few days trying to settle myself down and relax, but that wasn't coming easily. Chance finished his induction therapy in the hospital and was looking well enough to come home and get followed up and transfused as an outpatient. His follow-up bone marrow exam showed no definite detectable blasts, and that was good news. Julie wanted to work him up for possible bone marrow transplantation, but he would hear none of that, refusing to even consider it. The soft white hair fell out, and he had Dru shave off the little that was left. I glanced at him on the stairway one morning as I was running up and he was walking down. The light hit his face at a certain angle, and I took in a frightened, sharp breath. His facial resemblance to Jeremy was striking.

"Yeah, I look a little like him, don't I?" he said, a wry look on his face.

I nodded, the whole sordid night at Dru's house rushing back into my head.

Later that day I gave Dr. Katy a call. We decided to meet up at her office at seven in the evening; she had some wine there, and I would bring some dinner. I stopped at a small French bistro and saw some rotisserie chicken with some bread and cheese that looked good.

Her main office door was locked, so I rang the bell, and she let me in, leading me to her private office in the back. Boxes were piled up in the record and patient areas, with various supplies and office furnishings lying around ready to be packed. She was dressed casually in jeans and a plaid shirt with a corduroy jacket on top—and boots.

"Are you moving, Katy?"

"Claudia, I'm hanging it up. It's time, and I have plenty to keep me busy for however many more years the Lord is willing to give me." She sat down at her empty desk, and I pulled a chair up in front. "And that might not be very many, considering the wild and crazy life I've led."

She pulled a bottle of wine with two glasses out of her side desk drawer, pulled out an army knife, and opened the bottle. We ate and drank, and I felt more relaxed than I had in weeks. Then we sat back, sipping wine.

"So what will you do?" I asked.

"Maybe move back to the small ranch where I grew up. I've always loved the place, and no one else in the family is willing to look after it."

We were silent for a minute.

"You want to know what I did after you left," she said.

I nodded. "And about the guy who was there."

"I had some help," she said. "The guy took off—seemed awfully anxious to get out of there when he was spotted outside."

"By Joe?" I asked.

She nodded. "Joe was checking around while I found you and Dru. He saw the guy take off in a white van. And we think Kral was just borrowing the house."

"Did you recognize Kral?"

"Yeah—some people you'd just recognize no matter what. He was one of those." She looked deep in thought, and I wondered if she was thinking about my father and Kral. I decided I owed her a story, and I needed to get it out anyway. I told her everything, starting with the trip to San Francisco. Everything I could think of came out, sometimes out of sequence, but I managed to cover it all. Even Stephen. She listened without interrupting.

"Damn, I need another glass of wine," she said when I finally finished. We both had another, and I could see she was still taking it all in.

"Who would have thought that weirdo would discover a venom like that and then discover a drug reversing the effects of the mutation?"

We looked at each other, and I wondered if maybe my father had known or had any idea. She was wondering the same thing. She shook her head.

"He never mentioned anything like that to me—your father didn't."

"Well," I said, "we have what Chance and Kral have told us. We know Chance has the mutation. We still don't really know for sure that the venom caused the mutation or that the drug really works."

"But, my God, what if it's all true, Claudia? The man was a crazy genius."

"A real Moriarty," I said. "The medical version."

I put down my empty wine glass and took a deep breath. "Did you just leave him there?" I asked.

She nodded. "Killed by his own venom."

We ate for a minute.

"I didn't know you and Joe even knew each other that well."

"Honey, don't you remember seeing me playing poker with those guys—I played for years. The only woman they'd let play, even though I cleaned them out many times."

If I'd seen it, it was long forgotten. I wanted to ask her what to do if the police started asking questions about Kral or Jeremy or Chance or who knew what, then decided to tackle that when and if the time came. She'd said nothing about the police, and it seemed as though she wouldn't argue with my choices. She looked unwavering. She looked like a rock. I could lean on her if I needed to—at least as long as we were both still around.

"I guess you never found Tony, huh?"

"No—but I admit we didn't check every nook and cranny. We got the hell out of there, and obviously I didn't realize how—unusual he was—scientifically speaking. Not that I could have handled him anyway. I guess he slithered off somewhere."

Another thought popped into my head, one I'd been wondering about.

"Katy, I wonder if that was the real reversal drug Kral had at the house. I mean, why would he bring it there? It could have been anything in that canister, really."

She shook her head. "Maybe he thought Chance would show up, and he really meant to give him some. Who knows how his mind worked. Maybe he wasn't planning on killing you—just Dru. Interestingly enough, I found another vial of antivenom there after you left."

My mind was buzzing, considering the possibilities.

"Well," I said, "for Chance's sake, I hope the reversal drug was real. Maybe Kral had more stashed away somewhere."

"He must have had a more permanent place where he was living, Claudia. Maybe across the border?" She shrugged. "Maybe his son knows."

She got up and walked over to a chair her jacket was draped over. She opened a buttoned pocket and pulled out a letter envelope that had been folded into fours and placed it in my hand. I could feel what it was as I unfolded the envelope; then I pulled out two necklaces, one still locked together, with some dried blood on the tip.

"I didn't know what they meant, but I took them for you, Claudia. One was on the floor by Dru's chair, and one was in Kral's hand."

I put them in my pocket and got ready to drive home.

"Oh, and before you leave, take these too." She brought a small box over to me and put it on my lap. It was heavy. "One's yours and one is apparently Dru's. We found them before we left."

I took the box of guns and went home.

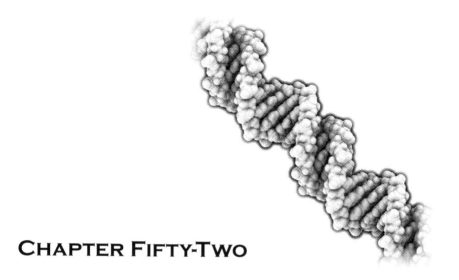

CHAPTER FIFTY-TWO

CHANCE DID WELL OVER THE next few weeks, with the chemotherapy killing off the blasts and his bone marrow gradually re-populating with normal cells until he needed no more transfusions. Julie and I were surprisingly pleased at his response, considering the mutation he had, but we tried in vain to convince him to get worked up for possible transplantation. At home, Dru and Chance would speak softly together, then break it off when I came in the room, and they seemed restless, obviously planning something. I wondered when they'd tell me, feeling like an outsider deeply enmeshed in their lives. I thought Chance conveyed a couple of guilty looks toward me, as though he wanted to say something, but he never did.

Most of my days were spent trying to decide if I could make a decision. I read whatever I could find on my father's bookshelf and tried to make my way through his book. I developed a somewhat unwelcome fascination regarding snakes, especially pit vipers and venoms, and began combing the Internet for more information. I never found any published articles by Samuel Kral regarding his work with snakes or venoms, or with the TP53 mutations for that matter. Chance said none of it was published and was obviously reluctant to discuss the subject of his father's research.

I tried to stay peripherally informed about the current research regarding potential substances that might reverse the effects of the

TP53 mutation and found it hard to believe Kral had discovered such a miraculous cure. Still, Chance had the mutation and hadn't developed a cancer until Kral's withdrawal of the so-called reversal drug.

We sat at the kitchen table after dinner one night, with rain pouring down and flooding lower streets during an unusually large deluge. The three necklaces were on the table, and Chance was looking at them closely, trying to detect differences among them. He shook his head.

"I always thought they were exactly alike, and I still don't see any differences. I don't know *how* he could tell them apart," he said, sliding them toward me.

"I think he was just bullshitting us," Dru said. "He was guessing."

"Put them away for now, Claudia," Chance said, pushing them against my fingertips. "We'll get back to them later."

They were on the verge of telling me something, I could tell. Dru looked at me with a sad expression on her face. "Cuz, we're taking off."

I can't say I was surprised.

"Taking off where?" I asked, my voice breaking slightly.

Dru looked at Chance, and he answered.

"I think we're going to Houston. I have a friend there I did some work with. He knows a chemist who can help me analyze the reversal drug—maybe make more of it. There's actually quite a bit of it spilled in that container—probably enough in the small one for some injections and in the larger one for analysis."

So he was still totally convinced about the drug. I couldn't blame him; ostensibly it had worked for years. But I was still hung up on my conventional therapies.

"Chance, you need consolidation chemotherapy for the next few months, at least. Just a few days a month to keep you in remission. You can't just go running off."

Dru looked alarmed, and Chance calmed her with a hand on her arm.

"Claudia, I can get it there. They *do* have hospitals, you, know."

I felt uneasy, but I thought maybe Dru could make sure it got done.

"And Kral—your father—didn't have more drug stashed away somewhere? Maybe in another house?"

He looked thoughtful for a second, and then shook his head. "Not that I know, but then, I certainly didn't know a hell of a lot about my own father—maybe didn't want to. And he moved around."

I wasn't really sure if that was a straight answer or not, but that was apparently all I was going to get.

"And by the way," he added, "my bills are paid."

So they had the money he'd mentioned.

"What about your house—and things, Dru?" I asked. It was my roundabout way of asking about the kids.

"Chance and I are going to paint and fix up the bedroom before we leave. Martin is coming down to sell it—or maybe to move down here with the kids. He can't seem to make up his mind yet. They'll be fine with him," she added, looking down and tracing the squares on the tablecloth with her finger.

"When are you leaving?"

"In a few days," she said, looking at Chance.

They weren't around much in their last days here. Chance was already due for his first round of consolidation therapy, and of course I worried. But it was *his* life. They left on a windy Thursday morning, she in her car and he following on his bike that he'd retrieved from who knows where. The canister was in a cooler in the back of her car. I went out into the street and hugged her, our hair collectively blowing around and blinding us. We both had tears coming down.

"Let me know," I said, as she got in her car. She nodded. Chance sat on his bike dressed in black with his helmet on—now a slightly narrower figure than before. I gave him a small wave, and he lifted his left index finger. Then they were gone.

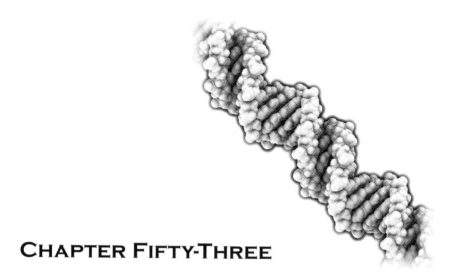

CHAPTER FIFTY-THREE

I SAT AROUND THROUGH THE weekend, finally coming to a decision. On Monday I gave Still a call, and we agreed I'd return to work in two weeks. He sounded relieved, but I could tell his voice was full of questions he would probably ask at some point—he wasn't shy about things like that. On Tuesday I drove into the hospital to find Julie. We had several subjects on which to catch up, none of which were particularly pleasant.

She walked into the office and dropped into her chair, looking a little ragged.

"Got any good news for me?" she asked.

"Yeah, I'll be back in two weeks. Can you hold out until then?"

"Just barely. It doesn't look like Jeff's coming back, at least not so far."

"Heard anything?"

"No body yet. The burned one they found by Blanco was some other unlucky bastard. The blood in the car was a match for Jeff's, though. From the rumors I hear, the police think he got caught up in some sort of Internet game that turned out to have some very unsavory characters involved. There may have been some big bucks involved too. They think he was going to meet somebody—or somebodies—and maybe he was robbed.

And then there are some alternative theories circulating about some kind of drug deal."

"Jeff into drugs? I still find that hard to believe."

She shrugged. "There were drugs at Jenna's place."

My heart tightened. He and Jenna both gone—it was all so unlikely.

"Any more word on Jenna?"

"Looks like a weird drug reaction, not an OD or anything like that. Still, it makes you wonder if Jeff's disappearance made her so depressed she took something. Gather ye rosebuds, Claud."

"Really."

"So Chance isn't coming back to see me for more chemo? I couldn't get him to schedule a follow-up appointment. His test for the TP53 mutation turned negative after therapy, by the way, but it needs to be monitored, obviously."

She was quiet for a few seconds. "And Stephen—Dr. Palmer—said he'd like to discuss Chance's genetics with you." She obviously didn't relish telling me the last part.

"Chance left town—with my cousin. He says he'll get the consolidation elsewhere. I guess we'll see." I shrugged. She frowned.

"Stephen and I are done, Julie. We pretty much had a falling out the last time I saw him. I don't think he has any high regard for me."

"Yeah. Well just remember that you owe me big-time the next time you talk to him—*bitch*."

We looked at each other and both laughed.

I drove home, not feeling in the mood to talk with Stephen that day. There were too many changes to think about, including no good news about Jeff. I'd lost a friend because of some stupid game, and Jenna was gone because of a horrible drug reaction. Gather ye rosebuds was appropriate advice. Life had turned from a given to a major crapshoot.

Walking into the master bedroom, I looked around for signs of Dru and Chance, but nothing personal was left behind. There was some dried dirt on the closet floor from Dru's muddy boots, and the feathered gown that she'd worn was half off the hanger. I walked out, leaving everything as it was. I took the boards out of the windows and opened the shades. The yard was in dire need of attention.

Sitting once again in my father's office, I stared at the safe, and then finally opened it. The Beretta was back in its spot. The white envelope sat there, and I pulled it out and placed the three necklaces in front of me on the desk. They looked exactly the same except for the trace of blood on the tip of Jeremy's. I chose one of the others, and—don't ask my why—I put it on, hoping it had belonged to Chance and not Kral.

I knew it was a strange thing to do—it should have repelled me. Yet I thought maybe they could mean something different—maybe represent a quest for something good.

Things eventually began to feel somewhat normal again after getting some help with the yard and giving the house a good scouring. I'd been thinking about my father and decided to give his attorney a call—something I'd planned on doing and then hadn't done after all. I asked for Jim Abrams and was surprised to hear he'd retired four years earlier, following a bad stroke. They gave me the name of his partner who'd taken over Jim's clients. On the phone, he seemed friendly enough and said he'd check my father's records in Jim's old files. Two days later he called me back, his voice sounding strained and tentative.

"Miss Ranelli, I found your father's records from this office. Was there anything in particular you wanted to know about?"

I wasn't sure where to begin. "Well, did you see anything out of the ordinary—any problems at work or with other people or anything?"

"Not really," he said. "I did find one thing, though, that might interest you." He hesitated. "It's a letter—unopened and addressed to you. It was stuck in between some other papers and probably got overlooked. A note on the envelope also stated it was to be opened only by you in the event of your father's death."

I sucked air in. "That was over five years ago."

"Yes, and I'm very sorry. You see, poor Jim apparently had some memory lapses back then. We weren't aware of it, and he seemed to be doing a fine job for his clients. He was a founding partner here. I believe this letter was misplaced and forgotten five years ago. Would you like to drop by and pick it up, or should I drop it off?"

I picked it up the next day and told him it was no big deal. What else could I say at that point? I opened the letter in dad's office late that night:

Dearest Claudia,

If you're reading this, it's obvious that I've moved on. I won't deluge you with maudlin thoughts except to say that you really have been the pride of my life. I know you're strong; please help your mother to be strong also. I've left you both in reasonable financial shape, not rich, but not bad; Jim Abrams will help you with that. There is one thing that has bothered me for quite some time. Years ago at the University I worked with a Dr. Samuel Kral, actually a genius of a geneticist but crazy as hell. I caught him doing what I thought were some pretty bizarre studies on unknowing volunteers—injecting experimental substances, possibly modified compounds capable of inducing mutations—I'm not sure what they were, but I reported him. He disappeared before any real investigation was done. He did say some threatening things to me the last day I saw him, but I've never heard any news of him since. I believe he was married with some children, God help them. Still, the whole thing bothers me, and if there ever was a Moriarty in my life, he was it.

Your mother never really understood the twisted character of this man the way I did, and I think she was fascinated with him in a small way—nothing that came between us, but she found it difficult to believe me, I could tell.

I don't think you will have any cause to be concerned about him, but if you should ever run across the man, please be careful. Notify the police if need be. There are two people I would trust with my life and yours, and they will always help you, if possible. One is Joe Picci, a long-time friend from the restaurant; the other is Dr. Katy, another good friend and one tough lady. Stay in touch with them at any rate; they're both good people in their own way.

PS: If you can't get through my book, I don't blame you. It's boring as hell. You know what's in the safe.

Love,
Your father

I went to the bathroom to dry my eyes and stared at the red-eyed, swollen creature in the mirror. The face looked pathetic, the green eyes a dull color. I lifted my bangs and examined the scar on my forehead. It could have been a lot worse, I thought, and seeing the letter sooner probably wouldn't have helped anything.

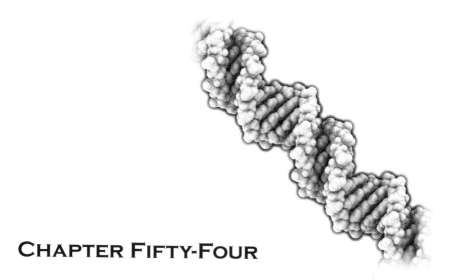

CHAPTER FIFTY-FOUR

IT'S A BRILLIANT MAY MORNING, and I'm up early for a change, feeling really groggy after all these days of abandoning my usual early morning schedule. I wonder if I really want to get used to this—but know I will. My green silk blouse looks like a good choice for the first day back. Maybe it'll bring some good luck and take some of the dullness from my eyes. I pull my hair back into a low ponytail and am forced to brush the bangs slightly to the side, since they're in bad need of a trimming. I grab my cell phone and purse and drive to the hospital, where my white coat still waits on the coat rack in our office. Stopping by his office to say hello to Still, I see that his face is full of questions, but I manage to escape without saying much. I spend time with Julie and some of the other staff, catching up on patients and re-organizing my desk, and the day is filled. By six, I'm tired but elated, happy to have gotten through my first day back with barely a thought directed to Dru or Chance or Jeremy or even Kral.

I stop in a restroom to straighten myself and see the chain of the necklace in the mirror. The two pieces are unlocked, and I can feel them move slightly as I walk. My fingers often glide over them when I'm thinking hard about something, until I realize I'm rubbing the snake between my fingers.

I take relaxed steps down the long corridors to the molecular biology department, turning the corner of the final hallway, stopping to stare at the line of faculty pictures hanging on the wall. Antonio Ranelli is in the top row, sitting with just a slight half-smile on his face, looking handsome in a white lab coat with a white shirt and striped tie underneath, and I feel pride swelling my head. Then I wonder what he would think of all that's happened—and my choices. I can't guess but have finally come to conclude that *I* can live with it; I just hope I don't tarnish the memory of him. I walk away, noting Kral's absence from the wall.

Slipping my hand into my left coat pocket, I feel something cold again. It's been sitting all day in a freezer on the ward. It's a small vial labeled with C911.2—one of the vials I took from Jeremy's cellar. When we were in the snake house at Jeremy's ranch, I saw the same number on Tony's empty cage, and this should be his venom—TNT, Kral had called it. This is one of two vials that I have, and I'm going to give this one to Stephen and see what he'll do with it. I suspect any geneticist would be interested in a venom that causes a specific mutation, and although this may not be Kral's greatest discovery (the reversal drug would certainly have that designation), this is half of the equation. I don't really plan on telling him the whole story—too many bodies unaccounted for—but we'll see how things go.

I also need a favor from him. Chance has said he doesn't know which venom he was given to use on me that night in San Francisco, but I have a feeling he thinks it was Tony's, and so do I. One thing I do know is that it got into my bloodstream. I've decided I might as well find out if it was Tony's venom and if I have the mutation. If I don't—fine. If I do, I'll take whatever comes and treat it, cope with it, like so many other patients do. Still, I'm hoping Chance will have luck in his hunt for the reversal drug.

He's expecting me, and when I knock on his hallway door it opens quickly. He's standing there, still wearing his white coat that makes the gray in his hair shimmer. I can't read his expression as he lets me in, and I sit in the chair facing his desk once again. I wonder where he'll sit, and he walks around to the front of the desk and sits on the edge, looking down at me. I think I can read some kindness in his eyes and maybe something else and begin to feel very warm. He leans forward and brushes a finger across my forehead, lightly feeling the new scar, then smiles.

"Did you get into another brawl during your time off, Claudia?"

I smile back. "Yeah, I got in a fight with a real—*snake*."

"You really should try to avoid people like that."

"Believe me, Stephen, I've learned my lesson."

My heat level is rising precipitously, as he stands and takes me by the shoulders, bringing us face to face. I close my eyes, and he softly kisses the scar on my forehead. We hold each other hard, and my mouth goes to his ear, brushing it with my lips.

"Stephen," I whisper.

He leans closer.

"Sequence me."

V W RAYNES

is the pen name of a physician practicing in Texas.

TP53 gene mutations are real, occurring in about half of all human cancers.

viperwomanraynes@gmail.com